AF485419

Steven LaChance's

A Novel

First Edition
First Printing, October 2024
Cover design by Rick Brandt
Edited by Rick Brandt
ISBN: 9798330428083

A few words to begin....

This book is about nightmares.

This book has been somewhat secret in its writing. In some ways, I have deliberately misled some people who might have showed an interest in what I have been working on. This was not without purpose. Sometimes, with more sensitive material, it is better to deflect from what I am working on to get the eyes off any research I might be doing. There are very few people who have even known this project existed or was ever a possibility for an upcoming book. The first writing I did of this manuscript I chose to put away years ago. I eventually completely discarded the first draft when I wasn't satisfied with the end result. I also felt the timing was not right for it to be given out for public consumption. Very little of that original manuscript exists within this version.
At that time, there was a rebirth of the popular nightmare film franchise. Numerous documentaries and books were being released on nightmares, shadow people and sleep paralysis cases. This story was not ready to share, and it was my feeling it might get lost in the onslaught of the sea of conjecture, entertainment and fantasy.

However, many things have changed over the past decade or so and I feel it is not only a perfect time to share it but an essential time as well. Something is going on and there seems to be a growing problem among people, which could be a direct link to the over-attention this type thing has been given. Or, on the other hand, it could be that people are just willing to discuss it more because the topics are more readily available. Either way, there is something evil and nefarious growing out there in both experience and sentiment. People are being attacked in their sleep. Seriously attacked.

I want you to take notice of something immediately before we continue. I need you to take notice because it is very important for your understanding about what you are going to read. You are not going to find the words "true story" anywhere on the cover of this book. However, here is the warning about what I am going to share with you that you must be given before we go any further due to the nature of what this book is about. Some of this book is very true and based on actual cases. Things like this have happened and are happening even at this moment as you read this. It is also known that this phenomenon can not only become viral upon hearing about it, but it is also a moving, feeding parasite in thought and in action.

This book is a conglomeration of ideas, cases, eyewitness accounts, research and personal experience. It is clear for those of you who have read the Screaming House books that I personally suffered numerous nightmare-type events and happenings during the haunting portion of my life. Dreams play a significant role in extreme haunting cases and seriously frightening paranormal events. I want you to have complete understanding that, even though the actual story portion of this book is fiction, it was based upon very real and true paranormal events and cases. Now that you understand this is based on an actual conglomeration of paranormal cases comes the second caveat you need understand before reading. It's a question you need to ask yourself. A very important question. Are you still sure you want to step into the world of Glow?

I'll give you a moment to decide.

If you are still reading this, I am going to assume that you have obviously answered, "Yes." I am glad you have decided to take this journey with me. By answering yes, it is important that you understand I hold no responsibility from this point forward for any nightmares or unexplained events you may believe are happening within in own your life because of reading this book. Yes, this a very real and significant warning. I feel like I need to make this clear because I saw, with the Screaming House books, that they could sometimes trigger claims of activity and events. My book on the Exorcist case was similar, with the same strange claims coming in.
Okay, I've done what I believe is responsible and my conscience is clear from this point forward. For those of you who are the praying sort, this might be good place for you stop and ask for prayers of protection.

I'll give you a moment to pray.

Amen.

I completely understand to some of you this is just a book. It is just a story for non-believers wanting a thrill in the night. That's okay, and I hope it fulfills exactly what you are seeking. But, for those of you who believe in the paranormal and the supernatural, this could be the opening of a new door. A door you might want to have kept closed. You have been warned.

About a decade ago I began hearing whispers in paranormal circles about a different type of occurrence. Then I started receiving messages from people claiming they were experiencing these things happening to either themselves personally or to someone they knew. I should clarify up front these cases all seemed to be fitting into the same type of constructs and circumstances. First, extremely frightening nightmares were the centerpiece of all the cases. Not just the simple type of nightmares, but with serious cases of sleep paralysis and sleepwalking, with a long list of nightmare-triggered symptoms and activity. Most of the cases surrounded young men - not all, but a vast majority - which I found to be very interesting.

It is known that 8% of the population at some time or another experiences sleep paralysis. It is also interesting to note that 28% of these cases are students. This also seemed to fit the age group I was seeing because all these cases seemed to be between seventeen and twenty-five years of age. Interestingly enough, all the activity began with some type of activity in the occult. The usual culprits were showing up in the cases - like spirit boards, seances and even visits to some type of mystic or self-deemed psychic for a consultation. Now I know there are some of you who are immediately going to try to dismiss this, but the fact remains all these cases began with some type of contact being initiated by the person afflicted. These are the characteristics of the cases, and I will not change that because some of you might feel uncomfortable with it. This is just the facts of what I was seeing. It has nothing to do with whether or not I believe in psychics, mystics or spirit boards. You just simply fill in the answers to the questions one after another on the proverbial paranormal activity worksheet. These were the answers. I don't want to say too much about the private particulars of the cases other than they existed. All the victims seemed to be normal and without any indications of mental illness or addiction. That was the disturbing part of this. They, for the most part, seemed like perfectly well-adjusted members of society - until this point of their lives. Until the nightmares began.

This book is more about outlining the steps of these cases than the individuals involved - how they match and differ in character from other types of haunting or demonic infestations (or whatever label you decide to give them). I prefer not to label the paranormal or the supernatural because I am not quite sure what to specifically call these dreams. It is sort of damned if you do damned if you don't situation when labeling these things. Call it a demon and it's the devil himself. Call it a ghost and its instantly Aunt Mary. See what I mean? So, I must give this some thought about what to refer to this moving forward.

In most of these cases, the supernatural culprit seems to have had a history. A history which slowly began to reveal itself within each case. The suicide of the victim was a very serious part of these events. I am not kidding when I tell you this is something which could lead to suicide, and, in fact, it has led to more than one death. The truth of the matter is there is no way of really tracking just how many deaths and suicides this type of occurrence has caused. It could be a whole lot more than we may want to believe. Especially concerning the fact that young male suicide rates have continually been on a steady climb over the past years. It is well accepted by the psychiatric community that nightmares are one of the leading symptoms connected to suicidal thoughts and tendencies. PTSD often has played an integral part of the life of many suicide victims. Continual horrific nightmares can cause serious PTSD. When you connect the PTSD and sleeplessness it is a recipe for trouble. 38% of people in the Unites States alone suffer from sleep disturbances, which lays fertile ground for sleep paralysis, hallucination and sleepwalking - stepping outside of the dream and impacting the waking life. Once this happens it's a scary, slippery slope. There have even been reports of people stepping out of windows in their sleep trying to escape the object of their nightmares. This is one thing Hollywood got right. It is an even more frightening thought when you consider the rise in suicide in young males and correlate that rise with the fact that nearly 20% of our youth are out there in the world having nightmares. Some of them are having these nightmares at least once a night and sometimes multiple times a night. In rare cases, every time they close their eyes to rest. Can you imagine if every single time you closed your eyes to sleep there was a monster waiting for you? Would that mess with your overall world - as you continue to slide further and further down into darkness with no one outside of your internal hell to help you? What would you do?

So, what is the point in all of this? It all seems to be backed up with statistics and sleep research. Here's the thing. All these cases had the usual nightmare claims we see in extreme paranormal cases. Most of the cases ultimately resulted in suicide. However, there was one single distinction which turned this research into these cases into something very different. The victims claimed their dreams were supernatural in nature and, even more frightening, the victims all described the same demon man in their dreams. Now this is where I began to get creeped out because I wasn't a stranger to this man. I have had my run-ins with him in my own dreams. You might remember the dream man coming through my bedroom window at night during my haunting.

Now keep this in mind. This is not part of the Italian conceptual art hoax in 2008. That hoax began with a website which asked the question, "Have you seen this man?" The website had an illustrated picture of a man's face. An ordinary looking man. The website went on to claim that people had been seeing the man pictured in their dreams since 2006. The website received over 9000 accounts of people claiming to see this man in their dreams. Some claimed the man's appearance was supernatural, others claimed he was just simply part of life. But, interestingly enough, none of the people claimed to have been dreaming of the man until after they were exposed to his picture. Of course, there was the religious theory that the man was indeed the face and manifestation of God. Four years later, in 2010, the creator of the website revealed it was all a hoax and part of a guerilla marketing campaign. However, it raised some serious questions about the power of suggestion in real life and its use in marketing. This story is not connected to that man.

Trust me when I tell you these events are not manifested in the silly Wes Craven sort of way, but could represent multiple demonic infestation-type events which are so unbearable they are causing young men to kill themselves. I know you must be thinking the same as I was - that the main goal of a demon, monster or whatever you would like to call it - is ultimately death. This idea that death and suicide was, and is, the goal of a demon was confirmed to me by one of the Pope's Exorcists years ago when I had the opportunity to sit down and talk with him about my own personal case and events which had been happening to me. If you have read any of the Screaming House books you will remember one of the centerpieces of my personal haunting were the nightmares. In fact, that is the reason I took an interest in these cases. All these cases had the markings of what the Church would call demonic. Like my friend Rosemary Ellen Guiley use to say to me, "Everything is connected." She was so right, and I have learned this lesson repeatedly through my years of dealing with the supernatural and the paranormal. Alien abduction cases often appear to be like what the Church would call demonic. Nightmares can often happen between whole groups of people who don't even know each other but describe, with disturbing details, the exact same thing.

For the sake of understanding from this point on in the book, we are going to label this entity as demonic and also something else you will later learn about within the story of the book itself. I have no other label for it, and it is just easier for the overall reader to refer to it in this way until its other possible origin is later revealed within the story. But, keep in mind, we do not know exactly what it is - demon, devil, ghost or just a weird fucking common dream. It just keeps it simple for everyone involved for outlining the characteristics of the cases. I must be honest about it and tell you they do follow the guidelines of a demonic type of supernatural event as set forth by the Roman Catholic Church.

What are these characteristics? There was always a clearly defined invitation period where the victim welcomed the occult into their life whether by use of spirit board, psychic reading or any other of the numerous forms people will use to try to contact the other side of the veil. It always seemed novel or fun to the victim at first. In one case with a spirit board, it presented itself as a very sympathetic character and slowly turned into the demon that seems to be a modern version of the fictional Captain Howdy character from the Exorcist.

Once contact was made, you can pretty much mark the steps and characteristics right off the demonic bingo card. However, there is a difference. The background the demon weaves through the dreams seems to be clearly more current than what we would particularly understand as biblical times. Seriously, the same tale appears in the same way in each of the cases with the same events being used repeatedly. It is almost as if the demon wants us to know he is the culprit. Of course, we can say with solid certainty that finding the real name is the end goal of the Exorcist's game, isn't it? We have all seen the Exorcist scream at the crescendo moment of a horror film, "Demon, give me your name." Why would the demon give away the game when he has such fertile ground to play on? Why would he make it easy to send him back to the bowels of hell? It wouldn't make sense, and, trust me, there is some sense in it all somewhere that is part of this riddle. I have a few ideas - if he truly is demonic - who he might be. I am sure those ideas might surprise you, but I am not ready to share them at this point - if I decide to evoke the name at all. There is always the possibility that he could be something different and new that we are not even considering. What if he is a psychotic interdimensional being who has no connection to religion or faith at all? What if his sole purpose is murder for murder's sake? What if that is how he gets his cosmic kicks?

Let's move forward from here with a little bit of caution. Even writing this in the middle of the day in my bright, sunny office I can feel a slight chill and the feeling someone is very interested in what I am writing and in what you are reading right now.

So here is the dilemma I am faced with while sharing this with you. What is the best way to share it with the utmost caution and respect given to everyone involved? I could write a book which would be a case-by-case study. The problem with that is most of these cases ended in death and apparent suicide. Out of respect for the families I think we need to tread lightly and handle this with sensitivity and care where they are concerned. This is one of the reasons that has kept me from sharing this for over a decade. I know the intense grief these families must be experiencing, even many years later. To easily follow the pattern of the nightmares, I have taken all the information I have been given over the years on these events and combined it into one story which contains fictional characters. This is the best and most protective way I can think of to ensure anonymity and the best protection for the survivors. Maybe others will come forward with their like experiences once this is published. That is completely up to them, and I have no desire to or have control of that. Who knows? My main goal here is to help others who might be dealing with this same thing. This is just telling the story. We are not alone. There is something going on when we sleep.

There are many of you who may have heard about the cases in Indonesia where over a hundred men died in their sleep and there were researchers who felt these unexplainable deaths were caused by some sort of night spirit. This is not a book about that case either, or about those cases which go by the Indonesian names: rep-repam, eureup-eureup, and tindihan. In fact, there are like cases all throughout the world of this type of night spirit attacks such as the one mentioned above and many others which are too numerous to list. Just for context, we have all heard of the Hag, Hat Man and, I would even include, the smiling Indrid Cold and the Greys from alien abductions into this grouping. In some way, like these other events, these cases have their own modus operandi which separates them completely and puts them into a classification of their own.

So, with all the above being stated and considered, it is once again time for me to step up and say, "Welcome to the Paranormal Road Show." There is something scary going on out there and I feel I have a responsibility to share it with you because if I don't, who will?

GLOW

<u>Part 1</u>

Moses

"I am your dwarf. I am the enemy within.
I am the boss of your dreams. See.
Your hand shakes. It is not palsy or booze.
It is your Doppelganger trying to get out.
Beware...Beware..."
-Anne Sexton

Chapter 1
Alex

His apartment was small. Not as small as it could have been, considering he was a poor working college student on a theater scholarship to an okay school, but certainly nothing like Havard or Yale by any means. But a good school, a state-run school none the less. For sure, it was one he would not have been able to afford without his scholarship or financial aid. He thought about something his mother had told him many times before, "Anything good in this life is worth working for." He laughed to himself as he added to the thought under his breath, "Because no one is going to give it to you."

He was living proof of a dedicated Midwestern work ethic. He lived in Missouri, in fact, or what he liked to refer to as the wonderful and blissful state of Misery. St. Louis, Missouri, to be exact - which, somehow, being a larger, more liberal city, seemed to deflect the fact he was at this moment in time, planted firmly in the middle of the country where dreams often went to die. He laughed at himself for having such melodramatic thoughts on a Friday afternoon.

His name was Alex. Alexander Mackenzie McAllister to be exact. His full name sounding way more prominent than he was. Those who knew him just called him Alex and it is true that his apartment was small. Very small, but he was lucky that it had separate rooms instead of one room like some of his friends who lived on campus in dorms, or the one-room studio flats which were spread around the city. He liked his one-bedroom walk-up and in fact, it felt, and had become, his home. It seemed to fit his lifestyle perfectly at this point in time. Alex flopped down on the couch and turned on the local news to see what was going on. The newscaster was speaking about some murder in the downtown area. A carjacking gone very bad, and one man ending up dead.

A woman's horrified screaming filled the room. Alex reached for his cell phone sitting on the coffee table in front of him, thinking he still needed to change his ringtone that had been the same since last Halloween. It was now firmly into the New Year. Just another of the many things he procrastinated away recently. Every time someone called it sounded like someone was being murdered.

"Hello?" he said with a somewhat tired voice.

After a slight pause the voice on the other end said, "Do you have Jesus, our Lord and Savior, in your life?"

Alex didn't even respond to the uninvited question and immediately ended the call, feeling irritated and a little more than put out by the interruption in his ever-so-important and rare moment of solitude. The ringtone of the phone had felt like it had sliced through his silence and into his body.

He lay back for a moment and somehow found humor and began laughing at the strange, spammy intrusion. Do I believe in Jesus? He had given this question some thought. Of course, he was sure everyone had to give it some thought at one point or another. At least he believed in - if not Jesus himself - then God or a higher power of some sort. Sure, he had given it some thought for a moment, once or twice. The end result of these thoughts was usually the same, just in the same way they were on this particular day. He decided that at the age of twenty-two he still wasn't sure what he believed completely. He did believe that there had to be another realm of consciousness. He understood the concept and the stability of energy. One of the most consistent aspects of the world was that energy never diminishes. With that understanding, he felt that since our bodies and our brains function on energy, or more specifically electrical impulses, it would only make sense; we are indeed part of a larger picture. He also could not discount his own experiences which he could never explain. Out-of-body sort of experiences he sometimes had when falling asleep or in his dreams. They were hard to explain, and even harder for him to completely comprehend.

The screaming woman of his mobile phone ringtone cut through his thoughts once more. He picked it up and answered it without even looking at the screen. He instinctively assumed it was the spam caller at it once again and he had something to say to them this time, "Hello?"

There was no immediate answer on the other side of the call, just like before, which really irritated Alex even more. "Listen I am a Satanist who is currently performing a blood sacrifice on a chicken while fucking a priest…"

A voice cut him off, "And how is that going for you?" Laughter on the other end of the line.

Alex could feel his heart drop into his stomach because he knew instantly it wasn't the spam caller, but his best friend Chuck.

"Oh man, umm, I have been getting these calls," Alex tried to explain.

Chuck just laughed and shrugged it off, "Hey, I get it man. I get them all the time too. Make sure you block the number bro and then you won't have to worry about them calling you back."

Alex laughed into the phone because he knew his friend was right.

"I know. I am just a little high-strung right now because I am buried in homework, and I just was trying to take a few moments to catch my breath and a few Z's, and I get this call. Mind you, this is not the first time. Last week it was window and siding sales calls. Why in the fuck would I need windows and siding?"

They both laughed. Alex continued, "I mean isn't there some type of qualifying information out there? It seems Alexa and Siri know more about my wants and needs than I do. I know all that fucking information must be kept somewhere. You would think there has to be some large clearing house of data somewhere that says, Alex McAllister doesn't need fucking windows, and he does not have the time or the inclination or even fucking need to believe in Jesus at this current time when he's trying to get through this fucking semester of school without flunking the fuck out. Hell, I don't even…"

Chuck busted out laughing, "Whoa you are strung out. Real quick bro and then I gotta jet. You want to get together tonight with a few friends and come over about nine and drink some beers?" Alex thought about it for a moment and decided an evening with friends might be exactly what he needed.

Alex took a deep cleansing breath and replied, "Yeah that sounds good man. Could be exactly the thing I need. You need me to bring anything?"

Chuck replied quickly "No just yourself. I have it all covered. Oh yeah, Bobby said he is going to bring this witchy psychic girl with him. We are going to see if we can get her to do something like tell our futures or something like that."

The idea of a witchy psychic girl piqued Alex's interest, "Sounds good to me. See you around nine."

Alex put his phone down once again and lay back on his couch thinking about what the night ahead could hold. It did sound like fun. It would be something out of the ordinary to break this never-ending semester rut he was in. As a matter of fact, he had been feeling somewhat down after they had finished last Fall's musical. More than just a little down. *Little Shop of Horrors* was a lot of fun to do, and he had the part of the Dentist which was perfect for him. Everyone he knew said he was perfect for the part. Maybe one of the best Dentists they had ever seen in Little Shop. This always made Alex wonder just how many times the average person saw Little Shop? He meant, of course, to make such a statement, and for it to be truthful, they would have to have seen at least three different productions. Just two would be way too few. Were they counting the film as one of these productions because that would skew things completely? I mean, in many ways the film is a different animal altogether, especially where the part of the Dentist is concerned. This was the useless musings of a starving actor craving positive reviews but also trying to qualify them when he got them.

Then, of course, there were the usual college show love affairs that seemed to happen with every show he, or anyone else did, for that matter. It was almost a prerequisite for college theater that at least half the cast needs to be fucking each other for the production to seem legitimate. Last Spring during *Barefoot in the Park*, Alex fell in love with one of the lighting crew. A strong, muscular guy who Alex would love to watch flex with even the smallest of moves. The guy had the arms of a God. At least that is what Alex thought and it must have been true because everyone else told him they had felt the same way.

"Just watch him flex those arms and pecs," Alex would whisper to his costar as things were getting changed and set.

These affairs usually started during the rehearsals and ended with the closing night party. Seriously, it was that predictable and never left Alex feeling too down but was always great drama fodder for those down-times between shows. That was until the production of Little Shop. For some reason his Little Shop affair was different. It was much more than just a tryst. Much more.

Alex fell head-over-heels in love for the actor who played the geeky Seymour. Well, in more precise terms, a cute twinkie blond guy named Ellis who played the nerdy Seymour. However, out of makeup and off the stage, Ellis was not geeky at all and was everything Alex thought he wanted and needed in this life. A great personality - and who the fuck is he fooling - Ellis also had great body.

Alex would tell his fellow actress who played Audrey. "He has the type of body only

Michealangelo could sculpt. He is a walking and living modern-day David."

Ellis was obviously a very good-looking guy who appeared innocent on the surface, but that innocence was only on the surface because Ellis was an absolute demon in bed who could go for hours. They had mind-blowing sex.

"We have the kind of sex that makes me feel like I have been in the literal presence of God himself," Alex would often tell his friends.

Alex was sure, because of his hot times between the sheets with Ellis, he completely understood the spiritual side of gay tantric sex. Whether the details of that were true or not, no one was ever completely sure. No one was exactly sure what tantra exactly was or even if Alex really knew himself. It sounded hot and mysterious. That was the exact effect Alex was after.

Yes, it is true that Alex fell deeply and truly in love with Ellis. A love Alex felt which would last long after the curtain on Little Shop had fallen. And of course, when it eventually didn't last and ended abruptly, the whole affair left Alex feeling used, and for the first time in a very long time, lost. The night of the Little Shop closing was the last night they were together. The next day Ellis was off with his next conquest, leaving Alex alone with a breakup playlist on his phone and finding himself whispering messages into Ellis' voicemail late at night after he had one too many drinks. There were a lot of nights after the affair ended Alex would have too many drinks.

"You told me you loved me," Alex would slur, crying into his phone which would never reply.

Alex called those first weeks of his sorrow as, "The Days of Gin and Regret."

He would say to his friends that he thought his affair might make an interesting play. Maybe even a musical like *Cabaret* or others which often featured tragic love stories. His friends were quick to tell him that no one wanted to hear about a hot time love affair during a second-rate college production run of *Little Shop of Horrors*. Well, that is, unless it was written as a gay porn story or filmed for an OnlyFans account. They all knew neither of those were an option for Alex. Alex was for the most part a good guy. He wasn't promiscuous by any means, but they all knew Alex could fall in love way too quickly.

They often would say to him, "Alex, you are tragic, and you thrive on that tragedy of your life to keep you going and feeling. We have seen you do this all before. You're an actor. Use these feelings in your work."

He knew they were right - or were they just giving him the actors excuse to help ease the pain and lessen the embarrassment? But, in the case of Ellis, Alex knew this was much more. Ellis was somehow different and left him living with this deep quiet ache that he was having a very hard time shaking. So much so, Alex was convinced that Ellis might have been his first real love, because nothing had hurt so badly after it had ended. Nothing had hurt this much before. Alex slowly fell to sleep thinking about Ellis. A deep sleep. Then, Alex began to dream.

Alex found himself walking through the downtown streets of the city. It was dark, and from the lack of activity, it was also very late at night. He was cold and he realized he was only half-dressed. He had a pair of jeans on and that was all. No shirt and no shoes. He knew he was paranoid and frightened, but he didn't know why. He rounded a corner onto Washington avenue and there, standing in the middle of the street, he could see the dark figure of a man. He couldn't see his face, but he instinctively knew that he needed to get away from him. Something deep in his gut told him this man was someone to fear. It was an instinctive and animalistic type of fear - much like a caged animal would feel. This was someone Alex needed to fear more than he feared anyone else in his life.

Alex turned on his feet and began to run the other way. He ran as fast as could, but every time he turned the corner the black figure of the man would be there. He ran and ran, but he couldn't get away from the man. Alex decided he had to hide. He had to find someplace to hide. That is when he saw an alley that jutted off to the side just ahead. Alex knew the area he was in. A friend of his had lived in a loft just up the street. Looking behind him Alex didn't see the man, so he quickly ran into the alley. At the end of the alley was a singular dumpster with nothing else surrounding it. It wasn't the best place for Alex to hide but he felt he had no other option. He needed to do something to get away from the man, and he had to do it fast. This was the only opportunity he had. Up to this point, at every turn he made the man was there waiting. This was his chance. The man wasn't waiting for him in the alley.

Alex ran to the dumpster, opened the lid and climbed in, quietly lowering the lid as softly as he could. Alex could feel the trash bags and wetness against his body as he shrank further into the darkness of the dumpster. The smell was unbearable.

"Here piggy piggy," a deep dark voice outside the bin suddenly said, sending shivers throughout Alex's entire body.

He knew in an instant it was the dark man and the man was in the alley. Alex was sure he had been found.

"Here piggy piggy." the voice came closer and continued to taunt him with his words.

Alex could feel his heart pounding within his chest as footsteps got closer and closer. Alex sunk further and further into the moisture and the stench of the trash around him as the sound of the man approached.

"Here piggy piggy," the voice came again - but this time it was different. Quieter, a low whisper, and it was obviously RIGHT THERE - just outside the lid of the dumpster where Alex was hiding.

Alex turned his body to sink deeper into the garbage. Maybe if he could cover himself with the trash bags it might help deflect any blows - or even the stabbing of a knife. He felt something which was almost like a baseball bat. A bat he could use as a weapon. Alex struggled to pull on the object harder and harder until it came loose. In the darkness of the dumpster Alex realized he was holding onto a severed human arm. He began to scream and scream as the lid of the dumpster flew open violently.

Alex jumped off his couch, screaming. A scream which later he was sure should have been heard throughout his building and out onto the street outside.

Alex sat back down on the couch with his head in his hands, "What in the fuck was that?"

Of course it had been a nightmare. Alex had nightmares before in his life, but he couldn't remember ever having a nightmare like this one. This one was different. It felt different. He had never woken from a nightmare so afraid for his life like this before. He was trembling and he couldn't shake off the fear he was feeling. He could feel his heart still pounding within his chest.

Of course, he kept telling himself over and over that he was being silly. Of course, he told himself that it was just a dream. Of course, he told himself it was just his mind reacting to the news story he had heard earlier about the missing guy they found in the dumpster in Tower Grove. Logic usually helps all of us to push our fears and the evil of our subconscious back into the right lane and under control. Reasoning, this time, did not help to slow the beating of his heart. Somehow this felt different. He couldn't put his finger on it, but Alex knew deep down that this felt like a warning. Like a warning shot had been fired. A warning. Yes, that was it. It felt like a warning. He sat for a moment getting his thoughts under control and then he got up to take a shower and get ready for his night out.

The hot water from the shower felt good as it flowed down Alex's naked back. He let himself feel more at ease as the memory of the nightmare began to wash down the drain along with his stress. It was amazing how much a hot shower could change your outlook on life and the world around you. The water felt good on his shoulders and the small of his back as it ran down to his ass.

This had been such a difficult semester for him. He had just felt so pushed all the time. So much so that everyone and everything seemed to be getting under his skin. This, along with the feelings of rejection from Ellis, were taking huge hits on his self-esteem. It was becoming very hard to put things in the hands of the universe and any sort of positivity was quickly short lived. These feelings of hurt and inadequacy just would not let him go. He turned around to face the spray of the shower. The hot water began hitting the front of his body, feeling at first as if it were pulsating hot fists pounding into his chest. As his muscles began to relax, the water turned into some type of wet massage. It felt good and Alex began to lose the world, closing his eyes. He reached down and began massaging his legs. He could feel himself getting excited as the spray from the shower began to hit the head of his cock, sending small shockwaves throughout his body. His nerve endings were waking up under the water. Alex slowly moved his hand to begin stroking his...

The sound of a screaming woman ripped through his bathroom. Suddenly his cell phone lying on the bathroom sink began to shriek once again, killing his mood and the moment instantly.

The phone call had been his friend Paul, who he shared a few different classes with. Paul had a question about one of their creative writing assignments and wanted to know if Alex was going to Chuck's that night for the get-together. Alex found himself looking forward to a good night out with his friends. This semester had not offered him too much time for socializing. He had a great group of friends who were all good guys. They really were a mixture of different types, with different backgrounds, likes, dislikes, preferences (and by preferences, he meant ALL preferences.) The one binding thing between all of them was a love of the arts. All forms, styles and types of art. Creation was a key motivating factor for all of them. One thing about being a young college student is that art could still be art for art's sake. Alex had a good handle on what his future would be when his art would become tied to his income. He also knew this time of his life was about learning and experimenting with his art. You can take chances with the art you create when you are not worried about it putting a roof over your head and food on your table. Art for art's sake is a freedom which is mainly given to the student or the very rich. And Alex would be quick to point out to you he was far from rich. He was the quintessential starving student and, yes, artist.

Alex walked into his bedroom dropping his towel on the way. He opened a drawer in his bureau looking at his underwear trying to decide on a style and color. A good collection of underwear is something he allowed himself to have no matter what. It was his private indulgence. Different cuts, styles, colors and sometimes just plain tightie-whities - whichever would give him a little extra bounce in his step on any given day. It wasn't really a fetish as much as a confidence booster. Let's face it, a nice jockstrap under a pair of jeans goes a long way in lifting one's spirit and, of course, balls. Alex laughed as he pulled on an electric blue jockstrap. He looked at himself in the mirror. He was satisfied with what he saw there. He looked good.

Whenever he had looked at himself and liked what he saw in the mirror he would remember something his grandmother use to tell him, "Baby, you are never going to be this young and look as good as you do at this very moment in time. One day you will look back and understand this. You will wonder where it all went - and are those lines on your face going to stay and get worse? So, enjoy yourself now because this is the best you are going to be today. Looks are fleeting baby. Every day is the last day you will look like this. Enjoy your days and enjoy those moments."

She was right, "Close your eyes grandma in heaven because at this moment your boy is feeling fucking sexy," he said jokingly as he started to laugh while slapping himself on the ass, making the sound of a loud smack.

He continued laughing while putting his pants on. He caught himself smiling and thought it was going to be a good night as he pulled on his jeans. It didn't take him long to finish getting ready and before he knew it, he was headed out the door to Chuck's.

Chapter 2
Contact

Chuck had one of the best living situations in the group of friends. His parents weren't necessarily rich, but they weren't exactly poor either. They were able to provide a good life for their only son while he was in college until he was on his feet in the world, working and able to fully support himself. And that was okay, because it was a luxury his parents were not able to have when they were growing up and just starting out on their own. They wanted the best for their son, and they wanted him to be happy. And happy is what Chuck was, for the most part of his life. There really was never any huge drama or things out of place. His life was normal without a lot of turbulence to rock things too much. 'Everything in its proper place' was a good definition of Chuck's life and had always been indicative of it. In fact, being an only child had way more perks than downsides. Sure, there is a whole lot of expectation put on an only child. It was true Chuck sometimes felt as if he was not completely living up to his parent's expectations. He just didn't have anyone or anything else to compare it to. There were television shows and movies which Chuck knew painted an unrealistic picture of a family. He knew he didn't fit into any of those 'son' character roles that he had seen. It was also true there were times when it was lonely growing up without any siblings. Looking back now, Chuck saw why his friends were, and are, so important to him because they helped to fill that missing void. Everything in place. Everything in place in Chuck's life and that included his friends, Alex, Bobby and Paul. They were Chuck's chosen brothers and that was all that mattered where they were concerned. Sometimes chosen family is just as important, or even more important, than your blood relatives.

Chuck lived in what they called a 'shotgun flat' on Shenandoah Avenue on the South side of St. Louis. It was an okay neighborhood and a nice central place to live within the city. It was right off Highway 44, which would take you anywhere you wanted to go in and outside of the city. It was near Tower Grove Park which had plenty of open area to run. It wasn't too far from nightlife or shopping. It wasn't a bad way to live. In fact, it was fucking perfect.

Shotgun houses were always rectangular and were usually no more than twelve feet wide, with a straight visual 'shot' from front to back. Chuck wasn't quite sure how wide his house was, because, come to think of it, he never decided to measure it before. He never had a need for that information. In St. Louis most of these houses were made from brick, and, in Chuck's case, his house was built in the mid 1920's. Due to the layout of the rooms from front to back, pocket doors were usually found to separate the rooms. This was also the case with Chuck's house, although he really didn't close them off too often unless maybe sometimes at bedtime. His house started with the living room right inside the front door. Then through a set of double pocket doors was Chuck's bedroom, then through another set of pocket doors the kitchen and then right off the kitchen was the bathroom at the back, behind what you would consider a regular type of house door. A white door, not that it fucking mattered or not, but most of the time in the city when Chuck saw a bathroom door in a house the motherfucker was white. Why white? He wasn't fucking sure even though it was just a useless observation. Useless, but for some weird reason true. Four rooms in a perfect line. That was what Chuck had. Four rooms in a perfect line, oh and of course a basement which he hoped to fix up someday. Something with a pool table and maybe a bar. A party room of sorts, but that was off in the future and something which remained in the back of his mind.

Alex parked his car in front of Chuck's house. He could tell he was one of the last of the group to arrive because the parking out front was tight and nearly non-existent. Of course, Paul was taking up two spaces with his pick-up, which irritated the shit out of Alex as he stepped out of the car onto the street. Walking onto the sidewalk he immediately heard his friends laughing inside the house as he knocked on the door while opening it and walking in. It was obvious to Alex that his friends decided to forego the convenience of edibles and instead light up a bong. Alex entered and saw the bong sitting firmly in the middle of the living room table along with his friends surrounding it. The room was full of the thick, sweet smoke which Alex had never really cared for. Now don't misunderstand Alex. He wasn't a prude. It wasn't that he looked down upon others who liked to partake of party favors, but in his case, he didn't like the way it made him feel, and, in the case of smoking, he found the smell almost unbearable. Being in a room with the smoke made his throat burn. He was sure that he had an allergy to smoke and tomorrow he would wake up still coughing and regretting being in the same room with it. Alex decided that Chuck was hoping he would loosen up and possibly get a contact high just by being in the same room. Chuck meant well, but the thick sickening sweet-smelling smoke made Alex physically uncomfortable.

Alex saw that everyone was sitting in the living room looking toward him has he walked in. After saying his hellos, Alex cut back through Chuck's bedroom into the kitchen to grab a beer from the fridge. He opened the refrigerator and pulled out a cold one as he felt Chuck's hand pat him on the back.

"Hey there bro, glad you made it." Alex thanked Chuck for inviting him and made a comment about needing a cold beer.

Chuck moved closer to Alex and whispered as if not to be overheard by the others in the other room. "This witchy chick Bobby brought is a trip. I mean, I just really can't figure her out. Is she a lesbian? Is she straight? I mean, is Bobby fucking her? Because we all know…"

Without a pause and in the same moment they both said in unison together, "Because Bobby will fuck anything with a hole." They both fist bumped and laughed out loud.

"Hey what's so funny you two?" Bobby said walking into the kitchen.

Alex and Chuck both continued laughing, walked out through the doorway into the bedroom and onward into the living room, "Just talking about the problem of too many mystery holes in the world," Chuck said. They left Bobby oblivious to them, while he dug in the fridge for a brew and a diet cola for his friend in the other room.

Alex and Chuck walked back into the living room. There they found Paul on the couch talking a blue streak, as usual, to this bohemian-looking girl who was trying to act interested in whatever he was incessantly talking about. You could clearly tell she was completely clueless and bored. This was not an unusual state of things for Paul who generally, if he was awake, was talking about something or another. Paul was the eternal expert on well, come to think of it, just about everything and anything you would want or could to talk about and even sometimes things no one gave a shit about.

"Why not give it a rest for a few minutes, professor," Chuck said to Paul entering the room, noticing Paul was clearly boring the literal fuck out the only female guest they had in the house.

Paul got up mumbling something about his full kidneys and needing to take a piss and the weather all at the same time while exiting the room through Chuck's bedroom. He cruised through the kitchen, where he passed Bobby on the way, and to the back of the house where the bathroom was located.

Chuck, playing a good host, hoping to possibly get laid by demonstrating his good manners and pleasant demeanor, introduced Alex by name to the strange-looking girl sitting on the couch. In truth, Chuck was high enough that he wasn't quite sure if he had introduced Alex by name or not when he had first arrived. Alex on the other hand was waiting for her name. By her looks Alex was expecting Chuck to say her name was Sabrina or Morgana or something witchy like that. It's a game Alex always played in his mind with himself when meeting someone new. You know how people usually resemble or fit into their name in some way? At least Alex felt most of us do. But have you ever met someone with who just did not conform or fit to their name at all? Someone who may look like a Pear, but they call them Apple. That sort of thing. How about a big brawly guy named Shirley? I mean, this could be a huge problem for someone and in Alex's mind he felt this was the case for the witchy girl sitting on the couch. Chuck then told him her name was Jane.

"Plain Jane" was something which instantly came to Alex's mind, and, to his surprise, the moment it did the witchy girl named Jane sitting on the couch looked at him and without him even uttering a single word she instantly responded, "Not Plain Jane. I am far from plain. I'm Jane. Just Jane. Jane is a family name. I'm named after my great grandmother."

Alex knew in some strange way he had just had his thoughts read by this girl and not only did this excite him, but it also confused him a bit as well.

The girl smiled at Alex's shocked expression, "Of course not... I.... but" Alex was obviously flustered as he blushed.

By the confused look on Chuck's face, you could tell he didn't have a clue as to what the fuck was going on between the two them and his thoughts immediately went back to deciding if Bobby was fucking this chick or not.

Jane laughed, "It's okay, blue is sexy," she said to Alex, confusing everyone in the room.

They felt it was strange for Jane to be saying this to a clearly gay Alex. There was no doubt what team Alex pitched or caught for.

Chuck decided he was not exactly sure he knew, or ever wanted to know, the answer to the top-or-bottom question concerning his friend. What the other guys didn't know was Jane calling Alex sexy was actually referring to the concealed electric blue jockstrap he was sporting under his jeans for support. Alex instantly knew she knew what she meant, and that made him turn even redder as they both began laugh.

"Touché," Alex said under his breath looking Jane directly in the eyes.

That is when her eyes caught his attention. He had never seen someone with such striking blue eyes before. A very deep blue that seemed to vibrate with energy. So vibrant, you would almost expect clouds and lightning bolts flashing within them. Alex sat down in a chair next to the couch still flustered by the whole experience and became rather quiet because he was sure he had just made a huge bumbling fool of himself. Jane sat back, smiling with a sigh, because it was clearly a checkmate, and she knew she was way ahead of the game where Alex was concerned.

To answer the burning question in the room, Jane and Bobby were just good friends, which Chuck was relieved to hear because it just might give him a fighting chance. Jane and Bobby had gone to high school together and, until recently, hadn't seen each other for two years. You see, Bobby moved to a different school district at the end of middle school, and it wasn't until college that all the boys completely reconnected. At any rate, Bobby had just reconnected with Jane after bumping into her at a local restaurant. To both of their surprise, Jane was his waitress and was also the manager, waiting tables because her server hadn't shown up that night for their shift.

To be clear, Jane was never physically or emotionally attracted to Bobby. He wasn't an unattractive guy he just wasn't her kind of attractive. Too clean-cut and all-American looking. Jane liked a tatted, rougher looking, bad boy sort of guy. Long hair was definitely a must. A man with long hair made Jane wet fast than any other feature. So, they remained friends and that was a great arrangement for both. The two of them could go for long periods of time not seeing each other and then they would reconnect, and it would be just like they had been hanging out all along. This was one of those times and they had been hanging out quite a bit again.

Jane knew Chuck was interested in her and she also knew Chuck was also somewhat of a ladies' man, which she clearly wanted nothing to do with. That was a recipe to end her long-time friendship with Bobby. She knew guys and she knew sleeping with Chuck would be like sleeping with Bobby's brother. Besides, the guys were close, and she would never step into a situation where it would make Bobby uncomfortable. Of course, being with Paul was completely out of the question and off the table because she could see he was someone she was only going to be able to take in small doses. Very small doses. In fact, the jury was still out whether she even liked him enough to be around him more than once.

These four guys were so completely different but somehow Jane admired and could see how their friendship worked. Jane could feel she would become an important part of their group as well, but she just couldn't pin down where and how she would fit into it all of it. She had the gift of knowing when she would have some type of future with people she met. She knew it, and it was never wrong. The universe didn't always reveal everything to her. Jane always felt that it would have been boring for the universe and her guides to let her in on everything. It was better if most visions - if you would like to call them that - came to her in glimpses and not smashing through her mind in full living technicolor one hundred percent of the time. That would be just too much and way too intense. Besides, she did enjoy having some uncertainty - which led to excitement. A book already written would be boring. Jane wanted the power to write her own book of life, or least give herself the impression she was.

Have your ever lived a moment when you somehow have this feeling or super knowledge that you are on the threshold of something which will change everything about you and your life? You often hear about car crash survivors who talk about knowing something was about to happen to them beforehand and even some who see the oncoming accident mere moments before it happens. For some reason, you have a feeling to turn right when you should have gone left. Plans fall through and something bad happens in the place where you had just been or where you planned on being. Often these moments seem brighter and crisper in our minds. Almost as if a hypersonic HD is switched on. It is not always a harbinger of bad luck and can be completely the opposite as well. It can be a prediction of something positive. Many new parents describe this knowing and feeling at the birth of a child. How much more of a life-changing moment can you experience other than bringing new life into the world? That's a life-changing moment and feeling. With that moment comes energy.

Jane sat on the couch looking at the guys talking back and forth. She was not really hearing what they were talking about. She knew this feeling, but she couldn't put her finger on what or why she was feeling it. But, looking at the guys laughing and joking, she knew something was coming. Something was getting ready to happen. Something significant.

She slightly jumped as Bobby turned the conversation toward her, "Jane? You with us?" Bobby asked with a smile, but she could tell by his eyes he knew something was up with her.

He knew when she got quiet it was usually because she was getting some type of message or feeling. Whatever you want to call it; something.

"Yeah of course I'm with you. I am just a little lost in my thoughts tonight, I guess." Jane said with an uncomfortable smile.

Bobby knew Jane well enough to know she was deep in thought for a reason. In his mind he thought maybe Paul had creeped her out a little earlier in the evening. Paul could be a little much to take at times and never knew when to shut the fuck up. Paul had absolutely the worst people skills and Bobby knew this. Earlier he saw Paul was clearly intent on bending Jane's ear. Of course, there was the obvious reason - they all were a touch high - and he knew Jane was most likely feeling some sort of paranoia in a room of new people. It was just in her nature, and he knew it. He didn't think much about the forced smile on her face when he brought her out of her thoughts because he knew it was just part of who Jane was. When they were in high school some of the kids thought Jane was stuck up or arrogant because they misread these quiet spells as her secretly thinking about how she did not like them. In fact,

that was ridiculous. The Jane he knew wasn't that
way at all. She was too grounded for arrogance,
but she was not a fool either. She had always
marched to her own drum, and however witchy his
friends might think Jane appeared to them now,
they had no idea how gothic and witchy her
adolescence was. Bobby laughed, remembering her
heavily lined eyes at the age of sixteen. Through
the years Jane took her persona from Halloween
horror show to a more sophisticated and grounded
bohemian woman. An earth mother of sorts, and it
fit her well. Hell, he still laughed when he thought
of his own geeky ass at sixteen. He and Jane were
no different than anyone else. We all change. Yes,
that was the truth of it. We all change.

Jane reached down next to the couch and
pulled out something from a large black bag she
had brought with her.

"You guys want to have a little fun?" she
asked as she laid an old, intricate spirit board onto
the coffee table in front of the guys.

They instantly got excited seeing it, "Do you
know how to work one of these things?" Paul
asked with excited interest sitting forward in his
chair.

"Of course," Jane replied with a giggle.

She had worked the board most of her life
because it was given to her by her grandmother.
She had taught Jane how to work the board years
ago - along with many other things.

"The idea is to talk to ghosts or something
along those lines. I mean, I have never done one
before, but I have seen them in movies and shit,'
said Paul in his usual run-on way of speaking.

"It opens up a doorway to the spirit world in
a way," Bobby said sitting on the floor moving
closer to the table and the board. "Jane is really

good at it, and we are in good hands if she is leading the communication," Bobby said with a wink to Jane.

Jane smiled back at him and was happy he was heading off the eventual questions which she knew Paul would dive into if Bobby hadn't addressed it first.

"Nothing to fear. We are in good hands," Bobby reiterated once again reaching to place his fingers on the triangular shaped planchette sitting on top of the board.

Jane saw him do this and immediately cut him off with a look at his hands and then a look toward Alex. Bobby seemed somewhat confused and maybe a little jealous because it was clear Jane was indicating she wanted to work the board with Alex. Jane had felt an immediate connection with Alex the moment she met him. She could instantly tune into his thoughts, and she was curious to examine this connection with him further. A session on the board would be a perfect way to further evaluate what was happening between them. Of course, she knew Alex was gay. This had nothing to do with sexual attraction. This was more on a spiritual level. A sexual connection and a spiritual connection were two very different things, and she clearly understood the difference.

There are a whole lot of people in this world who do not have a clue as to how those two things differ. They run around the world fucking their spiritual connections because they don't know any better. In fact, Jane felt this easily could be proven statistically with the fact almost half of all modern marriages ended in divorce. Well, at least forty percent. It was very rare for a couple to have both a spiritual and sexual connection. Those type of connections were rare, extremely rare. At least that is what she thought now, but hey, that could change.

"Here, come sit down on the other side of the table," Jane motioned to Alex.

Alex looked at her perplexed and then looked at Bobby, He wasn't sure if he wanted to even do this, and he didn't want to offend his friend, so he asked Bobby, "Are you okay with this?"

Bobby smiled making space for Alex at the coffee table across from Jane, "Sure man, I have done this way too many times. You give it a try. You're in good hands," he said looking from Alex to Jane.

Jane smiled and pulled a white candle from her bag. Alex knelt closer to the table.

"Why the candle?" Alex asked, as Jane put a flame to the wick to light it.

"You know Alex, I could write a whole book on candles and the importance of burning them for your life, your spirit, and, in this case, for communication with the other side of the veil. Think of the candle in this way; a candle symbolizes a person. The wax of the candle represents the physical body. The wick reflects the mind. And of course, the flame is then the spirit. The color of the candle is important too. In this case, the candle is white. I chose a white candle because it is sort of a catch-all candle that will help ground us, cleanse the area, help keep negative energies at bay and attract clarity in our communication with the spirit world. In doing this for the first time with you, I thought white might be best, instead of the normal brown candle I use for grounding," Jane explained.

Alex nodded his head in understanding. The color of this candle in the future would be something Jane would question time and time again in the days to come. Had she chosen the white candle wisely? Did it even make a difference or play a crucial role in the doorway she was about to open with Alex?

Chuck flipped off the light switch to the room leaving everyone sitting quietly in the candlelight. The group watched as Jane showed Alex how to gently place his hands on the triangular planchette in front of him.

"Now Alex, I need you to concentrate with me. I want you to do nothing but clear your mind and let the planchette begin to slowly move by itself on the board," Jane said softly, almost as if she was hypnotizing Alex and coaxing him into communication with the spirits.

The planchette didn't move over the board immediately. For an instant, Jane thought that maybe Alex wasn't going to be as compatible with her spirit as she originally thought. But, as soon as this unfounded fear hit her mind, the triangular planchette with its round hole began to move in a circular motion on top of the letters imprinted onto the board. Jane let the movement gain in momentum and strength.

Once she was sure the connection was strong, she asked her first question, "Is there someone here with us?" she always hated this part of the initial communication because it seemed so hokey and canned.

The planchette responded instantly moving over to the YES which was imprinted in the top left corner of the board. It then returned immediately back into its circular motion.

Chuck shivered a bit. Later he would tell Paul he could have sworn the temperature in the room had dropped a good ten to twenty degrees. An exaggeration on his part? Well, maybe, but the room did feel like it got cooler that night when the communication began.

"What is your name?" Jane asked, but the planchette continued in its circular motion, without answering.

Jane gave it a moment and asked again, "What is your name?" Again, the planchette continued moving in a circular motion without stopping to answer.

Understanding she wasn't getting a name Jane decided to ask, "Are you female?" The planchette swerved up to the NO imprinted on the top right-hand side of the board.

Paul excitedly whispered the obvious, "It's a man."

Chuck shot a glare in Paul's direction which clearly indicated, "Duh, motherfucker." Paul blushed a little, sitting with his back firmly against the couch.

What followed over the next few minutes was a barrage of questions. Some were answered by forming words with letters that Bobby would record on a notebook in front of them. At least it seemed as if it were just a few minutes. In fact, the session lasted over an hour. One question would lead into another, but never during this initial part of the questioning did the spirit want to communicate its name to the group. What they began to get instead was that, indeed, he was a man. He knew he was dead, and he said he died somewhere in the mid 1800's, from what they could gather. He claimed to have been a slave and when they asked him where he lived, he spelled out M-I-S-S-O-U-R-I.

The story began to come together. The group learned through the communication that the slave was sold, beaten, castrated and hung. Those four words were spelled out over and over again to the questions being thrown out to him. The communication seemed to be slowing and at that moment Jane decided to try for a name one more time.

"What is your name?" The planchette paused and then began to strategically move over letters on the board.

Alex, clearly excited and completely into the session, began reading the letters out loudly, M-O-S-E-S.

Everyone was clearly excited at the revelation of the name, and they all said, "Moses," looking excitedly at each other as they said it.

Then the planchette immediately went down off the bottom of the board passing over the imprinted word GOODBYE.

There were three strong knocks instantly at the front door breaking the spell. This startled the group, and they simultaneously jumped. Then, feeling silly, they began laughing together, exclaiming how it had scared the shit out of each of them.

Chuck got up casually and headed to answer the door turning on the light. He wasn't sure who it could be. It was starting to get a little late for people to just show up. He opened the front door, looking out onto the porch and into the night, but saw no one.

"There is no one there," Chuck said closing the door somewhat puzzled, turning to look at his friends.

"Probably some neighborhood kids playing Ding Dong Dash or in this case Knock Knock Dash," he said laughing.

Jane interrupted Chuck, "Not two. Three," Jane replied instantly. Chuck looking at her confused as he sat back down.

"Three. There were three knocks not two," Jane said seriously.

Chuck looked at her and replied with a slight bit of sarcasm in his voice, "Okay, three. What the fuck difference does it make how many times they knocked?"

Jane looking seriously at Chuck, "In the spirit world it does matter how many knocks there were. Spiritually, when you hear knocking on doors, it can either be a warning of danger, or even a reminder to be cautious. It just seems to me that three knocks coming at the instant the communication ended on the board with the 'GOODBYE' is something we should maybe pay attention to. Listen, it was most likely nothing. Some kids playing or someone got a wrong house number and realized it before you got to the door. But then again it could mean something. It could be a message, or Chuck you could have just invited something to step in here with us."

Chuck laughed nervously, "You can't be fucking serious? It was just some kids I promise you." Jane eventually nodded in agreement, feeling she was beginning to irritate Chuck with her questions.

When knocks come in threes Jane knew it was something wanting to come in, but exactly what, wasn't clear. She sat there thinking as the three guys passed the bong around between themselves, leaving out herself and Alex. Jane knew doorways were considered thresholds when dealing with spirit. Chuck opened a closed door after hearing knocking without taking the time to see if there was anyone standing there before opening it. That's asking for trouble. He had a peephole in the door, and there was a window next to the door and he didn't even bother to look. What the fuck was that all about? He could have been opening the door to anyone or anything. He might have just opened the door and let something in. Could it have been the slave Moses they had been communicating with? Sure, that was possible. Jane couldn't count how many times in her lifetime she has seen or heard about spirits entering through doors and windows into the physical world from the spiritual realm. How many urban legends and superstitions were there in the world about this? She began thinking about the vampire legends and how Dracula couldn't enter unless you opened the door and invited him in. Of course, Chuck didn't physically extend an invitation to the air, but just the simple act of opening the door and stepping onto the porch could be enough to say come on in.

Jane was a little freaked out and she was getting tired. She wanted to go home, knowing she would have to be the chauffer. Looking over at Bobby - who had clearly had one too many beers and one too many draws on the bong - she realized he was not getting behind the wheel with her in the car. She leaned over to tell Bobby she was ready to go. Alex agreed. He was also getting tired, and the party broke up quickly after that with everyone leaving. Within five minutes or so Chuck found himself alone, taking some beer bottles to throw away in the trash can in the kitchen. He looked around the kitchen and decided he would clean up and take the trash out in the morning. He turned off the kitchen light and walked back into his bedroom and on into the living room to make sure his front door was locked, and his alarm was set. He turned around to walk back into the bedroom and the kitchen light came on by itself. Of course it startled him, but he convinced himself he hadn't pulled the old kitchen light switch all the way down and it flipped back up on its own. He laughed turning the light off once again and got ready for bed.

Chapter 3
Nightmare

Alex was tired. It had been a great night with his friends. This was not unusual by any stretch of his imagination, because Alex usually had a great time with his friends. He loved their company, and, even within his darkest moments, they always seemed to raise his mood. Alex found himself humming a song he had just heard in the car on his way home as he fumbled for his apartment key. He finally found it through his increasingly tired and blurring eyes. He put the key into the lock and turned it. The lock opened immediately, and Alex stepped into his apartment, flipping on the light switch located next to the wall. He moved into the entryway closing and locking the door behind him. He put his keys and wallet on a small table inside the door.

Alex had found the night's whole spirit contact experience with Jane fascinating. He knew he liked Jane and was glad he had met her and could understand why Bobby had been friends with her for so long. He thought the whole board thing was interesting, even though he found himself outside of the situation, he wasn't sure what he believed about the entire experience. Sure, it was fun, and he had to admit it was something completely different for once. A great way to break the monotony of the busy droning on of his life this semester. The whole board thing had been so charged with adrenaline. Adrenaline and dopamine are powerful things, that when triggered in the body, can cause all sorts of feelings and reactions.

Alex continued thinking about it all, and he wondered if it all had been happening because of their simple desire of wanting it to be true. Of them wanting it to be real. You can say a whole lot about human nature where it was all concerned. The desire to be able to project your feelings about your own existence onto something else, even if it is just for a moment or two, is a powerful thing. It is simple projection. Everyone is constantly grappling with issues in their lives - day in and day out. Feelings are powerful things with an energy of their own. It is nice, even for a moment, to be able to give your feelings wings and let them be projected at you through something else. Some might even say it can be a type of healing in itself. Whatever the reason, it had felt somewhat cleansing for Alex.

However, there were a few things which sent the red flags running up the proverbial pole for Alex. He was now thinking (in the middle of the night after a few beers and most likely some kind of contact high) the whole sympathetic slave story that came out of the session seemed too stereotypical and melodramatic in so many ways. He struggled, trying to put the entire thing together in his own mind. The whole Moses idea was something you would expect from some type of low-budget horror film where people are fighting to save the soul of some slave who's haunting the plantation. Everyone has seen these cringe-worthy stories repeatedly.

Turn on your television any night of the week to any of the so-called haunted investigation reality tv shows and there will be someone on the screen selling drivel like this before running and screaming though darkened hallways and rooms. Alex could never understand why they were investigating the location in the first place if they were so damn frightened. It seemed illogical that if they were indeed there to investigate, why did they run away screaming any time something happened? Why were they even fucking doing it?

"Research my ass," Alex said under his breath slipping his shoes off.

These idiots never stayed in the room long enough to get a good look at anything. Alex giggled to himself at the thought of grown men running around screaming in the dark the first moment a slight breeze moved a door.

Alex opened the refrigerator and took a swig right out of the carton of milk which he found invitingly sitting on the shelf.

This was something which drove his mother insane when he lived at home. But now, it was an action of rebellion and toast to his independence, "Cheers," Alex said, laughing out loud as he toasted to the air with the carton.

He replaced the milk and closed the refrigerator. He walked into the living room and flopped down onto the couch, still thinking about the night. The whole slave story from the night ran through his mind on replay. The whole scenario just seemed way too convenient for him. It seemed like something too easy. Alex felt that everything about it was just so damn easily suggestive. Look, you begin getting these random words on this board and then a room full of people take them and run with them, fitting them into some sort of scenario. Sort of like a psychological word game. Now that made sense. He was sure he was onto it. It was making order from chaos.

People do it hundreds of times a day - just to keep moving - without going insane from all the chaos and nonsense they are surrounded by everywhere and at every angle. It makes sense to Alex that they had taken the chaos of these words and questions together and made it make some sort of logical sense. The human psyche craves order. The next thing you know, they came up with a male castrated slave with the name Moses. In fact, the name Moses had inherent problems of its own because it is just too convenient and too easy of a name pick for a slave, of all things, and it is not just because of its obvious biblical context.

Alex remembered from his American history classes that many slave owners named their male slaves things like Isaac, Abraham and yes, Moses. These names were so common that if anyone studied American history, which he had, it would be a name which could easily be brought up subconsciously as a slave name. Subconsciously being the key word in referring to all of it for Alex because he was sure, without a doubt, in the middle of the session, everyone believed it was indeed real. In the board session they believed they were talking to a slave named Moses because it gave some type of order to the chaos of the random words and leading questions.

Then, of course, there was the idea of castration which kept coming up over and over. This really didn't make a whole lot of sense to Alex. Slaves were human assets for the plantation owners. The fact that they could reproduce was considered a huge benefit. Think about it, each slave was worth a certain dollar amount. The engine of the slave trade was based upon the dollar and asset holdings. Every single outcome was economically positive for the plantation owner, and he would have made sure to protect his best interests at all costs. As cold and wrong as it was, it was economically advantageous for him that his slaves were able to reproduce. He would not damage what he considered an asset. It would be like a factory owner destroying the machines that produced his product. Alex was putting aside all the human factors in his mind. As stomach-churning as it all was, the slave owners considered their slaves property and not people at all. They would not typically castrate them because each young strong male slave was a possible money-making machine. You don't damage your own property and assets. You don't break the money maker. It was just not simply in the best interest of the slave owner.

The Arabs on the other hand did castrate their slaves, but in practice, it was just not something an American slave owner would do. It just seemed like something someone would come up with who didn't know better, but the fact remains "castration" was spelled out on the board not once, but a handful of times. There was, of course, a possibility the slave owner would castrate a male slave out of anger or for sadistic purposes. You cannot rule out crazy when dealing with people at any time in history. The questions kept rolling through Alex's mind one after another and in the quiet of the night those thoughts began to blur and, in that blur, they slowly began to turn into sleep. A deep sleep with Alex giving over and falling into the darkness of his dreams.

Alex found himself standing in a darkened room. There was a quiet sound of a slow, almost drawn-out dripping noise, which was the only thing to break the initial silence of his dream.

Drip, drip, drip.

The sound of liquid droplets hitting the floor.

In the darkness, Alex felt confused and frightened because he did not know where he was. Nothing looked familiar, and a slow growing panic began to set in as he looked for a way out - a way to escape being engulfed by the endless darkened room.

The sound of the dripping continued with in an almost rhythmic beat, which began to combine with the beating of Alex's own heart.

Drip thump, drip thump, drip thump.

Arms outstretched, Alex continued moving forward into the darkness. He was searching and searching - but finding nothing. The panic was setting in and he could feel the beating of his heart increasing with the pace of the dripping noise which continued to echo all around him.

Drip thump thump, drip thump thump, drip thump thump.

There was nothing there in the darkness he could discern. Nothing but the continual dripping and the sound of his heart.

Ever so slightly, in the distance, Alex began to hear something else within the sounds of his heartbeat-punctuated drips. It began softly at first, and then began to grow. The sound was faint, but audible.

Alex wasn't sure what it was, but he somehow instinctively knew he needed to follow it. It was the only thing he could do. He needed to find the source of the sound.

He began walking in the direction of the new sound which continued to grow. First, it sounded like a whisper and then turned into a faint cry. Alex was sure it was the sound of a man crying.

He continued searching in the vastness of the darkness until he saw two walls begin to rise in front of him. They rose so high he could not see where the top of them ended. They were jutting outward and where the two huge walls met in the middle it formed a triangle which, in return, formed a corner. In the corner of the meeting walls, Alex saw the source of the crying sounds he had been hearing. There, in a crouched position, was a shirtless, crying man. Alex could tell by his dress he was a slave. Alex slowly and cautiously walked up to the man and asked, "Hey, are you okay? Can I help you?"

No movement.

No answer.

Just crying.

Alex noticed the man's bloodied left hand was laying across his lap, hanging over the side of his leg. The source of the dripping sound became evident as Alex saw blood coming from his fingertips, falling into a puddle onto the floor.

Drip, drip, drip.

The man continued crying, unmoving and unstartled by Alex's words.

Drip, drip, drip.

"Seriously, can you answer me. Please sir. Do you know where we are?"

Nothing.

No reaction.

No movement.

The man continued sobbing and the blood continued to drip.

Drip, drip, drip.

Alex stepped forward now, standing right next to the man, looking down at him. Cautiously Alex reached down, lightly touching the man's shoulder.

"Hey, can I hel..."

Alex's words were cut off in an instant as the man sprung quickly into action. A scream began to grow from the man's now open and gaping mouth. His rotten teeth jutted out in all directions. He turned on Alex quickly and grabbed Alex's arm with both of his hands, his sharp fingernails digging into his flesh. The man's grip was painful as instant panic washed over Alex's entire body. The man's hands felt hot and wet on Alex's skin as the rusty smell of the man's blood filled the air. The momentum of grabbing Alex's arm spun the man around and Alex could see the crotch of his ragged pants. The pants were soaked in blood. Alex knew instantly the man had been castrated. Everything seemed to go in slow motion around Alex as he began to focus on the man's face. A slave's face.

The eyes.

"Oh my God, his eyes."

The eyes were nothing but glowing white!

"MOSES!" Alex screamed into the darkness.

Alex woke violently as he jumped up off his couch. He was fighting with the air trying to flee from his nightmare. In the violence of his flailing, Alex tripped, and his body came smashing down onto the coffee table in front of him sending books and magazines flying into the air. The legs of the table collapsed under the weight of his falling body. There was an instant searing pain to Alex's ribs causing him to scream even louder as he came completely out of the dream, crashing back into the world of the living.

<u>Chapter 4</u>
Hospital

Alex's eyes opened slowly to the world around him. The pain in his side became instantly intense as he woke from a restless sleep. The door to his hospital room opened swiftly and with it came a nurse, rushing in to check his vitals and give him a dose of pain medication. The one thing Alex noticed immediately about her was her kind face. She had kind and caring eyes. Alex could feel the medicine as it worked its way from the syringe into his IV and blissfully into the veins of his arm, replacing his pain with an overall welcomed numbness. Alex could clearly remember the events of the night before. He could remember the nightmare. He could remember waking up falling. The smashing of his body against the collapsing of the table. He remembered his frantic call for help to 911 and the rush to the hospital. He had two broken ribs and a punctured lung from his fall. He had a tube which ran from a hole in his side to a bag which trapped fluids so the air pumping in through a catheter could help reinflate his lung. It had been a serious fall, but he was going to be okay. That really was all that mattered to him at this moment. He was going to be okay. The medication not only helped him with the pain, but it also helped him to relax. Alex closed his eyes as the nurse continued about her business around the room.

Everything about last night seemed so surreal to him now. The whole evening had turned quickly into one bad dream leaving him damaged, hurting and scared.

He thought of the old nun from his childhood Catholic school saying, "You must deal with the consequences of your actions, young man."

Alex was never a favorite of the old bitter nun who clearly did not like him for whatever reason - of which he was never quite sure. However, as a child, it does cause confusion when an agent of God doesn't like you. This amused Alex as he thought about it because it had turned into a theme for him throughout his life. There was always someone claiming to be connected to Christ, God and the Holy Ghost who was convinced Alex was indeed one of the damned. Alex was sure that, even at a young age, the old nun had picked up on the fact he was gay. Sort of like a holy gaydar to uncover the sins of the wannabe buggers who the Church had condemned to eternal damnation. Of course he did not believe this. The sheer irony of the number of priests that were gay was not lost on Alex either. He also knew there was no invisible karmic price tag hanging around his neck because he happened to be gay. He knew he was gay, and he knew it at a very young age. It was never a decision for him. The decision was made for him by nature and God himself.

Alex sat up straighter as the nurse fluffed his pillows. He opened his eyes to see her as she spoke, "Comfortable?" Alex nodded yes to the nurse's kind smiling face.

"Good, you just rest," she said as Alex closed his eyes once more to the sound of the nurse checking his connections and tubes, emptying and changing various fluids.

He heard her footsteps as she walked into the bathroom. The medication had him completely relaxed and he felt as if he was sinking deeper and deeper into the mattress on the bed, almost as if his body and the mattress were becoming one. The nurse was back at his bedside once again as Alex opened his eyes slightly for an instant to see her. She smiled at him. He felt extremely thankful in this moment for this stranger whose entire intention was to care for him. He was a stranger to her and yet here they were. He reflected on that type of selflessness for a moment. Sure, he knew the nurse was paid for the work she did, but let's face it, this type of dedication to people took a lot more than just a paycheck. At least Alex hoped he wasn't just a paycheck. He preferred the idea this nurse was some sort of angel of mercy, or a Florence Nightingale if you will. This amused Alex because he was sure it was the drugs fueling his imagination.

"Alex?" The nurses voice cut through his thoughts. Alex slowly opened his eyes.
"Help me," the voice had changed. The white eyes of Moses were looking at him, through him. They were face to face with each other as Moses hovered over him.

Alex jumped as if he were falling with a startled sound coming from his lips as pain shot through his side. He blinked for a moment and Moses was no longer there.

The nurse's head peeked out of the bathroom doorway asking, "You alright hon?"

A confused Alex nodded to her, "Just a dream," he said sheepishly.

She nodded and smiled at him saying something about it being the medication and went back about her business. Alex lay in the bed with a tear falling from the corner of his eye because he knew it was not just the medication. He could feel this overwhelming feeling of not only fear but sadness rising within him. You might think he would be in a state of panic but even to Alex's surprise he wasn't. The panic demon was not something that was within him at all. This was something deeper. It's funny because panic is something you would usually associate with fear. This was not what Alex was feeling at all. This was a deep, more controlled fear he was feeling. This feeling was darker.

The nurse told him she would check back in on him in a bit and was out the door before Alex had the moment to react. She left him with his thoughts and the silence of the room. Alex lay thinking and his thoughts floated from one thing to another. He closed his eyes for a moment and when he opened them again Jane and Bobby were standing next to his bed looking down at him. Their faces were horror-stricken and worried, which seemed almost comical to Alex.

"It really looks a lot worse than it actually is," Alex struggled to speak through a dry throat.

He reached for the cup of water and ice on his tray and took a sip looking around the room. In the corner, Paul was sitting in a chair looking at him awkwardly.

Chuck was leaning on the window ledge looking at him, "You scared the fuck out of us bro."

Leave it to Chuck to get right to the point of things.

"I scared the fuck out of myself," Alex replied, pushing the buttons on the remote control on his bed to sit up a bit further.

"How long are you going to be in this... this... room?" Paul asked struggling to find the word hospital but not being sure if he even should say the word "hospital" in the first place.

Alex smiled at Paul being uncomfortable and wanting to put him at ease. "They say I should be able to go home in a few days. Once I get this hose removed from my side which is helping my lung to expand."

Alex noticed the color drain from Paul's face, "Trust me buddy it's going to be okay. It looks and sounds a lot worse than it is," Alex said soothingly hoping to calm his friend's nerves.

These guys were like his brothers. He knew if he was hurting, they were hurting as well. They were connected in that way. He was doing his best to relieve their worry.

Jane stood beside Alex lying in the bed. She wanted so much to open the conversation with him about what had happened to him the night before. But, standing there looking around the room she felt the whole scene had just too much of a fucked-up, Dorothy-waking-up-back-in-Kansas vibe. Asking what the fuck happened, seemed like it might be the wrong or inappropriate thing right now. But when did she ever worry about what was appropriate, and she was pretty fucking sure etiquette did not have this one covered. Fuck sensitivity, she wanted to know and for the past five minutes she had been standing there listening to the others trying to dance around it.

"Okay, since no one else is brave enough to ask the obvious question, I will. What the fuck happened last night?" There, she asked it, letting the cat out of the bag.

Chuck nearly fell off the side of the window ledge as all shocked eyes immediately went to Jane. It was so instantaneous and such a double take Alex had to laugh. A painful laugh.

"It hurts to laugh," Alex said holding onto his side.

Jane continued, "I'm sorry. But seriously what happened to you?"

Alex adjusted in the bed again as he began to tell them everything. About how he got home. What he had been thinking. How he fell asleep on the couch. The nightmare. Everything. They listened intently hanging on every word he had to say. You could tell by the looks on their faces Alex was scaring them, which wasn't his intention at all, but he really did not know how else to tell them. He was just giving them the facts. The fear on their faces was somehow strangely reassuring. He had been more worried that they would think he was freaking insane.

However, he knew in this moment they were understanding the seriousness of what he was saying, "Honestly, in some ways I feel as if I am losing my mind. I know what I have just told you sounds crazy, but it is what happened and is still happening."

When he finished telling the story there was nothing but silence between them. Everyone was trying to take it all in and understand it as fully as they could.

It was Bobby who finally broke the quiet, "Well, that is some serious fucked-up shit."

In an instant everyone wanted to talk at once. Ideas were shot back and forth. Everyone talking over each other. Everyone was talking, except Paul, who sat in the chair looking seriously at the floor.

The talking paused for a moment and Paul took the chance and spoke, "I am having dreams too. I have been dreaming about… well you know… I have been dreaming about Moses. I had a dream much like Alex's last night and then again this morning. I mean, I thought it was just my overactive imagination, but after hearing Alex's description of what is going on with him it is not too fucking different. I mean, shit, this is some fucked up crap and I am not sure I like it. I am not sure I like it at all."

The group sat in complete silence, listening as Paul emptied his thoughts.

Paul continued speaking turning toward Jane, "Seems to me, Jane, you have some fucking explaining to do. After all, this was your fucking idea with the spirit board and bullshit."

Bobby turned to Paul immediately as Jane grabbed his arm, "Now wait a damn minute. You are not going to lay this at her feet alone. You were there and you were just as excited as everyone else about jumping into it and using the board. You don't get to play fucking victim this time Paul. You couldn't fucking wait, but now you want to put the blame on her. It is not her fucking fault, you simpering fucking idiot. It is all our fault - and that includes you, too."

The anger was obviously growing within Paul as Bobby verbally lashed out at him.

Paul stood suddenly to his feet, pointing his finger, "Fuck you man. Fuck you and fuck her too."

Paul stormed out of the room leaving Jane holding tighter onto Bobby's arm whispering, "Let him go."

Jane understood that Paul would eventually come to his senses, and she didn't want Bobby to do something that would push their friendship to a point of no return. Words are something you sometimes cannot take back once they are said, and throwing punches would be even worse.

"I'll go talk to him," Chuck said calmly.

Chuck was usually a stabilizing force where Paul was concerned. He understood him better than most and could be way more tolerant of his outbursts than the others could.

"He doesn't mean what he is saying you guys. That was obviously fear talking. We need to give him a moment and give him the benefit of the doubt here. This has been a pretty fucked up twenty-four hours. We're all more than a little on edge." Chuck walked toward the door and out of the room.

Alex looked at Jane. Everyone seemed to be missing the most important and frightening point of what just happened. This wasn't about where to place the blame at all.

"He's dreaming about him too," Alex said.

Jane looked down at Alex sitting in the bed, "What?" She wasn't quite sure she had heard what he had just said.

"Jane, he is having the same fucking dreams. How does that fucking work?" Alex said looking at her seriously wanting some sort of answer.

Jane had no answer for him, but he was right. Something was alarmingly fucked up here and she knew deep in her gut it was just the beginning. Not even twenty-four hours after the first contact had been made and their world was already turning upside down. Upside down because of Moses.

<u>Chapter 5</u>
Healing

His alarm sounded, waking Alex from a deep, drug-induced sleep. Alex lay looking at his bedroom ceiling feeling grateful that he was at home, even though he had already been out of the hospital for a few weeks. The pain was still there but with each passing day it seemed to lessen. The pills didn't stop the barrage of nightmares, but they helped him get some rest in between. He needed the rest to heal. His injuries were healing. The throbbing pain he had felt in his side had now subsided. He lay there looking at the ceiling of his bedroom thinking about everything - and nothing at all - at the same time.

Is that possible? To think of everything and nothing at all at the same time? Alex felt indeed it was possible, due to his racing thoughts which never seemed to land on anything for any substantial length of time. Alex knew his concentration on just about everything had been completely off over the last few weeks. The only thing he could think of for any amount of time was Moses. Who was Moses and why was he occupying so much of his dreams and his waking thoughts?

The whole idea of Moses had become an obsession for him. Alex knew this, but what he couldn't figure out was why. The nightmares had not changed at all from when they first began. They played out in much the same way every single time without too much variance from their script.

Room. Dark. Drip. Walls. Corner. Crying. Man. Drip. Blood. Pain. White eyes. Moses.

The same scenario over and over. The nightmares were losing their ability to frighten him. It was much like watching the same horror film over and over when the predictable fright in them fades with each additional viewing. It was much the same for Alex and his nightmare of Moses. Over time the fear began to retreat leaving Alex with a skewed sense of just what in the fuck was happening to him and who in the fuck Moses was.

Alex began to spend hours at a time online, trying to find out everything he could, but again, Moses was a common name for a slave. Then there was the question in his mind about just how extensive the slave trade had been in St. Louis. This turned out to be an easier question to answer. Under Missouri law, slaves were considered property and were sold at auctions. This was a common practice in St. Louis. One of the largest and most prominent of these operations in the mid-1800s was known as Lynch's Slave Pen, owned by Bernard Lynch. It had been located in the area where Ballpark Village, Busch Stadium, high-rise condos and a parking garage now stood today. Here, enslaved people were put up for auction and sold to the highest bidder. They were subjected to all sorts of abuse during the process and often families were ripped apart, never to see each other again. They were stripped almost completely naked and treated like cattle.

Alex had to wonder if Moses had been sold on the auction block there. To Alex's shock, he found the St. Louis Jesuits were slave owners as well. He is not sure why this shocked him as much, but it did all the same. In fact, the St. Louis Jesuits had a slave name Moses who was purchased from a West Virginia planation and brought to St. Louis. As he dug deeper into the history of the slave trade, it struck him how determined the ancestors of these victims are - still fighting to this day to solidify their family members place in history. It is a history which they had to fight against unbelievable odds in order for it to be told.

Alex found the account of a man who was looking for information on his great-grandfather and family. He was finally able to track down where his great-grandfather and family had been kept as slaves. The house and the land in Georgia were still owned by the same family and had been passed down through the generations. The man went there to see if he could get answers from the family who still lived in the house today. He walked up to the front door and knocked. A white southern gentleman answered the door. He introduced himself and asked the man if he had any information about his family history that he could share with him. The old man told him to wait a moment and retreated into the house, emerging a few moments later with a handful of yellowing documents.

"You want your family history, well here it is," the old man said as he lit a match to the papers and sent them up in flames. "Now, take the ashes and get the hell off my land."

This is just one example of why slave history is so difficult to track down. In fact, in the case of Lynch's Slave Pen, the ancestors of the auctioned victims were still trying to get a memorial to remember the atrocities which were done to their families.

Alex was not naïve by any means. He knew racism was alive and well in the country and in fact it was thriving. Why was it so hard for these families to gather their history and be remembered? What purpose does it serve to keep it hidden? Is it shame or guilt on the part of the slave owner's ancestors? Questions like these came up repeatedly causing Alex to think. Alex thought about a trip he took to Berlin years ago with his family. The Holocaust is not ignored there at all. The names of the murdered are remembered and memorialized. You do not see flags and statues which glorify the people who imprisoned and killed the Jews for nothing more than being who they were. Alex couldn't understand the contrast with Germany embracing its difficult history versus the United States dealing with its own.

"Say their names," Alex found himself saying under his breath.

Saying their names was the only way to keep their memories alive and fighting for their history was the only way they could assure those memories would remain alive for future generations. Hiding the past does not mean the past did not happen and you cannot erase it even if you try. History has shown us time and time again it will almost always rise again. Alex thought about gay history in much the same way. It wasn't until he was an adult that he began researching and finding out everything he could about the history of the LGBTQ people who came before him. It made him defiant and angry when he would uncover example after example of exemplary role models who he wished he had known about when he was growing up.

"Say their names," came to his mind once again.

He could understand why these families felt the way they did. The attempt to erase a family's history is not only cruel, but inhumane. The ability to see ourselves in our past is very important.

Then Alex was sure he found what he was looking for. It felt like the whole world had tipped on his axis when he looked on the screen on front of him and saw a bill of sale for a slave named Moses. Alex knew it sounded crazy but deep down he knew this Moses was the Moses of his dreams. A chill ran completely through his body as he continued to read. The bill of sale put this Moses age around the age of twenty-six. It was deemed this Moses was a slave for life. He was sold for a total of $400. That was a high dollar amount, considering that slaves auctioned from Lynch's Slave Pen usually sold for $70 - $300. This Moses was seen to be very valuable. Of course, Alex was just going by a gut feeling. There was no way for sure to know if this was his Moses or not. But it gave him something to hang his hat on. It also cemented the idea of slavery in St. Louis and the possibility there had lived a slave named Moses. This answer would come as some sort of relief to his other four friends as well who were also having dreams about Moses.

All of the friends' dreams seemed to be alike. But all the dreams had small changes and additions to the locations and the scenarios. In Paul's dreams, Moses was always standing on a wood box with his hands tied behind his back, blood running down the front of his torn and ragged pants. In Chuck's dreams, a bloodied Moses was standing with a noose around his neck waiting for the floor of the gallows to fall out from beneath him. Bobby always found him crouched down in much the same way as Alex, except he was in a dark wood-like forest. Jane always found Moses laid out in a simple pine box coffin, hands over his chest. He lay there unmoving and weeping.

Even though all their dreams varied somewhat in some details, all the dreams were common in two very striking ways. First, Moses was always weeping when they each came upon him. Even in Jane's case, where she found him in the pine coffin, he was weeping. And second, his eyes were always open. White, glowing eyes with no iris or pupils - just two orbs of white. Alex thought about his friends, and he knew they were all having trouble dealing with what was happening to them. It was illogical and crazy, but the fact remained it was happening. Up to this point, no one had figured out a way to stop it.

Room. Dark. Drip. Walls. Corner. Crying. Man. Drip. Blood. Pain. White eyes. Moses.

The same basic pattern of Alex's dream was the same basic pattern of theirs. Why? Whatever the reason Alex knew all of them were regretting the night they had come in contact with Moses.

The frightened lady living inside Alex's cell phone screamed into the room. Damn, he still needed to change his ring tone. It scared the literal shit out of him every time he got a call.

Ellis' name was lighting up the screen. Alex reached over to where the cell lay on the bedside table, picking it up, "Hey Ellis."

"Alex? Alex? You gotta help me. I am sorry for everything. Everything, but you must help me Alex," Ellis was clearly distraught and crying.

"Help you? What do you mean help you, Ellis?" Alex said concerned.

This was the first time Alex had spoken to Ellis in months. But Alex could clearly tell there was something seriously wrong with him.

"He told me that you would be able to help me. He told me you could make it stop."

Ellis was almost pleading now through sobs, "You must make it stop Alex."

"Make what stop?" Alex asked.

"The dreams," the phone crackled and went dead in Alex's hand. Ellis was gone.

Alex was instantly in a panic because he knew something was terribly wrong. He was thinking about who he could call for help - when a knock at his front door split the silence of the room and the racing of his thoughts. Alex jumped up from his bed, quickly pulling on a pair of shorts on his way to the door. Alex looked through the peephole and he could see an upset Chuck pacing on the other side of the door. He opened the door to let Chuck in who quickly entered and was now pacing back and forth in Alex's living room.

"Alex, man, I have some very fucked-up news to tell you. You might want to sit down because this shit is really fucked up," Chuck was clearly upset and nervous.

Alex immediately thought it had something to do with one of the other three remaining friends.

"I don't need to sit down. Just tell me what's going on." Alex just wanted Chuck to come out with whatever it was.

Alex could tell by Chuck's expression and actions this was going to be bad news. Some real bad fucking news.

Chuck stopped pacing and looked Alex directly in the eyes. "It's Ellis, Alex. You are not going to bel..."

Alex, cutting him off, "I know. I was just talking to him. He is really fucking upset, and I am not sure what is going on with him. He just hung up on me before you got here."

"Alex, Ellis is dead. They found his body in a downtown dumpster early this morning. It's on all of the news." Chuck said bluntly.

Alex felt his knees go weak as he listened to Chuck.

"That's impossible, Chuck. I just talked to him!" Alex said fighting back tears. The room felt as if it were beginning to spin.

"I don't know who you spoke to, but that wasn't Ellis, Alex. Ellis is dead. They think he died a few days ago. They didn't give many details other than it appears to be a suicide and his body was found in a dumpster. He died from a self-inflicted gunshot wound."

Alex fell down onto his couch in shock, listening to Chuck. The sound of Chuck's words blended into the growing sound of his heartbeat in his chest, the impact moving his body to tears. Alex put his head into his hands looking at the floor. He knew he wasn't going crazy. This had to be some type of strange mistake. Occasionally, you will hear a story about someone who was assumed dead, waking up in a morgue. It could happen. It couldn't be any crazier than talking to a dead man. Seriously, there had to be some sort of logical explanation because if there wasn't one it would mean he had been speaking on the phone with a ghost and quite honestly Alex was not ready to take that leap. He had not been speaking to a fucking ghost.

<u>Chapter 6</u>

Black Roses

Black roses. All Alex could focus on were the black roses which covered the top of Ellis' casket. He wondered if they had a meaning. You know how red roses are supposed to mean love and yellow roses mean friendship? Do black Roses mean death? Alex was sure they had to have some meaning like that. What else could they mean?

Maybe it was something you sent your ex to say, "I hate you for what you did to me."

That seemed appropriate as Alex sat in the church waiting for the funeral service for Ellis to begin. He did hate what Ellis had done to him. Ellis broke his heart, but no matter how much after that breakup Alex tried to force himself, he could never force himself to hate Ellis.

How do you turn to hating someone you loved? The love switch just doesn't turn to off once one of the partners walks out. No, the hate takes time to fester, and not enough time had passed between the two of them for hate. Angry. Angry was the word that described how Alex had felt after Ellis ended their relationship. Alex had been angry. But even through the anger there was always a possibility a second chance might exist for them. But there was going to be no second

85

chances. They were over. This was final, and now Alex found himself feeling nothing but empty.

It was a closed casket. Sometimes it was just best that way and Alex was grateful for it. The last thing he needed was to be haunted by how much that thing in the box did not look like his ex-boyfriend. Ex-boyfriend? That caused Alex even more discomfort now when he thought about it. He will forever be the ex-boyfriend of the guy that committed suicide. People were bound to think it was somehow his fault.

You know the, "He pushed him too far and broke his heart," kind of thing.

No one would ever stop to think that maybe the shoe was on the other foot and just maybe it was Ellis who left him because he couldn't keep his dick in his pants? Of course not. Any sympathy anyone could have felt on Alex's behalf now laid inside that box with Ellis. Ellis' grieving mother walked down the aisle with his father. Alex had seen and talked with them outside before coming in. It was awkward and sad.

The most uncomfortable moment came when Ellis' mother asked, "Do you know what he meant in his note when he said, "He lied?" That is all it said. Nothing more. What did he mean by that?"

Alex was shocked at this because he had no idea he had left a note. He couldn't think about what it meant. Who had lied to him? Alex could feel her eyes glaring through him.

Ellis's mother continued, "He wasn't referring to you Alex, was he? You didn't lie to him, did you?" Alex took a step back because it was obvious she was becoming confrontational.

"I have no idea what he meant by that and who he was talking about. He was the one who broke it off with me months before. He wasn't referring to me," Alex looked directly into her eyes, the pain in he saw in her eyes was nearly unbearable for him to witness, and he fought back tears of his own.

Ellis' father took her by the arm gently, "Alex, why don't you go ahead and go in and find yourself a seat. The service should start soon." Alex nodded, turned and began walking away.

He heard Ellis' father whispering, "This is not the right time or place for this." Alex continued up the church steps pretending as if he never heard him.

Now here he was, sitting in the pew waiting as they walked past him down the aisle to the front of the church closer to the casket. Closer to what use to be their son and what Alex thought was now nothing more than a monster in the box. Alex was glad he was near the back of the church. He was far away from the monster. The monster who he once thought he loved. Alex had to wonder what Ellis meant by, "He lied."

Who lied to him? Was he talking about him? Alex had never lied to Ellis about anything. Alex had loved Ellis and in Alex's mind you didn't lie to those who you loved.

Then Alex remembered the phone call and Ellis saying to him, "He told me you could help me."

There it was again, "He."

Who was Ellis talking about and was this something Alex needed to worry about or fear? There is a lot of fucked-up crazies in this world. Was this one of them? Was it a hookup gone bad? And if so, was this someone they had both known? The thoughts were now racing through his mind.

All Alex could think about was the suicide note had also said, "He lied."

The actual service was exactly what you would have expected, and Alex was shocked just how little Ellis' parents knew about him. Ellis would have hated the entire thing. There was nothing of him in it. Alex was sure they would try to convince everyone that this is what their son would have wanted. This was not what he would have wanted. For one thing, Ellis would have never wanted to have his service in a church in the first place. Ellis did not believe in religion. Second, the music that was chosen were hymns. There was no personal touch. No one got up and said a few good words about him. Nothing but a sermon, a walk through the valley of the shadow of death, then over. Off to the cemetery.

Ellis would have wanted something completely different. He would have wanted his friends to stand and tell stories about him, even the embarrassing ones. He would have wanted it outside and not in the confines of a church. Ellis hated the church because of the brainwashing they had attempted to do to him when he was a child. He would have hated the idea of a church. He would have wanted the music to be Gaga and showtunes. How could Ellis's parents be so completely clueless about who their son was? Or maybe they did know him and it was all intentional. Maybe they really did know him, and they were embarrassed by him and now that he couldn't speak for himself, they could portray him as the beautiful angel they had always wanted him to be.

Ellis was no fucking angel. He was sexual and messy. He could piss Alex off more than anyone else in the world. He smoked pot, and on occasion would take Ecstasy, and that was okay - because that was also who Ellis was. Alex hated this idea of the manufactured memories people tried to pin on their loved ones when they died. The most fucked up thing about all of it was it erased who the person really was. They were erasing who he was. They were erasing Ellis.

Alex wanted to stand and scream, "You did not know him like I did." Alex began to sob as Ellis's mother walked by him sitting in the pew. She was glaring at him through her tears as she passed.

"You didn't know him like I did," kept repeating in Alex's mind.

Black roses, Alex decided, must be for a broken heart. Seemed fitting now because that is exactly what his heart was. Broken.

Chapter 7
Stumble Inn

Alex felt empty. Out of all the emotions he could have been feeling, empty was the one emotion Alex could hang his hat on. Alex wondered what he was supposed to be feeling in situations like these. How do you feel after your ex commits suicide and leaves a note that implicates you? What was the proper fucking feeling he should be having? It seemed the world has this set idea of emotions you are supposed to feel in any given situation. Being an actor, Alex understood this. Even though he had this understanding, Alex knew if he was playing this part, empty was not the emotion which would have come to mind as a choice for character motivation. What would be his motivation? Alex thought about it and the motivation he would have chosen would have to be anger… fucking pissed. But no matter how hard Alex tried to be angry with Ellis, all he could muster was a sense of emptiness. Of course, he understood that empty was a weird thing to feel in this situation.

What the fuck was wrong with him? To be completely void of all feeling toward something was not Alex's way at all. He thought about it for a moment. You know they always tell you in acting class to classify feelings as you experience them to be able to draw on them later for a character. In this case, Alex felt as if he were playing a mannequin or a robot because he was just going through the motions. He had been going through the motions all day long. It is how he got through the funeral. He wanted to just get fucking through it. It was a relief when it was finally over, and he could get in the car.

After the funeral was over, the group of friends decided to head over to their favorite local haunt, the Stumble Inn. The Stumble Inn was a favorite South City corner bar which was frequented by the city's artistic community. If you were an artist, musician, actor or any type of creative person, then you had graced the threshold of the Stumble Inn at least once. Inside its doors, between the old tacky fake neon Falstaff beer signs, Cardinal's memorabilia and the neon-accented painting of Jesus above the bar, many creative ideas had been realized, born and celebrated. It was always a lively place to drink and socialize. Saint Louis is one of those cities where there is a church on every street and a bar on every corner. The Stumble Inn fit comfortably into this tradition for decades and its inside showed the wear and tear of the years. The place had great eclectic bohemian energy, which the creative collective responded to positively.

Chuck came over to the big round oak table in the corner of the bar with two pitchers of beer. The four guys had gathered around the table after the funeral. The beer had been flowing now for a while and they were all beginning to feel a little more than just a little lubricated. The conversation became looser, leaving the funeral sobriety behind them. Talk turned to their lives and their thoughts on different things. None of them spoke about the funeral or Ellis or anything that had transpired that day. Alex was grateful to his friends for that, and he knew they were doing it for him. Paul was going on about something having to do with some one-act play he was working on where the entirety was told from the point of view of an ant. Chuck was trying way too hard to be understanding and kind after the argument they had weeks earlier. Emotions had run sky high that day and they both understood they almost ruined a very good friendship because of it. You can thank Chuck for pointing that out to both of them and smoothing things over the way he had always done. Chuck was often the great peacekeeper of the group. Now in the name of peace, Bobby found himself discussing the complexities of an ant's thoughts with Paul.

Jane walked up to the table. She had not gone to the funeral with the guys for the obvious reason that she had never met Ellis. She felt it would have been awkward, and quite frankly, Jane didn't like funerals. Even if she had known Ellis, it would have been unusual for her to attend. Jane felt that funerals were for the living and had nothing to do with the dead. In fact, she was sure, in her own mind, it might even be more painful for the dead to see all their loved ones gathered in one place grieving. Adjusting to your own death had to be difficult enough without that type of nonsense getting in the way. This is exactly why Jane didn't want a funeral when her own time came. Cremated and sprinkled someplace peaceful and beautiful is what she wanted. Peaceful. Done and dusted, literally. Besides, the whole funeral tradition was just too outdated and archaic for anyone really.

Jane was relieved when she walked up to the guys, and she saw they were laughing and joking. Well, three of them at least. She saw immediately that Alex was looking somewhat lost and disconnected from everyone.

She walked up behind him and put her hands on his shoulders and said, "Hey there good looking, got a seat for a lady?"

Alex looked up at her with a forced smile on his face, but he wasn't fooling her because she could see the pain he was trying to hide behind his eyes. At least that is what she felt.

The guys all stood up and offered Jane a seat at the table, pouring her a beer in a glass Chuck grabbed from the bar. The conversation continued from one topic to another the way it always did. Bobby said something funny, and they all laughed out loud.

The laugh was cut short when Alex looked up from his beer and said, "I'm still dreaming about Moses."

The name Moses instantly shut the group laughter down. Paul's laughter was the last one to fall off into a stifled and uncomfortable silence. Everyone became mute, looking at each other for a moment. An immediate seriousness moved across the group. Moses was the elephant that stood in the room among, between and around them. It was the one thing they all had in common. Saying his name was the one thing that could silence them all completely because they understood the name Moses because they all had been dreaming about the man.

"I said that I am still dreaming about Moses."

Jane, feeling if she had to say something in order to break the shock and awkwardness of the moment, reached over and took Alex's hand in hers, looked him in the eye and replied, "I am too."

The flood gate was opened and in a moment everyone at the table had admitted the same occurrence out loud. They were all still dreaming about Moses, and it wasn't just a one- or two-time type of thing. They were all dreaming about Moses every single night of the week and it was clear to them all that it was not stopping any time soon.

Chuck, trying to be reasonable as always, looked at Jane and asked, "What do you think we should do about it? I mean, Jane, you are the one with the most experience with these types of things. How do you think we should handle it? I don't know about the rest of you, but these dreams have got to stop. I'm not sleeping worth a shit, and it is starting to have a serious effect on my life."

Jane understood completely what he was talking about because the dreams were having the same impact upon her. In fact, the dreams were having the same impact on everyone sitting at the table. Jane had a solution that she had been waiting for the right time to bring up. She hadn't been sure if today would be right time because of the guys coming from a funeral and all, but Alex was the one to bring it up so, what the hell, here it goes.

Jane waited for a pause in the conversation about the dreams and then she said, "I think we should go see a psychic. Now I am not talking about just any psychic. I am talking about a good psychic. A real psychic."

She used the word psychic because she knew they would understand that more so than if she had used the word 'medium' to describe who she had in mind. None of the guys had ever been to, or even thought of, seeing a psychic before. Jane had their interest piqued and there were a lot of questions about who, what, when and where.

Jane went on to explain, "The psychic, more specifically a medium who I have in mind, is the real deal. She can, and does, speak with the dead. Her name is Jenny Star. She is very well known for this type of thing. I know of some people who have went to her for help with things like this and if you are really wanting to know something concerning the dead then Jenny is the one you want to go see. She can help us connect with Moses."

Paul jumped in almost immediately, "Wait a second, I am not sure about this. Connecting with the dead was what got us into this trouble in the first place."

Paul was making a good point to the group. But, after some conversation, they had all agreed the harm had already been done and they needed to do something about it. They all agreed they had caused the problem by trying to contact whoever with the board. Back and forth the conversation went from one worry to another.

Alex was the one who finally ended the debate, "Listen, I don't know if I believe this will help us or not, but what I do know is we have no other options at this time. We need to figure out how to get this to stop so we can move on with our lives. I don't know about you guys, but I feel like I have been stuck in a time warp every night for weeks and it will just not let me the fuck go. Every time I close my eyes he is there crying. Every single time, and it is starting to really fuck with me. I ended up hurt and in the hospital because of it, and even after that it continues, night after night.

We must do something and if Jane thinks this might work, then dammit, we have to try."

They all looked and listened intently to Alex. After all, Alex had been the one who was physically hurt when all of this began. He was making complete sense to them. One by one they all had to agree this might be the only option they had.

So, after everyone eventually agreed, Jane said, "Okay then, I will make us an appointment."

Chapter 8
Contact

The drive out to the far edges of the city limits seemed particularly long. All five of the friends piled together into Bobby's car on their way to see the mystical Jenny Star who Jane seemed to think could solve all the problems and be able to help them put Moses to rest. Or, at least, they hoped to get Moses out of their dreams and lives. It felt like some fucked up scene from a bad updated arthouse Oz scenario with all of them on the way to see the Wizard. They were a little higher strung than usual, partially because of nerves and partially because they lacked sleep. The dreams had remained consistent in frequency without changing in meaning for any of them. The same dream over and over every single time they attempted to sleep. Jane was in the back seat sitting in the middle between Alex and Paul feeding directions to Bobby who was trying very hard to concentrate on the road ahead through his nerves and exhaustion. It was true, they were a whole lot worse for the wear. The unspoken question which hung in the air between all of them was if they would find the help they needed to put things back to normal in their lives.

"Hang a left at the next street," Jane told Bobby from the back seat.

They turned onto a street that looked like what you would expect from the 'burbs. Identical house after house on street after street. One cookie cutter house followed by another. Alex always thought that this was the American dream everyone was supposedly striving for and quite honestly, he couldn't understand why. Alex thought about the old George Carlin stand-up routine, *"A place to put your stuff."* Jane heard Alex giggle slightly and looked at him, puzzled. Alex shook his head to signal it was nothing, and Jane once again looked forward.

At the next street, Bobby seemed lost and asked, "Are you sure this is the right turn, Jane?" Before them was a huge old cemetery on the right-hand side of the road.

"Yeah, the directions say her house is at the end of this street," replied Jane assuredly.

There were houses on the left side which faced the cemetery and there was one single house at the end of the street. It was the only house on the right side of the street. The back yard of this house was the cemetery.

"This shit is fucking creepy," Chuck said as Bobby pulled his car into the driveway and parked.

Chuck was right, it was creepy. A psychic medium who lived with her backyard butt-up against a cemetery. It gave the five of them all kinds of horror movie vibes and it was almost too much to be believed. There was nothing unusual about the house, which made it contrast even more with its surroundings. It was a very normal-looking house in a very normal-looking neighborhood. The house itself was one of those bi-level type homes which were popular in the eighties. It was very well kept with a nice, manicured lawn. It had new white siding with black trim and black shutters. The only thing out of place was the cemetery because everything else about the house itself screamed boringly fucking normal. They were not sure what they were expecting, but this certainly was not it.

Jane, flanked on both sides by the guys, reached out nervously and rang the doorbell. What they thought was strangely normal about the house was even more confusing when they got their first look at the medium. The door opened almost immediately. Standing in the doorway was a very attractive woman. They all assumed she was most likely somewhere in her middle thirties. She was dressed in business attire. It was obvious she had just gotten home from work.

Her smile was reassuring as she reached a hand toward Jane, "You must be Jane?" she asked.

She looked more fucking normal than the fucking normal white house she called home in front of the cemetery. Chuck had thought for sure the door would open to reveal an old gypsy woman. To his surprise, Jenny was far from old. As a matter of fact, she was not bad looking at all. She was kind of hot. She was someone Chuck might have even taken out, if he were a few years older. A thought he had not completely dismissed, because concessions could be made for age.

Polite introductions were made, and Jenny invited them into her house. The entrance to the front door was on a landing of a staircase that went up and down. Jenny motioned to everyone to head down the stairs to the place where she conducted readings. Jenny guided them into an all-white room. Everything in the room was white. Completely white. White and very modern. The furniture, the floors (which were of a whitewashed wood) and even the walls were painted white - even the fucking art hanging on the walls was also white. The all-white room gleamed with touches of chrome and metal.

Jenny directed them to sit at a large glass table which was centered in front of two large double-glass doors which revealed a view of the gravestones in the cemetery, no more than ten feet away. Jenny poured herself a quick drink from a decanter on the bar as everyone sat down and got comfortable. Jenny noticed Chuck watching her as she quickly downed it. Chuck was more than a little disappointed she didn't offer him a shot. At this point, he sure could use it. He was sure it must be tequila, and he loved tequila.

"Settles the nerves and opens the mind," she said to Chuck quietly with a wink almost as if she had read his thoughts,

In the center of the table was a black candle, already burning. The candle was the only item in the entire room which was not white or chrome of some sort. The color of the candle surprised Jane less than the boys because she knew it was there for protection and to help ban any negative energies. The contrast of everything against the backdrop of the cemetery was indeed unusual and caused more than one in the group to glance at each other with a shocked look on their face. They all sat down in the white chairs around the glass table. Jenny sat with her back to the glass door and the gravestones beyond. She made sure everyone was comfortable and settled.

Once everyone was quiet, she began, "Jane told me a lot about everything that has been going on with you all. I have been meditating and thinking about it since I talked with her. The good news is that I already have some impressions as to what is happening. What I am saying is, I have some answers for you all. It is easy to explain. You are dealing with what we call, for the lack of a better term, a spirit attachment. In this case, the slave Moses has attached to all of you. This, of course, is somewhat unusual, but not completely unheard of, either."

The five nodded as Jenny spoke.

Alex asked intently, "Attached?" Jenny nodded her head affirmatively toward him. "Do you have any idea why he has attached to us? Why us? What does he want from us?" Alex continued with his questioning of Jenny.

She could tell Alex was nervous by the way he rattled off the questions with no time for her to respond.

She let him finish rambling and then she looked at Alex seriously, "Well, there is no other way to say this."

Jenny took a deep breath and paused for a moment, formulating the best way to say what she needed to tell them.

Once she gathered her thoughts she continued, "When all five of you contacted him with the spirit board, you opened the spiritual door and invited him in. Now, he wants, let me rephrase this, he needs, your help. I want to stress the word needs because he is desperate. He is stuck in what I call the in-between. Others may call it purgatory and then others may even call it hell. Whatever you have heard it called before is not of importance. The point is, he is stuck, and he is demanding that you help him. Now here is the bad news. Until you do, he is not going away."

This caused a murmur within the group. The thought of him not going away was not an option for any of them. They needed him to go away. He must go away.

Jane, seeing and feeling the trepidation of the group, spoke up, "That is what we are doing here guys. Jenny is going to help him to move on, and in return, help us."

Jenny continued where Jane left off, "Jane is right. I can help you. What I need to do is to guide Moses out of the in-between and over to the other side. But to do this I am going to need your help. He has been stuck for a very long time and he does need our help. In order to accomplish this, I am going to have to contact him, but I am going to need your help to make this contact."

"What do you mean contact?" Alex asked.

Jenny continued, "What you would call a séance."

Paul was sure he wanted nothing to do with a séance. He had seen enough of this type of stuff on TV, and he was sure nothing good ever came of it. He was more than a little scared of the idea.

"I'm not sure I can do this you guys," Paul said looking at the others around the table.

Paul was frightened and it was obvious. Out of the entire group Paul was the one most afraid and it was clearly showing in this situation.

"What if we do this and we make it worse? What if we do this, and we end up inviting in something else and then we have two damn things we need to get rid of? It just seems to me that there are too many possibilities that this could go wrong," Paul said nervously.

Jenny had dealt with this type of fear many times. But time was of the essence here for them and her, she needed to respond quickly and firmly. She had to give him an immediate response, "If that is your choice then I can't help you.

I understand your hesitation, but trust me, when I tell you the only way to rid yourself of Moses is to help him. He is not going away on his own. Understand?"

Jenny looked intently at Paul as he weighed his decision. Paul looked around the table at his friends and he could tell they were willing to try anything at this point to make this all end.

Understanding that his friends were wanting to go ahead with the séance, Paul took a deep breath and reluctantly agreed by shaking his head, "Yes. I will do it."

"Okay let's go ahead," Jenny said as she closed the blackout curtains across the big double doors, blocking the view of the tombstones and the light outside.

She next switched off the lights to the room leaving the room completely dark except for the light emanating from the black candle flickering in the middle of the table.

"I need everyone to hold hands and let's take a moment of silence."

Everyone held hands around the table. Everyone settled into their chairs and into the silence of the room.

When Jenny was confident the group was ready, she continued, "I need everyone to breathe with me and slow our breathing down together and begin to relax. Breathe in slowly. Breathe out slowly," Jenny guided them softly and calmly.

"Again, breathe in slowly. Breathe out slowly," The room breathed together in silence as Jenny stared into the flame.

When she was sure everyone was breathing as one, she began to go into trance. She was ready to call the spirit forward.

"Dear Moses, beloved spirit, please move among us and speak through me. We are welcoming you with our open minds and our open hearts. Moses, let us help you," Jenny continued to concentrate on the flame as it began to grow and flicker.

Jenny's eyes began to glaze over in the flickering light, "Moses are you with us? Give me a sign you are with us," Jenny continued as a knock came from beneath the glass table.

The group was somewhat startled, and Jenny calmed them, "It's okay. He is with us. It is just his way of communicating."

Jenny was in complete control of the session at this point. She was experienced at keeping groups calm during the initial points of contact. She knew for most people this may be the first time they had an experience with the other side of the veil. In this case, she knew these five were somewhat shell-shocked with what had been happening with them. Sure, they had asked for it and invited it in. They opened the door to Moses and now it was clear to her Moses was going nowhere unless they could set him free to move on.

Jenny found Moses incredibly sad because she knew from her visions he had been enslaved in life and now he was still enslaved even in death.

Jenny let herself go deeper and deeper into the void, "Moses you can talk through me. It is completely okay, and I give you my permission to come into me to speak. I am a medium and you can use my body as a tool to communicate."

Jenny slowly bowed her head with her chin falling to touch her chest. Her breathing began to change. It became more audible and labored as she began to whisper in a voice which was not her own. She began to whisper in a male voice.

"He lied." Jenny spoke in a young man's voice and Alex knew immediately it was Ellis speaking though her.

"Ellis?" Alex said hoping for the moment to continue. There was so much that had gone unsaid between the two of them before Ellis took his own life.

"He lied." Ellis' voice came from Jenny's lips. Her head was still bowed as the words come out. Ellis sounded pained and Alex was sure he was crying.

"Who lied to you?" Alex asked with tears welling up in his own eyes. He couldn't believe he was hearing Ellis' voice. This was something he had not expected at all.

"Did Moses lie to you?" Jane asked out of nowhere in the somber voice of her own, fishing for an answer and hoping to provoke Moses. After all, Moses was the reason they were all here in the first place. She was a little irritated with Ellis showing up and hijacking her communication. They had come to speak to Moses and Jane was going to make sure that happened.

"He lied," Ellis replied again with no definitive answer. He continued crying through Jenny.

"Ellis, tell me what happened so I can help you. Who lied?' Alex was now also crying and begging Ellis for an answer.

Ellis' cries began to turn into a sobbing. A recognizable sobbing all five of them were very familiar with. The sobbing from their dreams. Jane sat up in her chair because she knew they were now in the presence of Moses.

"Moses?" Jane asked, cutting in to grasp the moment and hopefully help guide the session.

The sobbing turned into a laugh and then into a growl. "Moses?" A different guttural male voice came from the bowed head of the medium Jenny.

"Moses?" Jane continued asking.

"Are you Moses?" Jane was now pleading for answers because she was getting more than a little nervous.

"ARE YOU THE SLAVE MOSES?"

Another growling came from Jenny. She took a deep guttural breath and then a clear, male voice began to speak with a giggle. This was not Ellis. This was not Moses. This was something else.

"I lied. There is no Moses," the voice responded wickedly and with an almost toying intent.

In that instant Jane understood the meaning of it all. She knew she was now speaking to the one who had lied to Ellis, and it was now clear whatever this was had lied to them all.

"You are the one who lied," Jane forced the words out in a whispered voice.

The thing inside of Jenny was growling and laughing as Jane spoke, "You are the one who lied. You lied to all of us."

Jane's voice and her temper were rising above her fear, "Who are you?" Jane demanded from the laughing and growling thing which was occupying the medium.

Jenny's hands broke from the group's grasp. They all instinctively stood up and stepped back from the table. Once free, she began to slam her hands down upon the glass table as she punctuated her words.

"I AM GLOW," she said with a bang of both hands on the tabletop.

"GLOW," her hands slammed down.

"GLOW," her hands slammed down as she began to slowly raise her head.

"GLOW," once again her hands came down on the table through the evil laughs and growls.

"GLOW," banging down upon the table once again as her head continued to raise.

"GLOW." Her hands, now rolled into tight fists, slammed down again.

Then the entire group simultaneously saw the medium's eyes in the light of the flickering candle. White glowing eyes. White glowing eyes in the flicker of the flame, cutting through the darkness.

"GLOOOW," she screamed once more.

Her fists came down on the table for the last time with such a force it shattered the glass beneath them. One large piece of glass was propelled upward and stuck into the ceiling. The group shielded themselves from the smaller pieces as they flew past their heads. The shards of glass closest to Jenny sliced through the veins in her arms and neck.

She was flailing and screaming wildly now as the blood began to spray around the room. Chuck grabbed the curtains. Pulling them open, he illuminated the hysterical medium and the white room being spray painted with her bright red blood. A rusty, sweet smell filled the air as Bobby immediately yanked off his jacket and grabbed Jenny, trying to put pressure on her arms and neck to hold back the bleeding. He knew if he didn't slow the flow of blood down, she was going to bleed out very quickly. There was red dripping everywhere as Jane phoned in the call to 911. But they were too late.

As Bobby cradled Jenny in his blood-soaked jacket, she gurgled her last word from her dying lips, "Glow."

<u>Part 2</u>
Monster

I am the enemy within.
I am the boss of your dreams.
No. I am not the law in your mind,
the grandfather of watchfulness.
I am the law of your members,
the kindred of blackness and impulse.
-Anne Sexton

Chapter 9
Detective

It had been a long and exhausting day for Detective Vincent Rossi - one of those epic, no-win kind of days where nothing felt like it was going his way. We have all had those kind of I-should-have-never-gotten-out-of-bed type days. This was one of those days for Vincent. He had his share of open cases to dig through and it seemed everywhere he turned he was coming up against brick walls. All his leads seemed to be sending him to dead ends over and over again. He found himself tired and frustrated at times. He kept having to remind himself to let things roll and work through it all, instead of getting angry and working against it. Even though he tried, he kept feeling like he was leading an uphill battle. Life is exhausting if you try to live it constantly swimming upstream.

Vincent Rossi's life as a St. Louis homicide detective was neither easy nor ideal. It was long hours without much of anything happening. Sure, there were those days when you would solve a case, but those days had a lot of weeks of dead ends in between. For the most part, there were many times when Vincent would question if he had made the right career decision for himself at all. Sure, it was true that he always wanted to be a cop. From a very young age he did nothing other than eat, breathe, and sleep everything dealing with law enforcement. Vincent felt he was destined to be a cop without ever questioning his decision or how early in life he made it.

That was, until he was promoted to detective. Now, his choice in careers left him often bored and longing for more. He was beginning to think it might be the second biggest mistake of his life. Life had been much more satisfying and exciting back in the days when he was a uniformed officer. He enjoyed his time traveling the streets in his cruiser. He was a good cop and people in the neighborhoods he patrolled not only liked him, but also respected him. Oh, it was true in those days he had to be on his toes. Those days working the hard streets of downtown St. Louis could turn ugly very quickly and they often did. Vincent saw the darker side of the city. He understood the energy of death, pain and horror which pulsed through the city of St. Louis. His job as a cop was to assist in trying to keep the balance of it all. A balance that over the past years seemed to be tipping in all the wrong ways. St. Louis was considered the most dangerous city in the country and one of the most dangerous cities in the world, a badge it did not wear with honor. Sure, life patrolling the streets was tough at times, but the good far outweighed the bad. The neighborhoods were still tight-knit communities in a country where communities were falling apart as the world turned on itself. Vincent thought his life would be different once he made detective, but to his disappointment his promotion left him feeling a sense of loss. Sure, it was more money. Without question the extra money was nice and appreciated, but Vincent couldn't help feeling, in the tradeoff for a better salary, he left a lot behind. There were those darker moments when he felt as if he might have sold his soul and happiness for a suit and a few extra bucks.

It wasn't easy for an openly gay man to work his way through the obstacles, red tape and politics within the department. It took a lot for anyone to be promoted to detective in a city like St. Louis - let alone a gay man. It was no secret that the STLPD had factions within it which often made life harder for those in any type of minority. There had been instances of racial targeting and harassment throughout the years. The city overall was not fond of its police department and that standing within the overly diverse communities was a literal powder keg that could be lit and set off at any time.

None of this escaped Vincent. Vincent knew the relations between the LGBTQ community and the police had always been a strained one, and rightfully so. He understood you couldn't escape the bigotry and hate in the world as an openly gay man. Being gay was one of those things that Vincent knew made him somewhat of a loner within the department. At times Vincent felt he did not get his promotion to detective for his merit at all, but for the simple reason that he liked to suck cock. They were just needing to fill a quota, and for whatever reason, he was the first cocksucker that came to mind.

Vincent Rossi was a good-looking man. Some might even tell you he was a beautiful man. He stood about six-foot-two and weighed a solid 185 pounds. He was in shape, but it wasn't because he worked out all the time. Sure, he would go to the gym like everyone else, but his shape was due more to genetics than his workouts. His body was tight, strong and well- proportioned. Looking at him you could tell he was Italian with his olive complexion and sleepy blue eyes. Plus, his last name Rossi which was also a dead give-away. His hair was thick and black. He kept a closely shaved beard that accentuated the structure of his jawline. Yes, Vincent Rossi was a beautiful man, but behind those good looks and sleepy blue eyes resided a whole lot of sadness. Life for Vincent had not been easy. Like all of us, he had those dreams he never fully followed or that great love that was never fully realized. Vincent felt as if he might have seen all that humanity had to offer. If not all, then most. In some ways it had soured the man he was and how he dealt with the world. He understood human nature a little clearer than anyone would want to, or should have to, for that matter. Anything resembling innocence had been taken from Vincent in one way or another. His innocence had been gone longer than he cared to admit.

Vincent was a married man. He had married his husband Tim in 2015 following the landmark Supreme Court marriage equality case, Obergefell v. Hodges. The marriage had started off well, but recently Vincent had noticed Tim was becoming more distant, even secretive at times. One thing about Vincent's career as a detective was that he could always tell when someone was lying to him, including his husband. He knew without question Tim was keeping secrets from him. Sadness had seemed to become the tone of the day within his marriage. The overall feeling of the love they once shared was gone.

"Out to lunch," Vincent whispered to himself as he was driving through the streets of the city toward a crime scene.

Vincent's work hours were long, and he was gone most of the day, giving him very little time to pay attention to Tim and even less time to work on their struggling marriage. His whole life had become about his job and at times Vincent felt he was burning out. Without question he was burning out. That is how he felt much of the time, but then there would be those moments when everything would come together for him, and he would solve a case. Solving a case would always re-energize Vincent. He would always find himself in the moment rededicating himself to his career and he would once again stoke his internal drive to continue with it. In truth, Vincent was addicted to the adrenaline and dopamine release that solving a case would bring to him.

Vincent parked the car along the street as he arrived at his current crime scene. Red and blue lights from the patrol and emergency vehicles bounced off the white house in front of him and the cemetery headstones behind it, causing an eerie glow to emanate from its reflections. It was one of those creepy moments in his work he would not soon forget. It looked like something out of a twisted horror movie. It seemed everyone standing in the front yard looking toward the open front door was waiting for a killer to come bounding out - wielding a knife, an ax, a machete or maybe even a chainsaw with its loud motor echoing and screaming into the night. Reviewing the appearance of the scene, Vincent took note that within the group of officers, there were five people out of place and not in uniform. One of the five was a young female who was sitting on the curb with her head in her hands. She appeared to be crying and all of them appeared to be covered in what looked like drying blood.

Passing everyone without saying a word, Vincent walked up the front steps into the house, careful to not touch or disturb anything about or around the scene. The scene had already been secured and the criminal investigation team had already begun the collection of the evidence. From what Vincent could tell as he walked down the stairs into what once was a completely white room, there was plenty of evidence to collect. Blood and broken glass were everywhere. Amid the broken glass and blood splatter lay a single female victim. Looking at her, Vincent could tell the blood that covered the room was hers. She appeared to be a middle-aged woman. She was clearly deceased. She had lacerations mainly on both of her forearms and both of her hands. It was clear something horrible had happened to her. Something violent.

You didn't see this amount of blood spray from a simple act like stabbing or even a gunshot. Sure, the blood pooled, and in the case of gunshot, there was some splatter, but it was very focused. In this case, whatever happened had turned this woman into a human blood sprinkler. Obviously, she had not died of natural causes. There was nothing natural about the scene Vincent was standing in. The room came alive with the strobes from the flash of the cameras going off. Cameras which were recording every inch of the scene and the room. Pieces of glass and fingerprints were being meticulously gathered. Without question, at this point, the scene was clearly being treated as a homicide - until reason came along to classify it as something different. In Vincent's mind that seemed very unlikely, but he knew through his experience anything could happen with these cases. He also was painfully aware that sometimes you were never given the answers at all, and the leads would dry up. In that situation the case would become cold and filed away until some other evidence came along. Something else coming along was rare with these cold cases, but it could happen.

Vincent walked back out of the house and toward the officers who were attending to the five people he saw upon his arrival. He pulled the leading officer aside and told him that he wanted all five of the group brought in for questioning and everything on their person from this point onward was considered evidence. He wanted to make that clear because he did not want to lose anything during the transfer from point A to point B. Something horribly violent had happened to this woman and Vincent felt that either one, or all five, had committed a heinous act. Either that, or they were all witness to what caused the death and the vast amount of blood that was now sprayed across the scene. One thing for sure, all the white in the room was going to make the blood evidence much easier to track, measure and collect.

Vincent walked to his car and opened the door, getting in with a heavy sigh. It had been a long day, and he knew it was about to be an even longer night. He knew what he had to do next, and he dreaded making the call to his husband. He had already canceled one date with Tim this week. He missed a musical revival of *Sweeney Todd* playing at the famed Fox Theatre in St. Louis because he had two dead teens with gunshot wounds to their heads. They had been killed in what appeared to be execution-style with their hands tied behind their back. One shot each. Clean and precise.

Vincent knew he was in hot water already with his husband because they had those tickets for months ahead of time. Vincent had to laugh because the scene he had just walked out of made the vision of *Sweeney Todd* look like *Sunday in the Park with George*. Tonight, they were supposed to be going out for a late movie and a bite to eat afterwards. This was supposed to be his way of making up with Tim for missing the show. It was supposed to be his apology and now he knew he would be apologizing all over again. His apology date would now have to be put on hold because he had five suspects who needed to be processed and questioned. It was his job and his responsibility even though he knew Tim would be disappointed. He knew he wouldn't blame him for being angry with him. He felt like this would just end up being one more nail into the coffin of their dying marriage.

Vincent took a deep breath and said into his phone, "Call home."

Chapter 10

Interrogation

Vincent sat behind his computer at his desk. He had just spent hours interviewing the five young suspects involved in the death of the medium. It had been a very long night, and it was now dragging into the very early hours of the morning. He was still too wound-up to go home, and, in truth he wasn't ready to face the music waiting for him when he got there. Home meant dealing with a very unhappy husband. He was too tired to even think about dealing with that right now and, in truth, he was killing time so he wouldn't have to.

Sitting in front of his computer looking at the screen, he began going over, in his mind, the questioning of his current five suspects. They had all told him the same story. It didn't seem rehearsed, and the emotion was there with all of them. They went to the medium because they were having bad dreams, and the medium was going to help them overcome those dreams. The dreams had started because they had used a spirit board together. They went to the medium and they had a séance. The medium went into some sort of trance and broke the glass table in front of her by continually slamming her hands onto it in what they called some out-of-control possession. They said she showed extraordinary strength, which was clearly evident if she really did break the table with her hands. Half-inch annealed glass could be five times stronger than regular glass, but people often make the mistake that annealed glass cannot be broken. That is, until something does come along with enough strength to break it. Maybe the medium was trying to scare these kids by putting on a show and got more than she asked for - not knowing the glass could break. If she had only purchased a tempered glass table, it would have shattered into many small pieces instead of sharp, deadly shards.

But there was something else, something that was still eating at him. Sure, it was a fantastical story they all had told him. Hard to believe, but in truth, he had heard a lot of strange stories throughout the years, and he had seen people do the strangest of things. Especially those under the influence of substances. At this point, he was waiting for the victim's toxicology report to come back. It would not be unusual for someone to have extraordinary strength while under the influence. It would have taken a lot of strength to bust through a glass table like this one, unless of course it had already been weakened by some unseen hairline fractures. If this had been part of the medium's schtick, then that was possible. There was nothing found at the scene at this point to suggest drugs were involved, but we have all heard the stories of people who, for a single moment, suddenly have superhuman strength. A woman lifts a car to save her child who is stuck underneath it. A man leaps a great distance avoiding an oncoming bus. These stories were rare, but not unusual. Then, of course, in the case of being drug-induced, it was very possible. Vincent had seen videos of people under the influence of PCP or Flakka demonstrating amazing strength. Was the medium under the influence of something? In his mind, he expected something in her toxicology report to tell the story. Vincent also had trouble seeing these five friends being involved in something completely criminal and nefarious.

Vincent pulled the video of Alex McAllister up on his monitor. He spent a moment studying Alex. Young, good looking and seemingly intelligent. In many ways, Alex was Vincent's type, even though Vincent would never carry that attraction any further. It was just something that was part of his evaluation. Vincent imagined Alex was many people's type of guy. Good looking, sexy and fuckable. After all, he was a very good-looking young man who Vincent instantly could tell was gay. Not by anything outward, but it was something which Vincent just innately knew. Later, of course, this was confirmed.

It bothered Vincent that Alex looked as if he might be keeping something in. Something hidden he either didn't want to say or was afraid to say. Maybe some sort of secret? Interestingly enough, Alex had been connected to the recent strange dumpster suicide of the young man named Ellis. Alex had been dating that victim and then they had broken it off. Ellis' parents brought up Alex in a questioning way. It was more than obvious to Vincent that Ellis ended up no longer attracted to Alex, and, for a strange reason, the parents were either holding a grudge against Alex or believed Alex was indirectly responsible for their son's suicide. Logically, in Vincent's mind, that would have to make Alex his number one suspect out of the five. There were too many coincidences to believe that there was no connection between the two cases. Alex's involvement with both victims connected both cases without too much brain power given to it. But still, there was something about Alex which Vincent kept returning to. What was he missing?

Vincent put on his headphones and hit >PLAY.

He began watching his questioning of Alex on the video. He was watching for any body language changes that would suggest something was off. He was halfway through the video and there was nothing but a scared young man who had been witness to a horrific event. Vincent looked at Alex's hands, which showed a lot of nervousness. He noticed one of Alex's legs would nervously shake at times. There was no change in eye contact when Alex answered the important parts of the questions. No twitch or over-blinking of the eyes, and always direct eye contact. There was nothing that would be considered out of the ordinary. The young man's tone and demeanor fit with the words and the story he was telling. Especially at the more frightening parts of his testimony, he behaved exactly as any body language expert would describe as normal. At this point, there were tears running down the young man's face as he began to describe the last moments of the medium's life.

Alex became more emotional as he continued to speak on the video, "We were all holding hands. She, Jenny, broke her hands free from ours with both of her hands slamming down on the table in front of her. It was completely unexpected and for a moment I thought she could have been fucking with us. I really for a moment thought that this might all be some type of crazy joke. But it wasn't a joke because again and again her hands slammed down on the table in front of her. Her voice had changed completely as she slammed her hands down. A man's low voice. An 'evil voice' is how I would describe it. Like something you might have heard out of one of those bad horror movies. She said in this voice, "I am Glow." And then her hands kept coming down on the table over and over again as she began to scream in the man's voice, "Glow!" Over and over again. That is when she raised her head, and we saw that her face had changed. I don't know how to explain this to you, other than it was not her any longer. And her eyes, her eyes were completely white in the light of the candle. No iris or pupil. Nothing but white and they seemed to be glowing. And then, oh my God, and then her fists came down on the table one last time and the glass shattered. I felt the spray of blood hit my..."

There was a glitch in the video with a hiss and a flash of something. Vincent immediately stopped the playback of the file. He wasn't sure what it was, and he rewound it and hit >PLAY again.

"...oh my God and then her fists came down on the table one last moment and the glass shattered. I felt the spray of blood hit my..."

Again, the same hissing glitch and the flash of something which went by too quickly for Vincent to make out. Vincent stopped once again and rewound. This time he went frame by frame and sure enough the digital glitch was there. And then, on just one frame, was a blurred image. It appeared to Vincent as if someone were standing behind Alex with their hands on his shoulders. It appeared to be male.

Vincent rewound the video once again and hit >PLAY.

"And then, oh my God, and then her fists came down on the table one last moment and the glass shattered. I felt the spray of blood hit my face and that is when everything just went crazy. I mean, we all just lost it."

Vincent hit stop because the glitch was gone. He hit play, rewind and stop repeatedly but it was no longer there. Vincent was more than confused and more than a little creeped out by the whole thing. He tried to convince himself that he was just exhausted, so he shut his computer down and headed home. He was way too tired to continue, and he knew his husband would still be sleeping when he got there.

Vincent walked into the dark, deserted garage heading to his car. He had his keys in his hand and wasn't paying any particular attention to anything as he walked. His mind was still on trying to figure out what had happened to the video file that would cause just a glitch - and then for that glitch to just disappear. Maybe some type of strange digital bleed-through? Not permanent. The computer getting the pixels a little jumbled for a moment and then correcting itself. Stranger things have happened. Vincent kept formulating his justification as he walked to the driver's side of his car. He clicked the lock and began to open the door. Instantly, out of the corner of his eye, he caught some movement in a dark area of the garage. Vincent looked again quickly, and he saw there was an unmoving man standing in the darkness of the garage watching him. Vincent couldn't make out anything more than the outline of his body.

Vincent began to speak, "You startled me, man. What are you doing down here this late?"

The shadow immediately fled to the right as Vincent spoke to it. Instantly sensing danger, Vincent reached for his gun. Slowly and carefully, he began to search the garage. Minutes passed by as Vincent searched, but there was no one there. Finally, satisfied that the man was no longer there and that he had chased him away, Vincent retreated to the silence of his car. Starting his engine, exhausted, he began the drive home.

<u>Chapter 11</u>
Glow

Alex was exhausted as his naked body hit his bed and sank into the softness of his comforter. The police had given him a set of awful-looking clothes to change into because they took his own blood-spattered clothes as evidence. The idea they were being kept as evidence blew Alex's mind. He didn't know what they were looking for and as far as Alex could tell he was not a suspect or being considered as part of a crime. But then why did they want all of their clothing? The whole night had been some kind of nightmare.

Alex could hear the crying of a baby coming through the walls from the apartment next door. The sound, which usually would cause him to put on headphones, at this moment, felt reassuring. In a strange way it felt calming to him. The crying baby represented something normal to him and at this moment normal is exactly what he needed. He craved normalcy and the baby was helping to give him just that. There had been nothing normal about the night at all and Alex kept seeing the screaming medium in his head over and over. He kept seeing her distorted face and the whites of her eyes. The blood. So much blood. The still-crying baby brought him back out of it all once again, beckoning him to stay in this moment of normal and not let his mind wander toward the horror of it all. His mind calmed as he listened to the crying of the baby, and he began slowly... and... deeply... falling... to... sleep.

A noise in his bedroom caused Alex to open his eyes. He looked around the room and saw nothing. He lay back and looked at the ceiling and noticed the baby had stopped crying. The silence of the night without the crying child seemed almost unnatural to him. He needed noise. Alex listened intently to find something else he could focus his thoughts upon but there was nothing but silence. Silence and darkness. The only light coming into the room was coming in from the window at the foot of his bed. Sure, it was bad juju to have his feet facing toward the window instead of the door. His mother told him once that it was considered bad feng shui.

"Alex your feet should be facing the door. It is said you want your feet facing the direction they will remove your body when you are dead," his mother said.

Alex had looked at her like she had lost her mind. Who in the fuck says such a thing to someone? Alex wasn't sure if she knew what she was talking about or not, but the one thing he knew for sure was he would never be able to sleep with his head under a window. Bad funk shway or not, he wasn't sleeping with the window behind him. The thought of that just creeped him out completely. The idea someone could be watching him through the window while he slept was really too much to handle. It was a phobia he had all his life. Just like he couldn't sleep with closet door open or his foot or hand hanging off the bed. For Alex, that sort of thing was just craziness. Alex rolled onto his back looking at the ceiling. He was looking at the light over the bed which... needed... to... be... cleaned... Sleep washed over him once again.

The sound of movement in the darkness woke him. Alex tried to sit up to see where the noise was coming from, but he found, to his sudden alarm, that he couldn't move. He couldn't move any part of his body. No matter how hard he tried and struggled he could not move. He noticed everything in the room seemed darker, somehow different. As if it were a negative of itself. It was like nothing he had ever seen before and in the moment, he began to panic. He tried to move his arms, his legs, his head. Every part of his body was frozen, and his mind was now racing completely out control. Alex tried to scream but nothing would come out of his mouth. Not only was his complete body in paralysis, but so was his voice. Alex could feel tears begin to roll down the side of his cheeks and onto the pillow below his head. Was this it? Was this the end of his life? Was this a stroke? Or even worse, was this death itself? Or, even more terrifying, was he already dead?

Alex wanted to scream out, "I'm not dead. I'm not dead," but he was able to make no sound more than maybe a quiet grunt. A grunt no one would be able to hear.

No one was coming to his rescue. Another sound of movement came from within the room. This time it was at the foot of his bed. Alex found he could move his eyes to see. Only his eyes and nothing else, but at least it was some sort of blessing within his paralysis. Or maybe not a blessing at all, because standing at the foot of the bed was a shadowy figure of man. A man, who just stood there with the light of the window at his back - outlining him so he almost appeared as if he were a cut out from black construction paper - like the profile silhouette gifts they made in grade school for Mother's Day. This time the gift was for Alex and that gift was waiting at the end of his bed, carefully watching him. Studying him.

Alex struggled, trying to speak, but no words would come out of his mouth. Once again, a very silent grunt came out in the place of what should have been him asking, "What the fuck do you want?"

The man continued standing there, unmoving at the foot of his bed. Alex could feel his eyes upon his nude body, and, in that moment, he had never felt more naked and vulnerable in his life. He struggled to speak again but nothing would come out. Alex could feel his breathing increase as his pulse pounded in his head. The man just continued standing there unmoving. Motionless. The full extent of the situation began to become clear in Alex's mind. He was either already dead, or he would soon be, and there was nothing he could do about it. One way or another, Alex was convinced that it was death who was standing at the foot of his bed.

The man suddenly dropped below Alex's eyesight onto the floor. From what Alex could make out, the man was now on all fours and crawling.

"Oh, fuck now what is he doing?" Alex's panic-stricken thoughts were running through his mind just like the man who was now scurrying across his floor.

Scurrying like some oversized rat, searching for a bite of cheese.

Then, to his horror, Alex felt one hand reach up and drop onto the foot of his bed. And then the *other. The man was coming onto his bed and Alex was losing his mind to the fear because there was nothing he could do about it. Slowly and methodically the man began to crawl onto the bed. The outline of a head appeared into Alex's limited field of vision. It was a man's head which appeared to have long stringy hair. Next, Alex could make out a set of shoulders - and then a torso - coming onto the bed crawling almost serpent-like. Alex was still trying to scream, but nothing but a quiet grunt was able to escape through his lips. The man was coming closer and closer. Alex could feel the weight of the man's body on top of his as it made its way up toward his face. Alex was sure he felt lips brush against the head of his penis and then he could feel breathing on one nipple and then another as he was now seeing the top of the man's head as he came closer. Rape? Rape is what was going to happen? Alex was sure the man was going to rape him. Maybe he gave Alex something in his sleep to cause paralysis.*

Alex felt one of the man's hands go around his neck and then another. The man was now choking Alex as he began to sit up on Alex's body. Alex tried to struggle beneath his weight, but he could not move.

Alex tried to scream.

Nothing.

Nothing would come out and he couldn't move no matter how hard he tried. The man was now fully upright with his hands around Alex's neck. Alex could see the outline of his head as he leaned in closer and closer to Alex's own face. Suddenly the outline turned into revealing features and those features turned into a face. A face Alex recognized from earlier. It was the same face he had seen on the crazed medium. Then the man's eyes came into focus. The glowing white of the man's eyes cut through the darkness like lasers. White eyes. Then the voice broke the silence. Low, guttural and hissing.

"What's wrong, Alex? Can't move?" The smell of rancid milk and rotting flesh filled the room as he spoke.

Alex felt himself choking and gasping for air as the man's breath made his eyes water. His face came closer and closer. They were now nose to nose, and, to Alex's horror he was now looking into the glowing white abyss of his attacker's eyes.

"What's wrong, Alex? Can't scream?" the man said as he began to laugh and tighten his grip around Alex's throat. Face to face, Alex could smell the putrid odor of the man's breath even more.

"John Glow. That's my name and I have been watching you for a very long time." Suddenly Glow released his grip as Alex gasped for air.

"Let's play," Glow whispered with a wicked smile. And in an instant, Glow was off the bed and gone.

Alex heard his own screams as soon as he could feel the paralysis had lifted from his body. To his relief he could suddenly move again. Alex jumped from his bed and grabbed for the light switch. The room was flooded with the overhead light - but there was nothing there. There was no attacker. There was no threat. There were no glowing white eyes. There was no John Glow. Alex was completely alone, and he had never been more terrified in his life.

Deep down Alex knew this was just the beginning of something horrible. He knew without a doubt he was deep in danger and there was no one else that could help him. He was being terrorized by this man with glowing eyes and he knew without question there was nothing he could do about it. Alex grabbed a pair of gym shorts and t-shirt off the chair because he felt himself dangerously exposed. He had never felt more naked in his life. He needed to cover himself from unseen eyes that might be watching. He dressed quickly and then sat on his bed with his knees drawn up to his chest in the washed-out light of his room. He tried with everything he had within himself not to sleep.

In the other four friends' houses, John Glow was making his nightmare introductions to each of them, one by one. It was obvious to all of them, frightened in their own lighted bedrooms, that this was war. A war they all were completely incapable of fighting. One night, and all five of them had dreams of the same man. A man with white glowing eyes. This was nothing short of what must be the devil himself. All five of them came to the same conclusion - they must be damned, and it felt in the moment that no one was going to be able to get out of this alive.

<u>Chapter 12</u>
Convergence

Paul looked at himself in his bathroom mirror. He looked tired and there were dark circles which were beginning to show around his eyes. Sleep had become more and more infrequent because every time Paul closed his eyes Glow was there waiting for him in the darkness of his sleep. Horrible nightmares that often left self-inflicted marks and bruises on his body from trying to fight off his unseen intruder. Paul looked at the bruises on his torso from the continual one-sided fights with his attacker. His body was abused and was clearly showing the marks of that abuse. He was also having trouble keeping any food down long enough to matter. The cause, of course, was his nerves. He had always been a nervous sort. A real nervous sort who never really fit in. One of reasons why he was so close to Chuck and the other two guys was they had always accepted him the way he was. They were the first real friends he ever had. They understood him and were way more tolerant of his idiosyncrasies than anyone had ever been, including his parents. Paul fit in with his friends in a way he had never fit in before and that was something which made life so much easier for him to withstand.

Paul came from a well-to-do family. He was an only child who was often more of a burden to his parents than he ever was loved. His mother found him too dull on one hand and insipid on the other. *Insipid* was her label for him that would come up repeatedly in conversation with her through the years. After being told for years how dull, shallow and boring he was to her, Paul began to retreat within himself. It was a blessing when he was finally able to break free from her grasp and go to college. Even though college was in the same city where his parents lived, it was still freedom. Paul was able to live on his own, away from their judging glances and biting remarks.

Living on his own had provided Paul with an emotional freedom he had never experienced before. He loved to be messy if he wanted to be. He could do anything he wanted to do at any given moment, including jacking off in every single room of the house whenever he wanted to rub one out. He loved coming home and dropping his shoes and belongings at the door. Often, he would walk down the hall, undressing as he went. He could lay on his couch completely naked if he wanted to and no one was going to do anything about it. He loved this freedom. He was loving it, that was until all this nightmare business began. All this fucking bullshit with this - this John Glow thing.

Paul stood in the mirror looking at himself and he could see his hands were beginning to tremble once again in the same way they had when he lived at home. His nerves had caused his body to tremble uncontrollably but had stopped when he moved out of his parents' house and was living on his own. The trembling had now returned. Returned with his lack of sleep and the rise in the levels of his negative stress. He found himself beginning to retreat inside his shell much like the scared little turtle who hides when they feel threatened. There, hiding inside himself, he could not be hurt. It was all about that inner turmoil and pain with Paul. He would go to great lengths to avoid it because stress and negative emotions hurt him physically.

Then there was this morning.

All five of the friends had been having these horrific nightmares. All five of the friends were being visited by John Glow on a nightly basis. Paul was part of that five and he was no different. No different until this morning. Sure, he had been waking up bruised from the conflict in his dreams, but Paul summed those bruises up as something he had inflicted upon himself in his fear and struggle to wake up from his nightmares. Bruises from trying to free himself from the onslaught of the nightmare-fueled attack. Fighting with yourself and the nightstand can, and does, leave bruises. He was living fucking proof of that. He was positive his injuries were self-inflicted. That was how he justified it to himself anyway, and that was working for Paul. That was, until this morning. The nightmare he had this morning was very violent, and it had taken on an even more twisted, sexual and sadistic turn. Glow had been hurting him, hitting and choking. That sort of thing.

Paul found himself in his nightmare face down on his bed with his arms and legs stretched out toward the four posts of the bed. He couldn't see the restraints, but he was sure he had been tied down. Paul found himself able to move some. He was restrained but he could move. He could feel the weight of Glow's body on his back, and he could smell him and feel his breath taunting him on the nape of his neck. Paul then felt Glow move down his body toward his feet. He felt Glow pause, as his tongue brushed across his ass. Once. Twice. Three times.

"Mmmm," he could hear Glow enjoying the taste of his skin.

One more flick of his tongue, this time it went down Paul's crack and then - bite. The pain was shooting through Paul's body searing into his nerve endings and racing to his brain.

Glow was now violently biting him.

Biting and biting his ass.

Paul struggled to look over his right shoulder. There was enough give in the restraints that he could see Glow's face as he raised up. There was blood and flesh dripping and hanging from his mouth.

Paul woke up screaming and fighting right after he saw Glow leaning over to go in for another bite of his flesh.

It took a moment for Paul to stop fighting as he slammed back into the reality of his bedroom. He lay there panting and crying. He understood that he was safe - awake and safe for the moment. He lay there on his bed sobbing as he saw the sun shining through his bedroom window sending shafts of light into the room down onto the floor.

Bravery usually came with the rising of the sun, but this morning's light brought with it nothing but pain.

Paul struggled to his feet and looked into his full-length mirror. To his shock there were actual bite marks on his butt. Purplish bite marks which had already begun to bruise. The fear came over Paul in waves as he understood the seriousness and the meaning of those bite marks.

Paul understood Glow was getting stronger and was now able to physically hurt him in his dreams and in the living world as well. How was that even fucking possible? Paul was living in some sort of bad horror film. How could this be fucking happening to him?

He quickly began to connect the dots within his mind. If Glow was able to bruise him and hurt him in his dreams, then Glow was completely capable of killing him as well. His nightmares could take his life.

"My life," Paul whispered as he looked at his naked body one more time in the mirror, running his hands lightly over his now-bruising ass.

Paul called Alex almost immediately after finding the bruised bite marks. He was on the verge of a complete breakdown by this point and Alex could hear it in his voice. They both agreed they needed to get the five friends together as soon as possible. Paul needed to share with the others what he had experienced. It was one thing to have nightmares, but it was a completely different thing when your nightmares began to physically hurt you. The craziness of the idea that Glow was able to cause pain and bruising was something they both were trying to wrap their minds around and what it could mean to all of them. Alex hung up with Paul and immediately called the others to meet that evening at the Stumble Inn.

Paul went to his bathroom and began looking at his over-tired and worn face in the mirror of his medicine cabinet hanging over his sink. Paul was getting ready to meet his friends at the dive bar.

He once again looked at his tired eyes staring back at him from the mirror and whispered,

"God help me." He turned off the bathroom light and headed to his bedroom to get dressed.

It was a nice evening when Paul left to meet his friends at the bar. Happy hour was in full swing by the time he arrived at the Stumble Inn. His friends were gathered around their usual table in the corner. He could tell they were already deep in conversation. The strange thought crossed his mind that they looked like a convergence of the knights of the round table. Paul sort of giggled at the thought. He looked at Jane, all serious-talking and clearly ready to go to war. She would have to be Guinevere for sure. But Jane was no damsel in distress. No, not a damsel at all. Or, just maybe, she was a Lancelot type, because she sure had balls big enough to fill his shoes. What would be the correct pronoun for Jane in that case? Would she be considered a He or a They? Paul still found the whole pronoun thing very confusing. It was not that he had objected to it, he just hadn't figured it all out yet. He did know for sure that he was a He. However, he had not completely decided which team he batted for, or if it was just draft season. He amused himself with his colorful way of describing his possible bisexuality. He smiled to himself because it was nice to have a moment where he could have a normal thought. It had been weeks since there had been just one moment of normal for him. The group must have sensed him standing there watching them because in a moment they all looked up and greeted him with awkward smiles. Paul could tell by their forced smiles that Alex had already let the cat out of the bag.

"You seem to be in a better mood," Alex said to him with some relief, noticing the smile.

Paul knew they were expecting him to be a complete and total broken down mess when he arrived, but to their surprise, he wasn't. He felt almost good. The noise of Happy Hour, the laughing in the room, the music, all of it gave him a sense of security. It made him feel not so alone. Seeing his friends with their heads all together trying to solve what seemed unsolvable was a reassuring sight and he had found very little reassurance over the past weeks. In this moment he devoured it because it filled his craving for some type of normalcy. He wanted life to be normal once again and if this was as normal it was going to get then so be it. He was going to enjoy it.

"Will you go into the bathroom and show me? Well, um, you know, show me your, um like, show me your bruises?" Chuck said nervously.

Paul had to smile at Chuck's discomfort. It was not as if they had never seen each other's asses before. The only difference here was Chuck had never had to ask to see it before and it was making him more than uncomfortable in a weird straight-guy kind of way. In fact, they had decided before Paul arrived that Chuck had to be the one to look because he was the only completely straight guy of the bunch. Jane was out because she was a girl. Then of course Bobby could play on both teams and sometimes all teams at the same time, so that would be awkward. Of course, Alex was a screaming 'Mo' so that wouldn't be completely appropriate either. So that left Chuck, wishing for once in his life he wasn't straight because this was a burden that he was not sure he wanted to carry. Chuck also couldn't understand what sexual orientation had to do with it at all. For God's sake they were talking about Paul's ass. It is not like any of them was going to instantly tap that, even though it wasn't a bad ass, and Paul was somewhat good looking - in a geeky sort of way. His looks wouldn't be an issue at all. The fact that Paul would talk incessantly about the strangest bullshit would be the problem. Chuck could see Paul discussing the origins of the South African Bushmen as a bobbing head gave him a blow job, wishing he would just shut up and go with the moment. Paul definitely wasn't the kind of guy to just let it all go and lean into it.

Paul and Chuck both stepped into the larger handicapped stall in the men's bathroom. No one in the restroom thought anything of it. After all, it was the Stumble Inn, and the bathroom had seen its share of people stepping into stalls together throughout the years. It was no freaking big deal. Chuck closed the stall door and locked it with a large sigh as if he was telling anyone who may be in the bathroom this was a boring thing and not anything out of the ordinary was going on. Basically, Chuck's loud and long sigh was to announce to the room that they were not fucking and not going to fuck. In the meantime, Paul was loosening his belt, getting ready to, well literally, show his ass. Paul looked at Chuck who was looking at his feet. Paul turned with his back to Chuck and slowly dropped his pants and underwear.

"Oh my God," he could hear Chuck's reaction coming from behind.

"Yeah, I get that a lot," Paul quipped, trying to hide how invasive and humiliating it all felt.

'Oh my God' pretty much summed it all up for Paul. Chuck seemed to show no concern or any sort of empathy. Paul wasn't prepared for that, and he hurriedly pulled up his pants and began to buckle his belt. The color had left Chuck's face as Paul looked at him. Chuck wasn't someone who was easily rattled. Chuck was rattled, as the reality of their situation began to set in. Paul could tell in an instant that all of Chuck's concern was surrounding no one else but Chuck, without too much thought of Paul at all. There are those moments of clarity that show you where you stand with people who claim to be your friends. In one moment, Chuck had showed Paul it was all about Chuck. Chuck was the only one in the moment that mattered. He was wrapped up in himself. Paul's feelings were not only hurt, but he could also feel the anger rising within him.

"I don't know what to say man," was the only thing Chuck could say as they left the bathroom to rejoin the other friends who were anxiously waiting for them at the table.

When they walked up to the table Paul noticed Chuck nodded a yes toward the group. It irritated him because he knew the nod was a signal to them that Chuck had seen the actual purported bitemarks. Jesus Christ, like they didn't believe him. Paul sat uncomfortably onto the hard wooden chair. He could feel his anger continue rise. He sat back into the chair looking at the group.

"So, tell me, are you completely fucking satisfied now that someone has seen the bruised bitemarks on my fucking ass? Come on, it's like you didn't believe me. I know how it is. I know what you thought. You though crazy fucking Paul was coming unglued once again," Paul was clearly pissed, and the group knew it.

"I told you because I trusted you. Because of all people I thought you were the ones who would understand. I mean, goddammit, we are going through the same fucking thing here," Paul was glaring at each of them as he spoke.

"Hey, it wasn't that way at all," Jane jumped in to try to defuse the situation because other customers were beginning to take notice around them.

"I know exactly the way it is, you stupid fucking bitch. I know enough to know that all of this is your goddamn fault. I know that." Paul rose to his feet with his face getting redder and redder as he spoke.

There it was - out in the open - and there was no taking it back now. The other guys were trying to calm him, but nothing was going to change the fact they had showed their true selves to him. Nothing was going to change the fact that none of them trusted him enough to believe him.

"I am just crazy fucking Paul to you. You know what my biggest fucking mistake was? My biggest mistake was thinking all of you might be different from everyone else. I was so damn wrong. You are just fucking like them. You might even be worse. You know what - fuck this. Fuck you. FUCK ALL OF YOU!"

Paul was clearly on the move now and headed through the crowd to the door with Chuck following close behind. Chuck followed Paul all the way to his car. He had always been the one to be able to calm Paul down when he would lose control. He knew at this moment Paul was more out of control than he had ever seen him before. Chuck grabbed Paul's hand as it reached to open the car door.

"Hey man, it wasn't like that at all. You are seeing this in the wrong way bro," Chuck said sincerely, clearly pleading with Paul at this point not to leave.

"Don't you fucking touch me," Paul said and in one movement he slammed both hands into Chucks chest, knocking him to the ground.

Chuck was shocked by the brute force of the impact, and he hit the ground hard. When he was able to catch his breath and look up, Paul was already gone. Alex came running around the corner of the building to see Chuck on the ground and Paul driving away. He rushed to Chuck's side and helped him to his feet.

"Fuck them," Paul said as he drove away. The literal pain in his ass was a constant reminder of the nightmare he was living. Tears were streaming down his face.

Paul was driving erratically. He was trying to calm himself so he could just concentrate and drive. He knew he needed to find someplace to go. He knew he needed to hide and just get away from all of it. The one single place he knew he could go was his parents' downtown apartment. There he would be able to hide. It was a place where he could go figure this fucking shit out on his own because it was obvious no one else was going to help him. Hell, they couldn't even fucking trust him.

"Pieces of shit," Paul said under his breath as he continued weaving through the streets of the city toward downtown.

Thankfully, Paul knew his parents were gone on some fucking trip of some kind. They were always fucking gone. Paul was grateful for that because he knew he couldn't take any of his mother's "insipid" comments at this moment. He was sure this was a saving grace. A saving grace more for her than him because he would not be responsible if he decided to bust her wine glass up the side of her fucking ugly head. No, he was glad the bitch was gone, and she had taken his insignificant and pussy-whipped father with her. Max the doorman would be there and he would not let anyone in. No one would get in without his approval. There, Paul was completely sure he could be alone. There Paul could think.

Paul stopped at a stop sign at a crosswalk. There was an old man in the middle of the crossing. The man looked somewhat homeless with a dirty black overcoat and matted grey dreadlocks for hair.

Once the man was in front of Paul's car, he turned and brought both hands down hard upon the hood with a crazed scream, "GLOW!"

The man's eyes were nothing but crazy, glowing white orbs. Paul knew exactly who it was, and he put his foot on the gas, throwing the man off the hood of his car. He knew it was Glow and he was loose, and he was coming for him. To Paul's surprise, at the next intersection, there was the crazed dreadlocked man smiling once again as he raced by. The next intersection and the next were the same.

Paul drove faster through each consecutive intersection.

The fear was increasingly rising within himself as he sped through the streets, veering around to avoid the reappearing Glow, praying he would not be stopped by a cop. All the way into downtown he was followed by the crazed homeless man on every corner. The man had obviously been possessed with the essence of John Glow. Glow was loose and he was following Paul all the way home. Intersection by intersection and corner by corner there he was - white eyed and smiling.

Finally, Paul reached the safety of the garage at his parent's apartment house. He pulled into his father's parking space and turned off the car. He looked around the florescent-lit garage, but there was no one there with him. He waited a moment, looking to make sure he had not been followed.

He took a deep breath.

Maybe here he would be safe. Maybe here he could finally escape this living nightmare. He was crying heavily as he got out of the car and shut the door. Maybe here everyone would leave him alone. The long-time lobby doorman Max tried to greet Paul with a smile and greeting. He had known Paul all the young man's life. He was surprised and shocked as a tear-stained Paul brushed him and his greeting aside without saying a word.

The fear, the anxiety, the pain, the anger all began to somewhat subside and wash away as Paul stepped into the elevator and the door closed. He felt this was the right place for him to be. This is where he would be safe. He looked up at the number screen like a wounded animal as the elevator began to rise to the 36th floor.

Chapter 13
Alone

Paul felt as if his whole world was being held up by nothing more than a precarious layer of thin ice. As if, at any moment, the surface would crack, and everything would come crashing down around him as he drowned in the disaster of everything he was and everything he had ever known. He had known loneliness in his life, that was true. He knew how to handle being alone and now he even found himself craving the quiet of solitude and the calm of that aloneness. What he had never felt before was this fear that was now growing within him. He was afraid. Truly afraid for the first time in his life.

The elevator door opened on the 36th floor and Paul began the walk down the long hall toward his parent's apartment. They lived at the end the hall. It was the largest apartment on that level, which took up over a quarter of the 36th floor. Prime real estate. This was the place Paul had always known to be home. It was one of the first major modern high-rise apartments in the city when his parents bought it shortly before his birth.

Children were an afterthought for Paul's parents. In fact, they had waited until they had thriving careers before even considering having children. It was how they always thought of Paul. He was always last on their list of importance. Paul found out a long time ago his life remained calm and undisturbed as long as he didn't rock the boat.

He put the code into the lock on the door. His parents bought one of those digital locks a few years back and Paul appreciated the fact he didn't have to keep track of a key that he hardly ever used. He was grateful for that. Paul found it interesting that the code they had programmed into the door was his birth date. I mean, they most likely felt like it was a safe and difficult code for someone to figure out since they themselves had enough trouble remembering the year. Hard as that was for them to fucking remember, it irritated Paul they had reduced his birth year to nothing more than a security code for the fucking door. They most likely didn't even remember the significance of the number.

They obviously didn't, because every single damn birthday they would ask Paul, "How old are you this year?"

His mother even forgot his birth month completely once, thinking that it was August when it was actually January. How in the hell was she able to confuse the unbearable heat of a St. Louis August for a bitterly cold St. Louis January? It really was fucking remarkable when Paul thought about it.

The door unlocked easily with the code and Paul entered the apartment turning on lights as he went.

The apartment was impressive. His parents were big fans of a mid-century modern aesthetic combined with a love for contemporary art. The whole apartment looked like it had been staged for some type of fucking Architectural Digest photo shoot. Slick, and not feeling lived-in at all. You might even call it cold. Paul stepped into the living room and looked toward glass doors that led out to the balcony which overlooked the city. This whole side of the condo was nothing but a huge soaring wall of glass. It was an impressive view for sure, mixed in with a classic design.

There was a huge Warhol self-portrait overlooking the entire open living area on one wall, watching the activity of the world below very intently. Paul always thought the large, oversized portrait felt like an overly eccentric, wild, white-haired pagan god who was peering down upon him in judgment. It was as if the Warhol god could strike him down at any moment for being too loud, or not loud enough, for his parents to ignore. The goal was to blend into the room and not be part of the scene. It was quite the balancing act to make yourself be invisible, but the Warhol god was always there judging him to make sure that is what exactly happened.

There was an even larger Lichtenstein hanging on the other wall. She was a comic-book-looking girl crying into a phone. Paul had always wondered why she was so sad. What was the conversation she was having on that phone to make her cry like that for eternity? Maybe someone had died or maybe someone was telling her they didn't love her anymore. Or maybe, just maybe, she was watching Paul's life and was telling the person on the other end of that phone all about how sad and pathetic it was. Whatever she was saying, Paul felt a weird sort of kinship with her. He felt like he knew her. Like they understood each other. Unlike the Warhol god looking down with his severe and crazed judgement, the crying-phone-girl was his friend. They say, 'misery loves company' and that is what she brought to Paul. She understood his sadness because she understood her own. She was his friend because they shared misery.

Paul walked over to the bar kicking off his shoes to see if he could find a beer somewhere. To his disdain, when he opened the empty bar fridge there was nothing. His mother's white wine was kept in a cooler at the other end of the bar and his father had given into scotch many years ago. The scotch was most likely his father's attempt to deaden his madness – which stemmed from living with the witch that was his wife and Paul's mother. 'Witch' was a polite way for Paul to describe the woman who he found had nothing of value at all within her. Absolutely no goodness resided within the woman who had a pretentiousness, coldness and indifference to absolutely everyone and everything in the world.

Paul was used to them being gone. They had literally been gone most of his life in both a figurative and a literal sense. He had been raised by a series of nannies which were relationships that would always end fraught with contradiction. When he would start to get comfortable with a nanny, like children often will do, his mother would then swoop in with a fit of jealousy and replace her. To Paul it seemed that if she couldn't love him then no one was going to. It had nothing to do at all with Paul showing feelings for someone else instead of her. It had everything to do with the nanny showing him the love and compassion his mother either did not want or was unable to give to him. That substitution just would not do under her gaze and under her roof. It made Paul too visible, and just maybe there was a twinge of guilt within her, even though Paul felt for sure his mother was incapable of love or caring.

Paul's mother had none of the qualities you would expect from a mother. She was a beast. She made sure the nanny revolving door played out repeatedly throughout his childhood, leaving him feeling that if he showed love to anyone, they would leave him. If that didn't work, she would send them scurrying away.

He thought of his mother like the Queen of Hearts character in Alice in Wonderland, "How dare you show affection to the boy. Off with your head."

It was true the jealously was rooted in the reality that she did not like to share her things. Paul was nothing more than something she owned. Nothing of any real monetary value. In fact, it was the thing she owned which had the audacity to cost her. Paul was nothing but one huge expense and disappointment that bothered her at all times.

"Alexa, shuffle EDM music" Paul announced.

Music began to pump through the rooms' hidden sound system. Paul decided to pour himself some of his father's expensive scotch. Not because he liked scotch, but because he got the satisfaction that it would irritate his father to no end. It made the expensive smoky flavor taste even better and go down even easier. He took a sip of his drink and then headed outside to the balcony overlooking the city. The night wasn't too cold for the first time in a long time. It was spring in St. Louis. The best time of year to live in the city.

Paul walked over to the balcony and peered down into the street far below. The cars looked like small Hot Wheels vehicles as they zoomed back and forth. There were tiny people moving hurriedly through their lives, never suspecting that he was watching them from above, much like he was being watched by the Warhol god on the wall. He thought of a flea circus as he watched them scurrying below. He had never seen an actual flea circus and he had heard it was nothing more than mechanical things moving to give the appearance as if fleas were moving them. Paul smiled. The circus of the little things below were real, even though they were all programmed to act in very mechanical ways.

Paul took a deep breath and looked up.

He could see the St. Louis arch in the distance, floodlights illuminating its aluminum façade, making it glimmer and gleam as it soared up into the night sky. Paul thought of the lifetime of Fourth of Julys he spent standing in this spot looking at the arch, waiting for dusk. The balcony was a great place to watch fireworks during Fair St. Louis on the fourth. The arch was infamous for its huge, monster fireworks display.

Paul set his glass of scotch carefully on the rail which came up to about the height of his chest. He stretched his arms up to the sky looking up through all the light noise of the city toward the stars which lay beyond the glow of the atmosphere.

He took a large deep cleansing breath.

He was beginning to relax. He dropped his arms to his sides and noticed how tired he was getting. He wasn't sure if it was the scotch running through his veins, the trauma of the entire night, or both - but he was truly tired. He was hoping he would sleep well since there had been very little sleep recently. Deep down he felt this was the place to rest, as unhappy as it might have been for him growing up. Here he would be alone and protected. He found himself praying to the Warhol god that he would finally be able to sleep. He turned around on the balcony with his back to the city and began to...

"War," hissed Glow from his thin, taut lips.

Paul found himself standing face to face with glowing white eyes. This was the horrific face from his dreams and not the dreadlocked demon from the streets. He was standing face to face with the John Glow who haunted him in his nightmares and there was no one to help him. Not even the Lichtenstein phone girl looking out upon them crying into the phone. Now Paul understood her tears. They were tears of fear.

No one could hear him scream.

A personal war of manipulation and will was just beginning. Neither of them was leaving this balcony until it was over.

This was war.

A war Paul was incredibly inept to fight. He was just not equipped for the psychological onslaught which lay before him. The flea circus city continued moving beneath him, unaware of his danger and unable to help him from below. Glow had him expertly trapped like a lamb to the slaughter and Paul knew there was no escaping him.

Glow growled in delight because he had Paul exactly where he wanted him. This was not going to end well for Paul Fairchild. But for John Glow the calling card he was about to leave for the others would be epic.

Chapter 14
Velocity

Rapid acceleration, due to gravity, leads to high-velocity impact upon hitting the ground. The sudden deceleration of the human body during impact generates tremendous forces that can literally tear the human body apart. The body's major blood vessels rupture, bones shatter, internal organs crush and often lacerate. What may be even worse is the victim is alive and aware as they are falling to their almost guaranteed death. It is not the falling that kills them, but the impact below that brings with it an instant, slamming death.

SLAM.

LIGHTS OUT.

Most bodies will land flat for the initial impact.

Then, the body will bounce.

The human body will often bounce upon hitting the surface. Obviously, the odds are very good the victim is dead immediately at first impact and thankfully doesn't even feel the bounce.

There is blood.

An adult human body holds approximately 1.2 to 1.5 gallons of blood inside the body. The pattern of blood spatter is used to determine the height, force, and velocity of how a body fell.

In this case, a fall from the 36th floor.

Paul's body hit the pavement below and bounced. He was already dead from the initial impact of his body landing half-on and half-off the sidewalk, his back broken with his legs reaching into the street in a contorted position. Blood began to pool out from beneath his severely broken body as it landed a second time from the bounce. His right arm lay a distance away from his body after being severed by the extreme force of the initial impact. Paul's body was demolished.

Paul was dead.

It appeared to Vincent that every single emergency vehicle and squad car in the city was at the scene. The glare of the lights on the glass façade of the apartment building lit the streets and sent a strange glow throughout the neighborhood. Curious and shocked, neighbors were standing on their balconies looking at the chaos below. Vincent noticed an older man standing next to the front entrance of the building. He was the doorman who was on duty. He could tell the doorman was crying.

Vincent whispered to the officer attending to the doorman, "Let's get his statement and see if he saw anything unusual or knows anything about what went on here. We have a dead guy splattered across the sidewalk and street, and I want to know why."

The scene investigation team was already there gathering the evidence. They told Vincent they believed a male had fallen from a balcony on the 36th floor. At this point they thought it looked more like a suicide than a homicide. Vincent thought that was interesting. How could they reach any conclusions now – besides, it wasn't part their job anyway. That job belonged to him.

Vincent stepped into the elevator, and he began the journey upwards toward the apartment. At this point, they knew the victim was a young man who appeared to be in his early twenties or even early thirties. It was hard to distinguish his age due to the condition of the body. Vincent was a little irritated with himself because he forgot to ask if they had any identification on the victim. But obviously, no identification had been found yet or they would have been able to give him an exact age instead of making a guess. Damn. Vincent was hoping they were able to ensure an easy identification for the family. It was always easier on a family in that way. They liked to avoid having a family member identify a victim with this type of injuries in a morgue like you often see in the movies or on television. That rarely happened anymore - and for good reason. Seeing your loved one in that type of condition could fuck someone up for life.

Vincent walked down the hall toward all of the activity and an open door leading into an apartment. He noted immediately that, whoever this victim was, there was some type of connection to money. Big money, from what Vincent could tell, by his initial look at what had to be a five-million-dollar apartment at least. Vincent noticed the scotch decanter on the bar with the lid off, laying to the side. On the floor, completely out of place for the scene, was a pair of sneakers that had been kicked off and left where they fell. It was strange because this was the type of home where you didn't find anything just laying around. Everything here had a place and at this moment these somewhat dirty, worn Vans seemed very out of character for whomever owned the apartment.

Vincent looked around but found nothing else unusual. It didn't appear like anything had been disturbed. There was some electronic music playing in the background. The only major clue Vincent could find by simple sight alone, was a single patio chair that had been pulled up next to the balcony rail. Vincent felt it had likely assisted the victim to climb over the black metal railing and jump or fall to his death below.

Vincent walked toward the balcony in front of him. He stepped outside slowly taking in the scene. He first noticed a glass of scotch sitting on the balcony ledge which, height-wise, hit Vincent about mid chest. It seemed to Vincent an accident could most likely be ruled out. The only thing Vincent could see was the single chair, which was out of place, likely taken away from the glass table that was placed in the center of the balcony up against the wall. The back of the chair was facing toward the railing. Instantly, Vincent knew in his gut that the victim had used the chair to get over the balcony and plunge to his death. But why?

Vincent looked at the investigator taking prints.

"Make sure you get me some good impressions from the chair, the glass and the rail," Vincent said as he walked back into the apartment. That is when he saw a picture of a family on a shelf.

A family picture. It only had three people in it. None of the three people in the portrait were smiling and Vincent instantly got the impression that these people didn't love or like each other very much. It was an older man, an older woman and off to the right-hand side was a sad looking young man. Vincent immediately knew exactly who the young man was. It was one of the five suspects from his other case. The case with the dead medium.

Now there were three dead bodies. All three connected to Alexander McAllister. All three apparently taking their own lives. Okay, sure it was a little early to jump to conclusions on this current scene, but the facts were beginning to line up. All the facts were pointing directly at Alex. He knew all three of the victims. This was something more than just mere coincidence, but that something was not clear at this point in his investigation.

An investigator entered the apartment and approached Vincent.

"Well, the doorman has identified the victim. His name is…" the investigator stopped mid-sentence as Vincent raised his hand to stop him.

"His name is Paul Fairchild, and he is, or I should say was, a suspect in one of my other cases," replied Vincent as he wrote Paul's name into his notes.

The investigator looked at him perplexed as he asked, "Do you believe there is a connection?"

Vincent quickly replied, "Maybe. I'm headed downstairs to question the doorman for myself. This apparent suicide has just taken a very strange turn."

Vincent worked his way down to the lobby of the building where the doorman was now sitting with his head in his hands. Vincent felt sorry for him because he knew this guy was having one fucked-up work night. He also knew these doormen were sometimes very attached to the residents of their building.

Suddenly it hit Vincent. Paul Fairchild did not give this as his home address. Why? Vincent had a terrific memory, and this address would have stuck out immediately. After all, this is one of the most exclusive condo buildings in the city. Vincent thought it was much more likely that this was his parents' apartment, because he doubted the mousey Paul Fairchild could afford such an extravagant location. Well, that, and the family picture he had seen upstairs. Vincent took a deep breath and walked over to start questioning the older doorman.

The old guy was clearly rattled. Vincent noticed his hands were shaking and his voice somewhat quivered as he spoke. It was not unusual for people to be nervous when being questioned. He expected that. Vincent could tell he was looking into the face of loss and grief. Instinctively, this told Vincent the old guy had worked there for a long time and would be able to fill in a lot of missing pieces. It is amazing how much a person can tell you about themselves without even speaking. The way they dress says a lot about them. Are they well groomed? Vincent always looked their shoes. Clean and shiny shoes always told a lot about a person. Were the shoes leather or plastic? Are they looking into his eyes when they answer his questions? If they are not, try to figure out if it is because they are just nervous or self-conscious. Pay very close attention to what they are saying. Are they looking at you in the eye while answering a question but then they instantly break that eye contact and look down or away? This had always been a telling moment in many of his cases. What are they doing with their hands? Do they fidget when they talk? Did the person being questioned just cross their arms over their chest to close them off from you? Did you notice a gesture they keep repeating? Vincent had seen this political candidate once who would pull on his ear every time he lied. Every single time there was the ear-pulling, and every single time it turned out they were not telling the truth.

All these things mattered. They mattered a lot, and Vincent was a master at reading all the cues from a person and not just their words. Vincent had always thought this was something he learned instinctively from his experiences growing up gay. Being a gay man, you had to be sharp in reading people to be able to tell if you were in a safe situation or not. It was a survival skill. Reading a room correctly could sometimes save you from harm, or at least an unforgiving situation. Vincent was sure this was true. He knew for a fact gay men used eye contact and simple gestures to test out if another person was gay or not. That was fact and this wasn't some type of mythical gaydar they were using. Not at all. Gay men are experts at reading the non-verbal cues, especially the cues from other men. His focus turned back to the old doorman who was waiting for him nervously.

Vincent knew talking with the old guy was going to be difficult. He was sure the doorman was now wishing it had been his day off or he had called in sick. This guy was having one fucking bad night at work. He was nervous and overwhelmed with sadness and Vincent could see it and feel it radiating from him as he spoke. It was his job and the people in this building were something the doorman took very seriously. Vincent knew the old guy was trying to figure out in his head what he could have done differently that would have helped the now dead and broken young man lying in the street.

Vincent's first questions were the basic information-type questions. He wanted to set a conversational tone. The basic starter questions helped relax the old doorman a little and get him ready for the more difficult questions surrounding the death. Logical as this approach sounds, Vincent had seen many detectives who would just plow right into the meat of the matter, regardless of how the person they were questioning was feeling. Rarely was this insensitive approach as successful as giving the process a moment for the person to feel like it was just a conversation. You could literally see them relax when that happened. In the case of a suspect? Well, this process relaxed more than one suspect into misspeaking, which opened the door to a confession and their eventual conviction. The role of a questioner should always be as a listener more than anything else. You must know how to shut up and listen. You want them to do the talking as much as possible and the way you do that is to listen and keep your mouth shut.

"Name?" Vincent asked.

"Max. Max Washington, sir," the doorman replied.

In the process of a few minutes, Max shared with Vincent that he had worked there for a very long time, and he had also known the Fairchild family since they moved in almost 30 years ago. In fact, he had known Paul Fairchild for his whole life. He saw Paul the first day they brought him home as a baby. He also filled in some background. The parents were out of town, currently vacationing overseas. France, Max thought, but he wasn't completely sure. Vincent found out that Paul's parents were very wealthy. Paul's father was a successful stockbroker and Paul's mother was a high-ranking advertising executive who headed some of the city's largest beer accounts.

Vincent was interested in this type of background because wealth often played a big part in these cases. You would be surprised what people will do for a few dollars. The more zeroes you put on an amount someone has attained, the more inventive and elaborate these crimes could get. Vincent had to wonder if there was a financial connection somewhere and if Alex McAllister or any of the others were connected to it. None of it was making much sense. However, he knew he was missing something because, sure, coincidences can sometimes play into things, but he knew that was extremely rare.

There was something he was missing within all of this, but what was it?

Vincent knew it was time to drill the questioning down to the events of tonight. He asked the doorman what he had seen that evening. Then he sat back and assumed his role as a listener. Vincent took notes and listened intently while giving encouraging nods. Just let them talk and you will find out more than you ever wanted to or thought you needed to know.

"It had been a quiet evening you know. Not much going on. I had a few residents come in and out. Overall, it was a real quiet kind of night. Nothing that I would say was out of place. I knew every single person who came in and out of this building. This is my building. I have been here for thirty years. I know this building and I know the people who live in it. Then there was tonight. You know I think this might be the worst thing that has ever happened here in the whole time I have been here. We had a few suicides of course through the years. One of the lady residents took some pills and another, a man, well he cut his wrists in his bathtub. But this, this was different. This was out in the open for the world to see. Hard to cover up something like this and protect people from seeing such a thing. I know it will give me nightmares for the rest of my years. I will tell you that."

Max cleared his throat for a moment looking out to the front where the investigation was going full force around the victim.

Looking back at Vincent with tears in his eyes, Max continued with his story, "When Paul Fairchild walked into the lobby from the garage tonight, I could tell instantly there was something not right about him. I have known him all his life, so I am not a stranger to him or anything like that. He usually stops when he comes in to talk with me about life and tell me what he has got going on and all, well, with everything, you know. Just keeping me up to date about him and things like that. He has always been a good kid. I've always been quite fond of him. So, imagine tonight when I saw him upset like this. Yeah, he was very upset. To my surprise when I tried to talk to him, he just kind of rushed past me without saying a word. I could tell he was upset. It was obvious he was, or had been, crying. Of course, it upset me a little too you know. That is how these young people are these days. I didn't pry. I mean, I never pry into their lives because their lives are their business, and I always try to not pry. But I was worried about him. I can tell you something had really upset him. He wasn't behaving like himself at all. The elevator door opened for him immediately and in an instant, he was gone headed upstairs. It was about 8:30 or so. No one else came in or out of the building. It was an unusually quiet night. It was about an hour or so when I heard the commotion outside the front of the building. I thought maybe, just maybe, I thought I heard a scream, but I can't be sure because it all happened so fast you know. Maybe I am reaching and filling in what would make sense to me you know? I mean, you must try to find some kind of reason for why a young man with his whole life in front of him would do something like this. I mean, I just don't understand. Why would he do this?"

Max was holding back tears as he told the entire story of what he knew and had seen. It was difficult for him. He had done a good job of filling in the details for Vincent. The old guy wasn't a hostile witness by any means and Vincent knew if he thought of anything additional, he could easily get in touch with him and vice-versa. Vincent handed Max his business card with his number and once again headed out to the front entry of the building.

Vincent saw that things were moving along quickly with the on-scene investigation because they were already measuring the blood spatter. Even though Vincent was sure Paul had jumped from the balcony, the forensic evidence would help to back this up. At least he hoped it would help. Vincent walked over to the edge of the sidewalk, stopping at the curb. He took a few deep breaths.

He spoke to the attending investigators, "Will somebody see if there was some type of security footage that might help us figure this goddamn thing out?"

Someone agreed and was on the way to see if there was a CCTV video they could secure. Vincent stood on the curb looking forward, trying to tune out the chaos around him. Sometimes you had to take a moment and just shut the ugly out. And this scene was, without question, ugly.

Vincent inhaled the fresh cool night air.

The horror of the scene was in direct contrast with what was a very nice spring evening. Vincent noticed what appeared to be lightning flashing off in the distance. Some movement across the street caught his eye. There, standing opposite him on the other side of the street, was what appeared to be a homeless man with grey dreadlocks, wearing a dirty black trench coat.

He was laughing.

A crazy laugh.

Vincent and the man locked eyes for a quick moment. Then the man instantly stopped laughing and quickly walked away mumbling some type of nonsense to himself as he went. Vincent felt the hairs standing up on his arms as he watched the strange man walk into the darkness. The man darted off onto a side street out of sight and was gone. It all happened very quickly giving Vincent very little time to react.

Vincent stood on the curb and shook off the chill and thought to himself, "Did the man have white eyes? Man, that was some damn bad cataracts. It was amazing the creepy guy could see at all, let alone navigate the dark streets."

Vincent chuckled to himself shaking his head. He had already enough of this night, but he knew it was only just beginning for him. After a moment he took a deep breath and turned back to face the hurried, horrific scene behind him. The night was obviously getting to him. Vincent looked over and saw the investigators surrounding Paul's severed arm laying in the street, a good distance from the body.

"It must have been quite a bounce," Vincent whispered under his breath as he continued working the scene.

Chapter 15
Revelation

Alex couldn't sleep. It wasn't that he didn't want to sleep. Alex was terrified to sleep. Every time he dozed, even the slightest bit, Glow was there in the darkness waiting for him, ready to pounce. Glow never said much to him. The attack was always more physical than verbal.

Jane had told Alex she would have conversations with Glow. For Jane, part of her torture was Glow talking to her while he abused and raped her. She said it was the sick part of it all. He would often describe what he was going to do to her right before the act itself. Glow understood that, for Jane, the anticipation of pain was almost worse than the pain itself. So, he would sadistically savor her anticipation. Glow somehow instinctively knew for Jane the idea of being choked was just as frightening as the choking itself. He was inflicting pain differently with each individual. The pain was customized to cause the most efficiently effective emotional and physical damage. Yet, none of them could figure out how Glow knew so much about each of them to be able to personalize their torture.

With Alex, Glow just spoke in snippets of phrases to tease and accentuate his attack. He wouldn't let Alex know what he was going to do before he did it. He would just carry out the attack. He knew the 'not knowing' part of it was the greatest torture for Alex. The words he used were to make sure each act of violence was causing sufficient fear and pain. Glow would hit, choke, bite, scratch and cut his way onto and into Alex's body.

Yes, Alex was now also being violently raped.

With each involuntary penetration Alex was sinking deeper and deeper into the darkness of his helplessness. There was nothing he could do but pray the attack would end or he would wake up.

Meanwhile, Glow would continue thrusting his large member into Alex with a vengeance while laughing and ridiculing as he pushed. Alex would bite his lip because he knew Glow was wanting to hear him scream and react to the pain. Glow thrived on Alex's fear. It was almost as if he fed upon it like some kind of fucked-up, nightmarish vampire. Except this vampire fed on the adrenaline of fear, pain and deep sadness instead of blood.

The idea of some type of energy vampire made sense to Alex. Emotion is energy and a life-giving force. At least that was the way it felt. He wouldn't scream because he understood when he screamed the overly large penis would slam into him harder.

But why when he screamed?

Alex surmised that his pain and his fear of the pain was something Glow was feeding upon. It had nothing to do with the sex at all. It had everything to do with how Alex reacted to being helplessly, violently raped. Then there was tonight's attack.

Tonight's attack was different and even more disturbing. Tonight, Alex awoke from his nightmare naked. Alex had been completely clothed when he fell asleep. In Alex's mind he thought if maybe he stayed dressed Glow wouldn't be able to rape him. He felt that just maybe it would give him a fighting chance. Obviously, it didn't.

When Alex was aware of the nightmare happening, he was already naked on the bed with his legs spread completely apart with Glow's head between them, nibbling on his penis.
Alex was completely paralyzed unable to move.
Once Glow realized Alex was aware of what was happening to him, he then rolled Alex over onto his side and began to viciously dry fuck him with his enormous cock. Alex could still, even afterwards, feel the pain shooting through his body as it slammed in and out, rearranging his insides.
Glow had reveled in the fact that he shoved his dick in 'dry and rough.' He growled and hissed at Alex, telling him it was his favorite way to fuck his bitch boys.

Alex had woken up fighting with the air around him. It took a moment to understand that his nightmare was over. Slowly he began to settle down. His heart was beating wildly in his chest. Alex felt he needed to slow it down even more before he moved too quickly. He lay back upon his pillows taking deep breaths. He could sense the sweat on his naked body, and he could feel the wetness on his sheets. His heart had finally begun to slow, and after a moment Alex got up and walked into his bathroom to get a drink of water. He had knocked his glass of water off the bedside table during his waking fight.

The nightmares always ended this way with Alex coming out of them fighting. The second the paralysis lifted; Alex would begin to fight. He was sure the glass of water was also why his sheets were soaking wet. He stood in the bathroom doorway for a moment looking around the room. Nothing seemed out of place. He was alone. His pillows and blanket were thrown onto the floor. The sheets on his bed were covered in *blood*.

He stopped for a moment and looked again at his bed as the panic began to take hold.

"Blood?" Alex said out loud in a clearly distressed tone. "Real fucking blood, this was no fucking dream," he said out loud, clearly in distress.

Alex flipped the light switch on and his bedroom was flooded with bright white light from overhead. He now saw clearly there was blood smeared all over the white sheets on his bed. He saw, in one corner of the bed, a perfect, bloody handprint. Alex reached his shaking hand out to see if it matched his own. He held his hand just above the handprint. It didn't match. The handprint was not his and it was a man's. Alex instantly knew the handprint belonged to Glow.

"Oh my god, he can come out of my fucking dreams. "

Alex panicked immediately grabbing to inspect his genitals making sure there were no bite marks or bites taken out of anything. He needed to make sure there was no blood coming from there.

"Please God don't let it be coming from there."

After a very close inspection Alex was satisfied his penis and scrotum were fine and intact. Then, Alex reached behind to feel his buttocks. He felt wetness. Alex slowly brought his hand back around to see it and when he did it was covered in blood. Alex knew he was bleeding from the rectal attack and that frightened him even more.

Blood, real fucking blood was on his sheets and his body.

His blood.

Alex could then feel the real physical damage that had been caused leaving his insides bleeding from the attack. Alex knew enough about anal sex to know that bleeding could happen in rougher situations if not handled properly with patience, timing and lubricant. Alex also knew if the bleeding didn't subside soon, or the pain got any worse, he would have to go to the ER. The last thing Alex wanted to do was to go to the hospital again. There would be questions because it was obvious that Alex had been raped and he wasn't sure he would be able to explain it to someone without them thinking he was insane, or he had hurt himself with something like a broomstick.

"More like a fucking baseball bat," Alex said correcting his own thought out loud.

"They would think I was fucking insane," he said as he rushed naked into the bathroom.

Alex quickly jumped into the shower. He wanted to make sure the bleeding had stopped, and he was clean - in case he did have to go to the hospital. The hot shower felt good on his body. He stood under the water still shaking, trying to gain his composure and his thoughts. He watched some blood mix with the hot water and go down the drain. He wasn't quite sure if it was new or just left over from the attack. He stood under the water for a bit longer, making sure the water was running clear before getting out of the shower. Alex dried off and then took a tissue to check for any more blood. To his relief, there was nothing on the tissue. It appeared, for now, that he was going to be all right. Alex opened his medicine cabinet and took two ibuprofens for his pain. If that couldn't cut the pain, then he would need to worry.

Alex went into the bedroom, grabbed the soiled sheets off his bed and threw them into the washing machine that was hidden in a closet in his kitchen. He then came back into the bedroom and put fresh sheets onto the bed. He dressed quickly, grabbing a clean pair of gym shorts and a tee from his dresser drawer. The clothing felt like an armor to him for the moment. Being naked made him feel weak and vulnerable. For the first time in a very long time Alex didn't feel comfortable in his own skin. He felt dirty, and, as if for some reason, he had done something, whatever that something was, to cause it all. All of this was his own fucking fault, and no one needed to tell him it wasn't.

This wasn't fucking happening to him because they used a goddamn spirit board. There had to be another cause for this. This seemed way too personal for it to be caused from just one session with the board. No, this was something else. He was sure of it. He was sure it had all been set in motion even before Ellis committed suicide. Alex was sure it was Glow who had caused Ellis' death. Ellis had told him somebody lied, and Alex was sure without a doubt now that somebody was John fucking Glow. He felt for sure that Glow was carrying out some type of cosmic retribution. But Alex didn't have a clue about what that was, why or what it even might be.

Alex knew he wasn't going to be able to sleep any more that night. He walked over to his desk in his living room. The pain forced Alex to gently sink into his office chair in front of his computer, feeling more helpless and alone than he had ever felt in his life.

He looked around the room.

On one wall he had framed musical showcards from many of the shows he had seen through the years. On another wall, above his desk, was the huge screaming face jumping off the movie poster for Pink Floyd's *The Wall*. Alex studied the screaming face carefully. He thought it now seemed even more appropriate hanging over his desk than it ever had before. The screaming face felt like a portrait of his own living nightmare. It was a good illustration of how frightened and out of control he felt.

The one thing about all of it that Alex hated more than anything was relinquishing his control.

He refused to be a victim.

The one thing Alex hated more than anything else were people who loved playing the victim as a badge of honor for the world to see. He was not going to be one of those people. Alex refused to let the world view him as a victim. Even in this situation. He was not some kind of goddamn victim. He had to figure this out. He was not going to just roll over and let this continue. Alex adjusted his sore ass in his chair, moaning slightly as the pain shot through his rectum. He was not going to be some fuck boy for this cosmic mother fucker.

Alex put the words SLEEP ATTACK into his browsers search bar and hit >ENTER.

There was all sorts of medical information which came up first. It discussed sleep studies, sleep apnea and narcolepsy among many other things. Alex immediately ruled out most of it in his mind because if he had a medical condition then all his friends had the same condition as well. This seemed very unlikely to Alex because they were all experiencing the same nightmares and sleep paralysis. Glow was in all their dreams, and it was almost as if Glow had used Moses to entice them into it all.

"Almost?" Alex whispered to himself.

There was no almost about it. Glow had used the fucking slave Moses to play on their sympathy to seal the deal they were making with the devil. But then again, he reminded himself of Ellis. Alex's mind was racing wildly from one thought to another. He had to force himself to concentrate. He needed to force himself to stay with and on his original line of thought.

All five of them dreamt about the slave Moses and described him in detail. It was that collective buy-in to Moses that somehow made it easier for Glow to attach and then attack them. There wasn't a medical condition which caused this. No, a medical solution would only make sense if it had been just one in the group who had been having the nightmares. Five people having the same type of nightmare with the same symptoms seemed highly unlikely. Alex was resigned to the fact that he could easily rule out all possible medical causes.

So, if it was not something medical then there was no other option left other than for it to be something supernatural - as crazy as that seemed. Alex was quickly running out of justifications for it all and trying to blame it on anything concrete in this world just didn't add up in one way or another. He was sure, whatever this was, it was not part of their understanding of the world around them. He looked again at the computer screen, and something stood out about sleep paralysis and shadow people which caught his attention.

Alex put SHADOW PEOPLE into this browser and hit >ENTER.

Surprisingly, there were a lot of articles about these nighttime visitors called Shadow People. There were pages and pages of this stuff with people sharing their personal stories. But nothing Alex was reading seemed to be similar enough to fit John Glow completely. First, Glow was not a shadow. Just the opposite.

Glow's facial features flashed in Alex's mind for a moment.

No, Glow was not some type of shadow person or Hat Man. The Hat Man he read about always appeared as a shadowy outline and was clearly wearing a wide-brimmed hat.

Glow's face flashed in his mind once again.

Alex then began to drill down on Glow's appearance within his mind. The most frightening aspect of Glow were his glowing white eyes. It was the most memorable of his features. Glow's eyes almost reflected the light as if they were some type of white mirrored metal. He also had long stringy hair - what Alex thought was brown or black. It was clearly unkept. There was also something about Glow's face that seemed familiar to Alex. It was almost as if Alex had met or seen him before.

"What was it about the face? Why was his face so damn familiar?"

Then it hit him. The face resembled the face of the Italian Jesus. As if Michealangelo's or DaVinci's Jesus had gone mad. Alex could not believe how fucking cliché that was, but it was clearly the look the motherfucker was going for. Glow wanted to look like Evil Jesus.

Alex put SLEEP DEMON into the browser's search bar and hit >ENTER.

Pages and pages of information came up on his screen.

<u>Sleep Paralysis Demon: What's Really Going on Here?</u>

<u>What to Know About Sleep Paralysis and Demons</u>

<u>What is my Sleep Paralysis Demon?</u>

<u>What's a Sleep Paralysis Demon? What to Know</u>

Page after page, Alex read everything he could, but even though he felt he was indeed getting closer to an understanding, nothing seemed to completely fit their situation. He was able to rule out the Night Hag completely. Alex was painfully sure that Glow was presenting himself as a male because he knew that his huge penis was not just his imagination. Alex read about sexual nightmare attacks. He read about the Incubus and Succubus. Yeah, Glow could almost fit as an Incubus. The Incubus is an evil spirit who sexually attacks sleeping victims, causing sleep paralysis. Mostly, the attack is upon women. Men are generally believed to be attacked by a Succubus, the female counterpart.

The name Incubus is derived from Latin. The word incubare, which means 'to lie on top of' while incubo means 'nightmare'. Sure, to that extent, it seemed to fit. The Incubus' genitalia were described as usually being overly large and hard. The attack could be violent, but there were also reports of the attack being sexually exciting and satisfying for some. The Incubus seemed very close to describing Glow, but it still wasn't a complete match.

Then Alex came across information about a research study on sleep paralysis initiated by a Dr. Jalal Baland, which had been conducted in Egypt and Türkiye. The Turkish portion of the study is what Alex found to be particularly interesting. In Türkiye, there were 59 participants in the study. Out of the 59 people, 51 of them had the same nightmare in which they encountered the same supernatural entity. The majority of those who encountered this entity believed it was a being known as Karabasan, a vicious djinn that paralyzes its victims in their sleep to attack them.

"Djinn?" The name djinn stuck out to Alex in the text.

"What in the hell was a djinn?"

Alex put DJINN into his browser and pressed >ENTER.

To his surprise, there was a lot of information about the djinn and Alex began a deep dive into everything he could read about them. He learned that the word djinn came from the Arabic word jinn which literally means 'hidden from sight'.

The idea of the Arabian Nights-type genie shares the same Arabic root, which Alex thought was very interesting, He found that in pre-Islamic Arabia, the djinn were spirits who were both feared and admired. The djinn were ancient creatures who have been feared, written about and discussed for a very long time in Middle Eastern cultures. The djinn had inspired poets. They could control the weather. The Quran depicts them as neither good nor evil, but they can choose their actions. They have free will.

According to Muslim demonology, the djinn were spirits who inhabited the earth. They could assume various forms. They also could exercise supernatural power. The true form of the djinn was unknown because they couldn't appear to humans in their original form. However, they were able to shapeshift into human or animal forms. Arab lore said they had superhuman strength and speed. Some teachings believed they were immortal beings, created at the beginning of time, that can mimic human voice and even possess people like demons do. On and on Alex read. The more he read the more he became convinced Glow was indeed one of these ancient creatures.

"John Glow is a djinn."

This made complete fucking sense to Alex. Glow could shapeshift because he was a djinn.

"What about the slave Moses?"

Moses wasn't some slave. Moses was Glow himself. It had been Glow all along manipulating them in their sleep. He was playing with them much like a predator who plays with its food before devouring it. The more Alex read the more nervous he became. He felt as if the walls were beginning to close in around him and their opportunities for escape from Glow were becoming less and less of a possibility.

Alex was convinced that John Glow chose to appear as the Italian white Jesus deliberately because he was more ancient than the bible itself.

"Christ walked this earth thousands of years after Glow's creation."

This was Glow's way of pointing out the visual irony.

"How fucking dare people put Christ above his ancient self?"

John Glow chose the name John to sarcastically refer to the book of John in the bible. Glow was a reference to the Morning Star - Lucifer himself. Alex was sure the connections were deliberate, not in a literal sense, but his way of poking sticks at the idea of Christianity. Alex felt that if he himself were an ancient being the whole idea of Christianity would be something to not only laugh at but despise as well. This felt right to Alex.

It was also clear to Alex that Glow chose the slave Moses because of the ideas of captivity and servitude. In literature the genie is always a creature in service to mortal man. You know, the whole fucking three wish thing and all. Alex had read the Arabian Nights. He knew the genie lore and had seen the popular culture glorification of them as the jolly old souls who were put on this earth to gleefully service men. This idea of slave-like servitude would anger Glow's ancient ego.

"Of course, it did."

And if Alex thought about it, rightfully so. It wasn't as if Alex was feeling sympathy toward his attacker but gaining an understanding of who John Glow was and how he worked - what made the motherfucker tick. It was obvious to Alex that Glow would be in service to no human because they were inferior to him in every way.

"The idea of servitude would make him furious."

That is why the slave Moses appeared castrated in all their dreams. The idea of servitude to a lowly mortal man would be a castrating abomination to Glow's ego and sensibility because he was the superior being over man.

"Moses was a metaphor for Glow to give a huge finger to the world."

The nerve to think this ancient being who had walked the earth since the beginning of time would bow down and serve men would be fucking outrageously nonsensical to John Glow.

"But what about his eyes?"

Alex was sure the white glowing eyes were not a choice. He read a lot of about the djinn shapeshifting and there was always something off about their appearance. It was almost like there was a cosmic law that they had to have something about their true form remaining when they shapeshifted in order to give themselves away. In essence, they were not allowed to be a perfect copy without flaws to show who they really were.

"The white eyes were something Glow could not control."

In the research, Alex was finding that the djinn would have white, black or even metallic eyes. This was the obvious thing Glow could not conceal. It was the universe's way of marking him as a djinn - a heads up for those who would encounter his self-created counterfeit form.

The next article is what really bothered Alex. The article examined whether the djinn could harm humans or not.

"Could a djinn kill someone?"

To Alex's relief there appeared to be no instances where the djinn had killed a human, unprovoked. There was some type of judgement which was connected to the djinn. Some form of retribution for them killing humans. It was unclear what this judgement was or how it was handed down. The major consensus was the judgement would come from an overlord of the djinn or God himself. But in truth, the way we understand God could be a completely different thing from the reality of the djinn. Because of this judgement, the djinn was more likely to drive their human interest toward insanity, suicide, or both.

"Suicide? Was the medium's death really a suicide?"

Alex knew what he saw in her séance room that night, but of course there was no way he could have known what was going on within her mind.

"Was the slamming of her hands down onto the glass table an attempt to get the djinn to leave her body? Was it her own self-defense that killed her? Then there was Ellis. Is that why he shot himself alone in that dumpster? What or who was he hiding from? Was he trying to escape something? Was he trying to escape from John Glow?"

Then there was himself and the group. Alex knew, the more they were attacked and the less they were able to sleep, the less their chances of survival were. A lot had been studied about sleep deprivation on the individual and their psyche. If they knew and understood the motive, then maybe, just maybe they would be...

A knock came at his apartment door causing Alex to jump as his concentration was shattered. Alex laughed at his own reaction to the knock as he got up from his computer and walked over to the door. It was very late at night (or early in the morning) for someone to come over. Alex peered through the peep hole in the door and there stood the handsome Detective Vincent Rossi on the other side. Vincent was ready to knock again when Alex opened the door leaving Vincent's hand in midair with no place to go.

Vincent felt a little silly with his hand in the air and blushed slightly as his hand dropped back to his side.

"Would it be alright with you if I came in for a moment to speak with you?" Vincent asked nervously, somewhat stumbling over his words.

"I know it's a strange hour, but this really couldn't wait." Vincent continued trying to explain himself for his late-night visit.

Alex nodded with a yes and let Vincent into his apartment - just inside the front door and no further. Alex couldn't help but notice Vincent's cologne and how good he smelled. Of course, it hadn't been lost on Alex that Vincent Rossi was a very handsome man. He was a very good-looking man and when those eyes looked directly into Alex's, they would make him not only nervous, but he could feel himself blush. However, good looking or not, he was still a possible threat to Alex.

They both stood facing each other inside the small entry to the apartment as Vincent began to talk nervously once again. He knew he was giving Alex some very bad news -never a part of his job he ever got used to doing.

"Alex, I need to tell you that your friend Paul Fairchild is dead," Vincent said nervously as Alex felt his knees go weak.

"What are you talking about dead? I just saw him. What do you mean dead?" Alex could feel the panic and the grief rising into his throat. This couldn't be happening. Paul couldn't be dead.

"We believe he committed suicide. Alex, at this time, the evidence suggests he jumped from his parent's apartment building on the 36th floor," Vincent said, trying to convey empathy with his tone.

Vincent tried to give the facts carefully while paying very close attention to Alex's reaction to the news. His reaction might give Vincent a clue if Alex might be involved in some way. Vincent was aware it might be viewed as him being cruel or seemingly emotionless at the loss of Alex's friend. The very last thing Vincent wanted was Alex to be involved in a crime in some way. There was something he really liked about Alex. Vincent couldn't put his finger on it, but he found himself attracted to Alex. Of course, he was testing Alex, and this was a test. It was essential for Vincent to observe Alex's reaction to the news of his friends passing to make sure he was telling the truth, and he was not involved. Vincent was using his instincts here and they rarely led him down a wrong path.

Alex could barely speak as he felt the sound being sucked out of the room. He felt the room beginning to spin around him, "Oh my God."

Alex felt the world slipping away from him as he dropped to the floor passing out at Vincent's feet. Vincent quickly dropped to his knees catching Alex's head in the palm of his right hand and effortlessly and gently kept it from hitting the floor.

Chapter 16
Connections

    Vincent could not remember a time when he had someone pass out on him after delivering them bad news. It was never an easy thing for him to do, but this reaction was sort of new to him. He was sure that it must have happened before to another cop delivering the news, but for him this was new. He had seen people completely shut down and he had also seen people completely emotionally break down, but this was the first time someone had actually passed out once the news was delivered. But there he was, finding himself down on his knees in the entry of the young man's apartment, holding Alex's head in his hands waiting for him to come back around. It didn't take long for Alex's eyes to flutter open as he begin to speak.

    "Oh… what…" The world was slowly coming back to Alex with confusion - half in and half out of his foggy mind.

    Alex began to focus on the face in front of him. He was almost expecting white eyes but instead the eyes that were coming into focus were blue. Blue eyes, and he could feel the warm hands gently holding his head.

    "Take your time Alex. It's okay. You just fainted. Nothing to be worried about. I am here and I have you." Vincent said as soothingly as he could.

Vincent almost looked somewhat angelic to Alex with the entry ceiling light illuminating him from behind with a soft glow. Except for his short hair, Vincent could have passed for Jesus with his worried, sweet face. At least this time the face appeared like a good Italian Jesus. Alex kept focusing on the concerned face in front of him as he became fully aware of his surroundings. Then he remembered Paul. Then he remembered that Paul was gone. Then he began to cry.

Vincent, sensing the seriousness of the situation, wrapped his arms around Alex pulling him close to his chest. There was nothing he could say now that would matter or stop the flow of tears. Vincent knew instinctively it was best to let Alex cry for a moment and work through the initial shock of it all. Alex continued to cry into his chest as Vincent pulled him even closer. They stayed this way until Alex's sobbing began to subside. Two men holding onto each other in the middle of the floor, in the middle of the night.

Slowly, Alex backed away from Vincent's hold, looking into his blue eyes once more through his tears. Alex felt as if these blue eyes were really seeing him and understood precisely what he was feeling. Then an uncomfortable feeling set in, along with regret.

"I'm sorry. I didn't mean to..." Vincent cut Alex off because he wanted to spare him any sort of awkwardness or embarrassment.

"It's okay Alex. You have just been given quite a shock. It's a natural response. The tears meant you loved someone, and that is okay. I am just glad I was here to catch you," Vincent said caringly.

Vincent was truly glad he had been there. Vincent was also glad that he got to see what he felt deep in his gut already. His gut had told him Alex was not involved with any of this in a criminal sense. Vincent thought he could even be considered a victim, caught in the middle of some type of weird shit storm. Vincent couldn't put his finger on what was going on, but he knew he needed to get Alex's total, unfiltered story.

"You want me to help you up and get you over to the couch?" Vincent asked. Alex shook his head in agreement.

Vincent could tell Alex was still a little dizzy and confused as he wobbled on his feet. Vincent helped him up and over to the couch and down.

There was a side chair that faced the couch that Vincent motioned to as he asked, "Is it okay if I sit with you for a moment?"

Vincent knew he did not want to leave Alex alone just yet. He wanted to make sure Alex was indeed okay. At first, they sat in mostly silence as Alex slowly came back to full reality. Vincent could see the shock was still there but at least now he was becoming more and more lucid.

"Alex, would it be okay if I talked to you and discussed this? It would be off the record of course. I will not put anything we talk about here into a report or anything. It will be just between the two of us. I won't record it. But, Alex, I need your help here because I must tell you I think there is something serious going on and you might know what that something might be. I must tell you that I don't believe you have done anything wrong. I promise you that you are not a suspect. But I need you to trust me enough to tell me in your own words what is happening. Why are there three deaths and why you are connected with all three of these victims?"

Alex paid very close attention to what Vincent was saying to him. Sure, Alex was still nervous and not fully sure if he could trust him or not. In truth, Alex knew he was running out of options and maybe talking about it to someone on the outside would help. He looked into Vincent's eyes as he spoke to him. The eyes were supposed to be the windows to the soul. Vincent's beautiful blue eyes seemed to care. So, Alex agreed to tell his story and Vincent listened intently as Alex began to take Vincent through everything from Ellis to Jenny the psychic and now Paul. Vincent listened intently as Alex took him through the entire story and his feelings about each of the events and, finally, the last time Alex saw Paul.

"I came around the corner of the bar in time to see Paul's car driving away. Chuck was on the ground, and I could tell by how he was acting their fight had gotten physical. You need to understand this was not something that usually happened between the two of them. Chuck was always able to calm Paul down. Not this time. Chuck told me Paul pushed him hard to the ground. It seemed odd, but Chuck was somewhat hurt, and the palms of his hands were scratched from landing on the pavement. One of his hands was bleeding a little. So, I helped him into the bar where the others were waiting, where we could clean him up. That was the last time any of us saw Paul alive," Alex felt the word alive stick in his throat as he fought back the tears which were now welling up in his eyes.

"Are you okay?" Vincent asked carefully reaching his hand over, touching Alex's knee for a brief moment in a gesture of caring and understanding.

Alex could feel electricity coming from Vincent's hand as he touched him - or was it just wishful thinking? Either way, Alex could tell Vincent did care.

Vincent hung on every word while Alex told him about the crazy story which included the slave Moses and the name John Glow. This was the second time Vincent heard about the nightmares, but this time Alex was more relaxed and filled it in with a lot more detail.

"Could you tell me some more about this John Glow? Anything you could tell me that might help me make more sense of this?" Vincent asked cautiously.

He didn't want to give Alex the impression that he didn't believe him. Strangely, he did believe him. As crazy and outrageous as the story was, Vincent could tell Alex believed in it fully. Was it some sort of hysteria all five had been involved in? Were they feeding and adding to the frenzy between each other? And the psychic? What Vincent hadn't told Alex was that the psychic had somewhat of a shady past. A few drug arrests and some fraud charges. She had been married before and there had been a few domestic disturbance calls. She had divorced her husband a few years back, but it seemed her troubles had continued. There were red flags everywhere where Jenny Star the psychic was concerned, or, as she was legally known as, Margaret Tolson. Vincent had logical questions going through his mind, and, at this point, Vincent was looking for a plausible explanation. Anything that would make some sense of it all and how they were connected. In order to do that he needed to know more about who John Glow was.

Alex took a deep breath and began filling in all the details about John Glow. Alex self-consciously hesitated as he began to describe the sexual abuse to Vincent. Vincent could immediately read his hesitation and stopped him from continuing.

"Stop right there for a moment, Alex. I need to let you know something before you continue. I'm gay. So, anything you need to tell me about this is going to be okay. I'm gay and I am married to a man. Sex between two men is not something foreign to me and it is not like you are telling this to some straight cop that would not understand. I get it."

Vincent could see the uneasiness leave Alex's face as he continued. It made it a lot easier for Alex knowing that Vincent understood what he was describing, especially when it came to the explanation of the anal penetration and the blood he found on his body and sheets. At times when Alex explained the attacks, he would pause, trying to hold back tears. But there were other times when he couldn't hold them back at all. Vincent gave him the time to let it pass until he could continue to speak. The whole time Alex told him about the physical attacks he kept his eyes glued to the look on Alex's face. Vincent had enough experience with rape victims to know that Alex was indeed a victim. Most rape victims will have a certain look in their eyes and on their face when they describe their attack. It really is somewhat of a disassociated deer-in-the-headlights sort of look. Alex had this look when he spoke about what John Glow had done to him. Vincent had no idea what had happened to this guy, but it was very clear that something happened to him and that something was pretty fucking horrific.

Alex finished telling his account up until the point where Vincent knocked on his door. By the time he finished, Vincent could hear the birds outside as light began to shine into the room through the living room window. They both sat in silence for a moment. Alex was relieved, feeling he was able to finally unload it all to Vincent, who was carefully thinking about everything he had been told.

Vincent slowly began to speak, choosing his words carefully, "You know, doing the job I do doesn't leave a lot of room for what I believe or not believe to be true. Often, I must just follow the facts of the situation. I am telling you this because I do believe you, and I do believe something is happening to you. Now, on the other side of things, here is what the facts are and what those facts are telling me. I know I have three victims. One victim an apparent accidental death and the other two suicides. Nothing out of any of the investigations of the scenes or the victims have pointed into the direction of foul play or any sort of homicide at this moment. All of you knew the victims. All were present for what we believe was the accidental death. One of the victims was an ex-boyfriend of yours that you had recently broken up with. We know that it was hard on you because during the investigation of his suicide we read your DMs and heard your voice messages to him. This obviously caused the parents to suspect you as a person with a possible motive. However, there was absolutely nothing about the scene which indicated any more than a fatal self-inflicted gunshot wound. Then there is Paul, who was clearly alone at the time of his death. I am sure any surveillance footage that is collected from the scene will also demonstrate that, because we have an eyewitness to the fact

Paul arrived at his parent's apartment alone. The only thing putting up a red flag here factually is that you all knew each other. Okay, simply knowing the victims is not going to get anyone brought in on any charges. See what I mean?"

Alex was hanging onto Vincent's every word and responded with, "Yes. I see that and I also know all of this to be true."

In truth Alex was relieved to hear Vincent say that none of them were being considered a suspect.

"You said you were researching when I arrived here to your apartment. You mentioned you found something that made sense to you. Could you take me through all the things you learned and how you think it might explain any of this?" Vincent sat back in his chair once again as Alex began to talk, filling in the process and the details of what he found while researching online.

At times, Alex would get excited, talking very quickly with his hands gesturing wildly. When he would go too fast for Vincent to keep up, he would stop him for a moment and have Alex slow down and repeat what he had just said with a clearer and more detailed explanation. When Alex was finished telling Vincent everything, he looked at Vincent searching for some sort of validation. Vincent took a deep breath leaning forward in his chair.

"So, what you are telling me is that you think John Glow is not even human but some type of supernatural being based on the beliefs of Middle Eastern cultures?" Vincent asked carefully, not wanting to give Alex the impression he didn't believe him.

Alex responded to the question with, "Yes. I believe John Glow is what is known in Middle Eastern culture and religion as a djinn."

Vincent realized that Alex believed in what he was saying. And why shouldn't he? Vincent had spent his entire life dealing with (and being put down) by people who thought he was going to burn in hell because a man in the sky had told them so. If they could believe in the Father, Son and Holy Ghost then why couldn't someone believe in a djinn? However, within the confines of the law and his investigations, the idea of some sort of djinn was not going to fit into any constructs of the law. Vincent could easily follow the dots of the logic as Alex connected them. He could follow Alex's line of thinking and concluded why Alex believed this to be true. Ancient lore and religion, and Alex's belief in both, wasn't any better of an explanation than what he already had to go on. So, why the fuck not? It's not that Vincent believed the supernatural was involved with the cases. Vincent felt assured in the end that wasn't going to flesh out. However, Vincent had been around long enough to know even the craziest aspects of a case could not be overlooked. And this, well, this was one crazy aspect for sure.

Chapter 17
Toxic

Vincent was exhausted but decided to stop by his office anyway on his way home. The day shifts were already coming in when he arrived. He sat at his desk putting his head in his hands, closing his eyes for just a moment. It was 9:30 a.m. and his workday had started at 3 p.m. yesterday.

It had been quite a night which started with Paul Fairchild's suicide and ended with delivering the news and questioning Alex McAllister at his apartment. Vincent had made sure Alex was doing okay before he left. The news of Paul's suicide had been hard on Alex. It was an emotional moment for sure, but in the aftermath of it all, Alex had opened up, giving him a lot to think about and digest. Things always seem worse in the dark hours of the night. Vincent had to wonder if that had any influence on the conversation he had with Alex. The whole conversation was not only emotional, but it tuned out Alex had been hiding some pretty off-the-chain stuff. Regardless, he did get a lot of information about the cases and how they might be connecting.

Vincent now understood more about Ellis and his relationship with Alex. At first, Vincent thought Ellis might have taken his life because of his breakup with Alex. You know the story of the jilted and distraught boyfriend who couldn't live without the other. Vincent had to laugh at his own romanticism of the two-Romeos scenario. Ellis's mother had told him Alex was the one to break off the relationship. That was until Vincent learned Ellis had actually been the one to break it off with Alex. The mother, as it turned out, was pushing a false narrative. Alex's private text messages and voice messages had already communicated the reality of the breakup. After talking with Alex tonight he now knew just how brutal and uncaring Ellis had been toward Alex at the end of the relationship. He literally just cut Alex completely out of his life without a second thought.

It really bothered Vincent the mother had tried to pin the suicide on Alex when it was her son who had been a complete and total asshole in the relationship. This bothered Vincent a lot. This is not the kind of guilt trip you should put on another person. But he also knew the nature of mothers. After all, he was Italian, and he knew how they could be about their sons. Vincent remembered this kid named Joey who lived on his street when he was growing up. According to Joey's mother, if Joey wasn't the second coming of Christ, he was at least a Saint in the living flesh.

In truth, Joey was a small-time thief at the age of twelve who, every time he got caught, you could hear his mother exclaiming to whomever would listen, "Not my Joey. My Joey wouldn't do anything like that. My Joey is a good boy."

A few years later Vincent heard Joey was serving a life sentence in the State prison for murder. That is how these mothers were with their boys and Ellis' mother was no different from the others. Even though Vincent wasn't sure if she was Italian or not, she fit into this stereotype.

Alex had also filled in more detail concerning the night of Margaret Tolson's (aka Jenny the Medium's) accidental death. Now that was one crazy fucking story. What a fucked-up thing to be a witness to. Vincent hadn't told Alex anything about what he had found out about the medium and her life. He felt as if it was maybe better to save that information until later. The department hadn't released any information at the family's request. Vincent couldn't have been sure if they were worried at the prospect of media attention, or they were embarrassed by Margaret's antics and the way her troubled life ended.

Sometimes it was hard to tell what a family was thinking. As far as the media were concerned, her name was given out as the alias she began using after her divorce - Jenny Star. It wasn't a legal name change. She most likely felt it was a more interesting name for what Vincent was sure was a psychic scam she was running out of her house. She was on the easy take, and she most likely saw this group of friends coming from a mile away. They were easy fucking targets for a skilled con artist like Margaret Tolson aka Jenny Star.

Then there was the newest addition to the mess, Paul Fairchild. Up until the time Vincent talked to Alex, he thought he would be dealing with Paul Fairchild's parents for quite some time. He had mentally buckled in for the ride of outraged rich parents who would go on a campaign of how their son had been murdered and no one was going to do anything about it. Even though it was an obvious suicide, Vincent had seen families try to protect their loved one's name in this way. Like in some way their loved one's suicide had shown weakness and was now a black spot they needed to remove by having some poor sap pay the price in prison.

However, after Alex told him how messed-up Paul was from the lack of care and attention he had gotten from his parents his whole life, Vincent no longer thought he would be hearing much from them. Vincent had seen enough of this rich type come through the departments. They either cared too much and demanded justice, or, in Paul's case, they were most likely so unbothered he was gone they would let it go as a suicide without much more care. They would consider his existence already a black spot on their name. The suicide just helped scrub away what they most likely felt was already there. Poor bastard would leave the world without too much fanfare or as much as a decent goodbye. Best to deal with that black spot removal as quickly and as quietly as possible. It seemed to Vincent, from what Alex had told him, Paul's few friends and the doorman were most likely the only ones who cared for the poor guy. That reminded Vincent that when he came into work next, he needed to look and see if there was any surveillance footage that caught anything of interest. Nowadays, it was next to impossible to off yourself without some type of camera somewhere catching you doing it. Even cameras inside houses were catching this shit on film. You could make a whole new run of *Faces of Death* with that type of gathered footage alone.

Vincent laughed at his own morbid sense of humor as he raised his head up from his desk. He looked at his emails for a moment and saw the toxicology report had come in on Margaret Tolson. Vincent opened it up and read the results. To his surprise, the results were very interesting. Margaret Tolson had levels of Dimethyltryptamine

(DMT) in her system at the time of her death. Well, Margaret Tolson the medium was full of surprises. It is virtually impossible to overdose on DMT, but there was enough in her system to cause hallucinations.

Now this, Vincent thought, was fucking interesting. Vincent quickly pulled up his written transcripts of the five friends' statements of what happened at the scene to see if anyone had mentioned anything he had missed that might be a clue. It was Charles Parker, who the friends called Chuck, that said something of interest.

Chuck said, "She was standing at the bar talking to all of us as she poured herself something out of what looked like a liquor decanter before beginning the séance."

Chuck just thought she was taking a shot of tequila or something to loosen herself up. In fact, Margaret Tolson had casually said something like this to Chuck as she went to sit at the table. The only reason Chuck even noticed it was because he could have used a shot of tequila too to calm his nerves and he thought it was rude she hadn't offered. Other than that Chuck thought it was no big deal.

Vincent was instantly embarrassed that he hadn't caught it as something of interest as Chuck said it. With this type of accidental death, the consumption of any unknown substance should have been of interest. Vincent had asked for toxicology to be done on her remains as soon as possible in order to satisfy his quest for any missing pieces of the puzzle. That was a good move. The right move. But still, he should have caught this in Chuck's testimony of what he observed. Vincent had been overly tired the night of her death and his mind was preoccupied with his pissed-off husband who was waiting for him at home. Still, there was no excuse. He was a better detective than that.

Chuck had been the second-to-last of the friends he questioned. Thumbing through all of their statements Vincent realized that Chuck was the only one who noticed her taking a shot before she began. She must have done it very casually, so no one thought anything of it. But why DMT? How did the DMT play into what she was doing? Obviously, she felt it did something for her or she would have never ingested a substance like this while getting ready to put on a show and carry out a scam. It seemed to Vincent she would have wanted to be on her toes and in complete control of the situation.

"Put on a show," Vincent whispered under his breath.

That idea stuck with him in the moment. That was it, she was putting on a goddamn show. Vincent knew something about narcotics. After all, it was a requirement in his training. And of course, he had been exposed to almost every substance you could think of while working the streets. The streets were full of junkies and dealers. Sometimes people got out of hand.

DMT came with a whole unique set of questions. This was not just a substance you ran into or heard about on the streets. Recently, Vincent had heard a lot about people who travel to South America for these ayahuasca tea ceremonies to get in touch with their spiritual side. It was a type of DMT they were using for those rituals. In fact, Vincent saw a whole exposé documentary which, he remembered, was produced by Lisa Ling. Not that who produced it or was starring in it mattered. In fact, he had seen a growing number of news reports on the subject. All the reports involved people who would come out of these sessions claiming they had seen the face of God - or more. The next obvious question - was it possible that Maragret Tolson figured out a way not to only ingest it for herself but to somehow transfer it onto the five friends in powder form?

Vincent shot off an email immediately asking for a toxicology report on Paul Fairchild. He didn't want to ask the group to take a test because the DMT only lasts in the system for about 24 hours in urine and for only few hours in saliva. So, any traces from them would have already left their systems. Vincent wanted to check to see if Paul had any traces of it in his system because it would explain a lot about his suicide if he did. Meaning, Paul would have had exposure to DMT right before his jump. Vincent hit send on the toxicology request and quickly pulled up some information on DMT, just as a refresher, since it was a substance that was obviously connected to these cases.

Dimethyltryptamine is a compound which can be found in various plants and animals. It is used as a mind-altering drug. It causes those who ingest it to hallucinate and see things that are not there. There are some who believe that DMT can open doors to other dimensions and beings. Some say it is a religious experience and many have claimed they have been in the presence of, or have seen, the face of God while on a DMT trip. DMT has been around for a very long time. It was used for hundreds of years by different cultures for rituals and such. It is an active ingredient found in ayahuasca tea, which is native to South America. It can also be synthesized in a lab setting. DMT also goes by the name Dimitri, Businessman's Special, the Spirit Molecule, and Elf Spice. It had also been found in a new designer drug hitting the streets lately called Black Pope, which had been causing a lot of problems for the city.

Black Pope was not just DMT, but contained a laundry list of compounds, that when combined in a lab setting, became a very potent and dangerous substance. People used it recreationally. The high from regular synthetic DMT on the streets only lasts for about fifteen minutes to an hour. The effects of ayahuasca tea lasts up to six hours. Black Pope, on the other hand, could cause a high that could last for about twelve hours. Black Pope behaved more like LSD in that respect. There were some rumors Black Pope may have been related to an earlier government experimental LSD known as the Monkey. There had been a lot of speculation through the years about the government's research into psychedelics and a lot of those stories had become part of urban legend. So much so, it was almost impossible to distinguish between fact and fiction.

Black Pope was the new designer drug on the streets. It was rumored to have come out of Singapore or China. It was no secret that the Chinese had fueled the spread of Flakka in the US. However, that had been greatly reduced over the years. Black Pope was not going away any time soon. A lot of the dance clubs in St. Louis had become easy places to score Black Pope, like most of other types of illegal substances. In fact, Vincent recently had a case at an infamous St. Louis club known as Sanctuary.

Sanctuary was a huge venue that had opened in an old downtown church. On one night Vincent got called to a scene there when someone who had been 'riding the Pope' shot up a group of six people with a gun outside on the front steps of the club. The suspect claimed he did it because they were coming to hurt him. Of course, they weren't, and it was all in his mind due to the drug. One of the downsides of Black Pope is that it can cause extreme paranoia. This guy's drug induced paranoia left six people senselessly dead on the steps of Sanctuary for doing nothing more than being in the wrong place at the wrong time. Yeah, Black Pope was bad news and causing some serious problems. It was very different from the regular DMT they had usually seen on the streets and in the clubs. Of course, DMT and other hallucinogenic drugs were on the rise because there had been numerous reports lately they may have some psychological and health benefits. However, the risks far outweighed any benefit they might have. That included DMT.

The synthetic drug Margaret Tolson had ingested was indeed not Black Pope. What Margaret had ingested was the average synthetic DMT they had been seeing on the streets for years. While thinking about it, Vincent dispatched officers to the Tolson scene to bring any decanters they could find near or on the bar in the house to be sent to the lab for analysis. They also needed to bring someone onto the scene to see if there were any traces of DMT in a powder form remaining on the shattered shards of glass from the table or anywhere around the room. He could not rule out she had drugged the entire group in some way. Especially, after the strange conversation he had with Alex just a few hours ago. Vincent was grateful the case was still open, and details of the scene had not been released back to her family.

"Why DMT, Margaret Tolson?" Vincent asked himself out loud as he pulled up more information.

Vincent began sorting through a plethora of information on how DMT was used for spiritual, ritual and psychic purposes in hopes he could find something that would help him connect the dots. He found something interesting that talked about DMT being used to open a doorway between a medium and the other planes. That would make a lot of fucking sense. Maybe Margaret Tolson was really trying to contact the slave Moses and was using the drug because she thought it would help her to accomplish it. If that was the case, it had backfired on her completely. She hallucinated something completely different and in doing so not only killed herself but planted the seeds for the others to believe in Glow as well. Vincent continued reading even though he was very exhausted. Now this is where it got really fucking creepy. On the following page Vincent read that it was also believed DMT could be ingested to open a doorway (or in this case the article called it a portal) with the ancient beings known as the djinn.

"Djinn," Vincent stopped and reread aloud this time.

"What the fuck?"

Chapter 18
The Visit

Vincent was exhausted by the time he reached home. It was already a little past noon. He was grateful his husband Tim was at work and would not return until after six in the evening. Vincent figured it gave him between five and six hours to get some sleep. He would get up and leave the house for work before Tim arrived home, avoiding any sort of scene or confrontation. Vincent's nerves were raw, and he just could not handle any sort of dramatic scene between him and Tim at the moment.

Vincent walked into the bedroom. It was cool and dark in there. There was a fan turning overhead which kept the air moving in the room. He completely undressed and threw his clothes across a chair and climbed underneath his comforter, completely naked. The bed and softness of his sheets felt good on his body. He took some cleansing breaths as he began to decompress from the previous long night into the morning.

Suicides were never easy cases and were often pretty sad scenes to work. Even though, Vincent felt he had taken a lot of good steps with his caseload. Things seemed to be moving in the right direction. His work usually was a mixed bag kind of thing. You could be dealing with the most horrific of scenes in one moment and the next have an incredible breakthrough of sorts that often could and would lead to solving a case. Vincent hoped he had those kinds of breakthroughs tonight.

Then, for some reason which Vincent couldn't explain, he thought of Alex McAllister and how vulnerable he appeared to him last night. The vulnerability shouldn't have surprised Vincent at all because he had picked up on it the first time he met Alex. Vincent had to admit he felt an attraction toward Alex. Of course, it was an attraction he would never act upon because he was a married man. Even though he and Tim were going through a difficult time Vincent knew he would never cheat on him. Vincent loved Tim and he wouldn't hurt him in that way.

Now, if he had been single and a little younger, the situation would be much different. There was something about Alex he felt strongly attracted to. Obviously, Alex was that good-looking actor type with a great body and a gleaming white smile. But for Vincent it was more than just a physical thing. Vincent laughed to himself staring at the ceiling because he knew if he were single, he wouldn't kick Alex out of his bed at all. In fact, he might even be the one to take his hand and lay him down there. He imagined for a moment what sex might be like between the two of them. Vincent was sure it would be a lot of romance. Hot, but romantic was the best type of sex for Vincent. The connection of the body, the feel of a touch, deep kisses, looking into someone's eyes at the moment of climax that was the sort of thing which really turned Vincent on. He was a true romantic in every sense of the word. Vincent could feel himself beginning to get hard beneath his sheets.

"Not now," Vincent said under his breath with a sigh.

Even though his body was begging for release Vincent knew he needed sleep more. Vincent took a series of deep cleansing breaths once again to put the world and Alex McAllister out of his mind. He needed to completely shut down and open himself up to some much-needed and well-deserved sleep. He pulled the comforter over his shoulder up to his chin and rolled over to his side. In a very short time Vincent was sleeping.

Vincent opened his eyes because he could feel the air from the fan above cooling his naked body. He was on his back looking up at the spinning ceiling fan blades. He was cold and could feel the goosebumps on his legs and arms forming. He reached for his comforter to pull it up over his body.

Wait a second.

He couldn't move his arms.

No matter how hard he struggled he could not move them.

He couldn't move his legs or his head.

No matter how hard he tried or struggled, Vincent found he was completely paralyzed and could not move. He lay there in a panic trying to fight against whatever was happening to him, but it didn't take long to understand it was useless.

Lying there, looking at the ceiling, he heard a noise next to the bed.

A noise that sounded like it could be someone crawling on all fours toward the chair which was positioned in the corner of the bedroom. Not necessarily crawling, but almost scurrying like a rat caught in the night.

Vincent found he could shift his eyes to follow the sound of the movement. The top back of the chair was visible enough for him to see, if he concentrated with his eyes looking downward and over to the right.

The room was still very dark, so he wasn't seeing clearly at all. He saw something rising in the darkness. A figure rising off of his bedroom floor between the bed and the chair. The form looked like it might be male as it rose. All Vincent could see was just an outline in the darkness of the room. More than just seeing it, Vincent could feel it.

His heart was beating faster, and his entire body was tingling, like an electrical charge was running up and down, raising the hairs on his legs and arms as it went.

He then saw a flicker of something white.

He saw a flicker of something white in the area where the eyes would be on this form's face.

Then he saw the eyes fully open.

They were completely glowing white.

Vincent was now fully aware of who this was and what was happening to him. He tried struggling to break free once again as the form crossed to the chair. As Vincent watched, unable to move, the form sat down with only the glowing white eyes visible and blinking as they contrasted with the darkness.

"You might want to stop struggling, Vincent. It isn't going to help you, and it is just going to exhaust you and weaken you even more than you already are," Glow's voice hissed and growled from the chair in the corner of the room.

Vincent found that he couldn't make a sound or say a word even though he tried with everything he had. Nothing but a soft grunt sound would come out.

"Cat got your tongue?" Glow asked with a giggle, already knowing the answer to his question.

"Trust me, Vincent. I know the answer even if you were able to answer me which, of course, I have made sure you can't. I just cannot stand the idea of having to listen to you go on. And my, do you go on and on." Glow's voice rose in volume and intensity as he spoke, his rancid breath filling the air around Vincent and the room.

"I have been listening to you of late and you are nothing but so fucking full of yourself Vincent. I have not come here and put all this effort into talking with you because I want you to reply. I don't want to hear you, Vincent. I don't want to hear you at all," Glow continued as Vincent once again tried to scream.

Glow giggled watching him struggle as the tears began to form in the corners of Vincent's eyes.

"I don't want to hear you scream either. I want you to listen to me. First, I must tell you that it really pisses me off that you don't believe in me. I am not some fucking Santa Claus or boogeyman childhood fantasy that you can turn on and off at will. Yes, Vincent, I am John Glow and the one thing that Alex McAllister has gotten right in his whole rotten fucking boring life. I… am… a djinn. He was completely right about that," Glow said with an evil laugh.

Vincent understood the danger he was in. He knew that if Glow was a djinn he was dealing with an ancient being who had been around for a very long time. Glow was clearly confident and in full control of whatever the purpose was of this meeting. All Vincent could do was watch and listen.

"I am the one you have heard called John Glow. Now, whether that is my real name or not is really nothing of your concern. But at this point, think of it as my given 'Christian' name to be used." Glow giggled on the word Christian causing Vincent to remember how Alex thought the name was blasphemous and a proverbial finger to the idea of Christ.

"I am sure you would like to know why I am here, right Vincent? Well, I am here because I thought it was time to meet you in person. We have been observing you for a very long time. It just so happens the universe caused us to intersect with you at this particular moment. The truth is, we had planned on doing that much later and in very different ways," Glow went on in an almost matter-of-fact tone.

"Oh, Vincent the plans the dark universe has for you my friend are really something special. Me? I am just dropping in to let you know the ball is already rolling downhill and there is nothing you can do to stop it. The train has left the station. The plan is set in motion. The time is ticking on the bomb. Well, you get the point," Glow laughed as he stood up walking to the side of the bed next to where Vincent was laying.

Vincent was now able to see him more clearly. Glow's image was exactly the way Alex had described him. A crazed, glowing-eyed, Italian-looking Jesus. Vincent felt Glow's hand begin to rub up and down his leg, up and across his pelvis and across his abdomen back and forth in slow teasing sort of motions.

"Shit is about to get real Vincent. Shit is about to get very fucking real," Glow giggled as he continued running his cold hand over Vincent's naked body.

"Oh, I would like a piece of that," Glow said as he pinched Vincent's nipple hard.

"Or a piece of this," Glow said laughing as he grabbed Vincent's genitals in his hand and squeezed causing pain to shoot through Vincent's entire body as his nerve endings fired with the discomfort.

"Oh, I think I want some of this," Glow giggled as he brought his hand up to Vincent's abdomen and began once again rubbing his hand back forth across it. Glow stopped his hand for a quick moment to look Vincent in the eyes.

"Vincent, the reason I am here is that you don't believe in me. I must tell you that your disbelief and show of arrogance is an outrageous insult to me. It is true you are not part of this now. You are inserting yourself into something that has nothing to do with you. You, Vincent, have much larger problems on the way. The monster of fate has something completely different planned for you my friend," Glow said as he once again began rubbing his cold hand from Vincent's abdomen to his pelvis and back.

"My role here with you right now is to gain some common ground with you Vincent. Get us on the right foot. To make it crystal fucking clear to you that you need to butt the fuck out. Because Vincent, trust me when I tell you, I always get my way." With this, Glow smiled a wicked smile, leaned over and bit Vincent's abdomen just above his navel.

Vincent could feel the sharpness of Glow's teeth as he bit into his flesh, drawing blood. Glow raised his head with blood seeping down from the sides of his mouth leaning closely into Vincent's face and said one word, laughing.

He said, "War."

Vincent woke up suddenly and instinctively rolled into the fetal position. His hands cupped over his abdomen where he could feel the pain from John Glow's bite. Expecting blood and a deep bite mark, Vincent moved his hands away, but there was nothing there. He was completely unharmed and intact. Vincent looked around the room. He was completely alone. There was no one there. It was nothing but some kind of fucked-up bad dream. Vincent lay there calming himself and reasoning it all away. He convinced himself it was all just a nightmare and nothing more.

<u>Part 3</u>
War

"One can't build little white picket fences
to keep the nightmares out."
-Anne Sexton

Chapter 19
Bobby

Bobby was sitting on the back porch swing at his grandparents' Marthasville, Missouri farm. He was swinging back and forth the way he had always done when he was a boy.

It was a nice night.

Quiet and calm.

There was a breeze causing the field of corn to look like waves as it moved back and forth. It was difficult for him to see clearly, but Bobby noticed the moon rising on the back edge of the field.

A huge harvest moon.

The orangish-red moon continued to rise, glowing and casting its light onto the cornfield, bringing it more and more into focus.

Bobby was humming to himself - some song he knew when he was a child while watching the big full harvest moon rise.

"Jimmy crack corn and I don't care..."

He stopped singing in mid-verse.

Through the moon's illumination there was a flicker of something coming from the middle of the field.

Bobby concentrated toward the flicker as he started hearing a sound.

Swish. Chop.

Swish. Chop.

It was the sound of something chopping through the stalks of corn in the field. Bobby strained his eyes so he could see more clearly. His eyes began watering as he stared. He wiped them off with the sleeve of his shirt.

Swish. Chop.

Swish. Chop.

He pulled his sleeve away. Looking toward the flicker of light coming from the field, he saw a man.

Swish. Chop.

Swish. Chop.

He could clearly see there was a man in the middle of the field.

Swish. Chop.

Swish Chop.

The moon had now risen even more, and Bobby could see the man was holding something in his hands, bringing it up with a swish and then bringing it down with a chop.

Swish. Chop.

Swish. Chop.

The man was cutting the cornfield stalks with a scythe.

Swish. Chop

Swish. Chop.

The man was moving slowly to the side. He looked like the vision of death himself bringing the corn down around his feet with the screams of the cutting action.

Swish. Chop. Swish. Chop.

Swish Chop. Swish Chop.

The man was working faster. Bobby could see the man was shirtless wearing nothing but ratty

bib overalls that were fastened at one shoulder. He
was working faster and faster.

Swish. Chop. Swish Chop. Swish Chop.

The man turned his head and looked toward
Bobby.

"Oh my God," Bobby could see the glowing
of the man's white eyes.

Swish. Chop. Swish Chop. Swish Chop.

It was John Glow - swinging the scythe
faster and faster. He was working toward
something which appeared now to Bobby, lined up
in a row in the field. A taller, straight line of
something in the shadows of darkness, illuminated
by the rising light of the moon.

Swish. Chop. Swish Chop. Swish Chop.

The harvest moon fully rose above the field
and Bobby clearly saw that the neat, shadowy row
was actually PEOPLE. Not just any people, but a
lineup of everyone Bobby loved in his life. Lined up,
standing and staring forward in a trance. Glow was
working even faster chopping with a vengeance as
he came nearer.

Swish Chop. Swish Chop. Swish Chop. Swish
Chop.

Glow was now laughing wildly as he worked
toward the row of people standing in the field. The
full reality of what was happening washed over
Bobby as Glow began to chop even faster.

Chop. Chop. Chop. Chop. Chop. Chop. Chop.

Bobby jumped off the swing and began
running toward the field to stop the chopping. No
matter how fast he tried to run, it seemed as if the
field and those he loved were getting further and
further away from him.

Chop. Chop. Chop. Chop. Chop. Chop. Chop.

Bobby was screaming, "STOP, don't you hurt them!" But Glow just continued chopping faster and faster.

Chop. Chop. Chop. Chop. Chop. Chop. Chop.

Bobby finally reached the field, and he began to furiously fight through the rows of corn to get to his loved ones. He saw them fully and clearly standing in a row. They were entranced, waiting patiently to be harvested. He saw Glow wildly chopping his way closer and closer to them with the scythe.

Chop. Chop. Chop. Chop. Chop. Chop. Chop.

Bobby could see that his mother was the first in the line waiting to be taken down by the swinging of the scythe. He screamed frantically as he ran closer and closer. Glow looked at him with complete contempt and disgust at Bobby's futile fight against what was inevitable. Glow became even more crazed as his white eyes gleamed into the night and his laugh echoed along with the sound of his chop.

Chop. Chop. Chop. Chop. Chop. Chop. Chop.

"Don't you hurt my mother!" Bobby screamed as Glow slashed the scythe back and down violently to chop Bobby's mother's body in half.

Bobby woke up screaming in his bed. His breathing was fast and heavy. Sweat covered his naked chest. Bobby threw back the covers to cool down. He lay there, catching his breath and trying not to concentrate on the dream. He needed to calm his mind. He felt something as he moved his feet. Looking downward toward his feet, he saw that they were covered with mud. Covered in mud from the cornfield he had been running through moments before in his nightmare.

Bobby would sleep no more that night.

The next morning Bobby felt more exhausted than he had ever felt in his life. He was not able to sleep after the dream, the mud and the corn. What used to seem unbelievable to him had now become very real. The nightmares were continuing and getting any kind of quality sleep had become less and less of a possibility. In fact, all of his friends were dealing with the same type of nightmare events. They were all having nightly Glow visits. They were all being physically abused. They were all also being sexually abused at times as well. Their bodies had bite marks and bruises all over them. The actual penetrative rape happened more often with Chuck than with the others. Bobby felt this was because Chuck was the one of the remaining friends who was completely heterosexual. Bobby was sure it would be an extra charge of shits and giggles for Glow to attack Chuck because it was an invasion of his body and an attack in the most personal and sexual of ways.

Bobby worried about Chuck more than the other two because Chuck had also taken Paul's death the hardest. After all, Chuck was Paul's closest friend. Bobby knew it weighed heavily on Chuck that his last moments with Paul were spent fighting. They had never fought like that before. Chuck claimed he couldn't get the image of Paul's angry face and the actual feeling of Paul's hands on his chest to go away. He claimed it was some strange sort of sensory memory where he could feel the entire confrontation all over again. Chuck said it kept playing over and over in his mind, wiping away anything good about their friendship.

Yeah, Bobby was worried about all of them, but he was really worried about Chuck. It seemed to Bobby that Chuck was clearly at a breaking point. Both the violent night attacks and Paul's death were taking a toll on Chuck, more so than the others. None of them were in good shape but Chuck was the one who seemed closest to breaking. Bobby had become so worried that he had snuck into Chuck's bedroom and took the handgun out of the dresser because he was worried, he might - well, you know. Bobby then gave the gun to Alex for safe keeping. Bobby knew the gun would be in safe hands with Alex.

Alex had always seemed the most stable one of them all. Even in the insanity of all of this, Alex seemed to be holding up better - or at least better at hiding his fear and emotions from everyone else. The one thing Bobby was sure of is that Alex didn't like guns and would never use a gun in under any circumstances. Bobby knew it had to be Alex because things were getting bad enough that he didn't even trust himself with one. He felt he could even envision a moment when he would have no other option but to use a gun on himself. Chuck couldn't be far behind him either. For God's sake, it didn't take a fucking genius to understand how dangerous sleep deprivation had become for all of them.

It had been over two weeks since Paul's death. His death had been ruled a suicide after the police viewed all the available surveillance footage from in and around the apartment and the building on that night. Paul had been completely alone at the time of his death. The security footage clearly showed him alone on the balcony of his parents' apartment. It showed him turn around and stop as if he saw someone or something.

But there was no one there.

This was the moment Paul began speaking and crying into the air. He was speaking to himself and there was good reason to believe he was having some sort of breakdown. You could clearly see Paul becoming more and more emotional and agitated as the footage went forward. At one point, near his last moments, he was screaming and crying at nothing but air. It was as if he was arguing and trying to reason with someone who simply was not there. Then almost as quickly as Paul's episode began, it seemed to stop, as a blank expression came over his face and in his eyes.

It was almost as if that was the moment when Paul died. The moment when his expressions went to blank nothingness. Then, without emotion, Paul robotically grabbed a chair from the nearby table and brought it over to the balcony. Without looking back, he climbed up onto the chair. He moved very methodically, as if he were climbing some stairs. Paul stepped onto the balcony edge and stepped off into the air and the darkness below. He didn't hesitate and he didn't look back or down. It appeared like he was climbing a staircase to nowhere and then in an instant he was just gone. The camera in front of the building caught the actual moment of his death.

The toxicology report said Paul showed a little alcohol within his blood, but not enough to impair or influence his thinking. There were no drugs found in his system. It was funny that they thought his suicide might have been caused by drugs. Of course, the police thought something like that had to be drug related. It seemed they were trying to connect the death of the medium and Paul's suicide together with something. They clearly thought drug use might be the common dominator between the two deaths.

According to the police, the medium had levels of synthetic DMT in her system at the time of her death. Of course, the idea Paul was high on DMT was squelched when his toxicology came back clean. There were no traces of DMT or drugs of any kind in his blood at the time of his death. Whatever the circumstances and reasons may have been for both of these deaths, drugs were not the connection. The reasons both Paul Fairchild and Margaret Tolson (aka Jenny Star) had for their behavior on the nights of their deaths went to their graves with them.

Both cases were officially closed.

Paul's death was labeled suicide, and the medium's death was labeled accidental due to the influence of a controlled substance. Bobby thought it was pretty fucked up because DMT has the same drug classification as heroine and ecstasy. Why would she do something like that right before the séance began? It just didn't make sense to Bobby.

There wasn't a funeral for Paul, in fact his parents didn't even release an obituary. Paul was cremated and interred, with his parents being the only ones allowed to be present. Bobby and the others were told there would be a private service for only the parents and to please respect their wishes and not contact them again. Bobby was shocked at the coldness of Paul's parent's attitude and actions. Of course, they behaved in the way that should have been expected, or what Paul would have expected from them. Paul always claimed that he was more of a burden than anything else to them. You know, people will talk about their families, but you never think it is as bad as what they claim it is. However, in Paul's case, it was as bad as what he claimed. These people were fucking heartless.

It really bothered Bobby how quickly they worked at silencing Paul's memory. Out of sight out of mind. Their cruelty was so much they wouldn't let his friends say goodbye to him in any traditional sense. Without an obituary being shared, it was impossible for the group to know where his ashes were being kept to even pay respects on their own. It really bothered all of them. They felt Paul had been erased and they were afraid if Glow could do that to Paul, then it was also a possible outcome for each of them. The group began retreating into their fear and pain further and further, emotionally separating from each other.

It bothered Bobby that the other guys didn't see the value of the support they could give each other. He found it frustrating they were leaving him to not only mourn Paul, but the group they once were as well. Bobby felt like he was mourning the loss of their friendship. What was once the most supportive aspect of all their lives was slowly dying like a cancer. A slow and painful demise without sleep or recourse. It is not that they didn't see each other, because they did. But when they did, it felt forced. It was painful for all of them because there was now always going to be that empty chair at the table where Paul once sat going on about something crazy. Bobby missed those ramblings and that good kind of crazy. But now, even when they were together, it was as if they all were not actually there.

Bobby felt lucky that he still had Jane to lean on. Jane wasn't going anywhere. They had missed each other's company too much when they lost track of each other before. Bobby felt Jane brought a stability to his life he had been missing. Not in an attraction sort of way. He never found himself physically or sexually attracted to Jane.

Sure, even though Bobby felt he was fluid with his sexuality, Jane was not even close to his type. Jane felt too much like his sister to be considered anything else. Besides, lately Bobby had been seeing way more men than women. So much so, he felt guilty about the quick hookups he had been having with the guys on his phone apps. It was a perfect fit for him now during the chaos of everything. No attachment and no strings. Bobby was not capable of giving anyone else any sort of emotional attachment. It became a parade of faceless torsos who he would choose from. Meet. Do the deed and go.

Bobby found humor in the fact that he was even interested in sex, considering the nightly Glow assaults he was dealing with. Although the dreams weren't always sexual, he found it strange that the more Glow raped him, the more promiscuous he became within the waking world. It was as if he had to take all this anger out on someone else. He needed to be assertive and take back his sexual control somehow. Bobby found he was always the top these days. It was as if the act of him penetrating another would give him back the parts of himself that Glow was attempting to strip away from him. It seemed to Bobby that it was all very Freudian, but he kind of understood it. He now knew the girls who the boys called 'loose' in high school were the abused ones trying to take back their power. Sex, to those girls, gave them a hidden strength over the abuser they had at home. Well, it made complete sense to him, and he liked the idea that the sex was helping to give back what he was losing. It was his way of giving the finger to John Glow.

Chapter 20
Kitchen

Jane was now sitting across from Bobby at her kitchen table. Bobby was surprised she managed to fit a table into the kitchen at all - in spite of all of the pillows and shit she had on the floor. And it was a normal-looking table. One of those tables you would see in a '50s diner. You know, the red laminate and chrome type with matching chairs. It's presence among Jane's shrines, mandalas and incense burners was a complete fucking contradiction that Bobby had a very hard time wrapping his mind around. Of course, Jane had always been a contradiction - so he just went with it, occasionally stopping to notice something which stood out and left him puzzled. The kitchen table was one of those puzzles.

"You know what we need to do?" Jane asked sitting at the table.

"What do we need to do?" Bobby said, responding in a seemingly unmotivated and depressed tone.

"We need to get out and be among people, Bobby. We have spent too much time holed up mourning Paul and worrying about this Glow shit. Did you ever think that maybe if we stop devoting so much energy to over-thinking this, maybe things could turn around? There is a lot to be said about the power of positive energy and thinking. We cannot change the energy around us by hiding away, Bobby." She reached across the table and took one of his hands into hers and looked into his eyes.

He looked back at her and squeezed her hand, nodding reluctantly in agreement. Of course, he knew she was most likely right. Jane was a huge believer in the laws of attraction, and she had taught Bobby a lot about how what you feed into the universe is what you get in return. Maybe all of this was some major kind of mind fuck they were bringing down upon themselves just because they wouldn't let it go. Give it back to the universe and let it sort it all out. Jane was right, they did need to change the energy around them.

"My cousin who lives in Tulum is home for a visit. Some friends are getting together and throwing him a party. We should go, Bobby. It's the right kind of people we need to be around right now," Jane said with a reassuring smile.

Jane's cousin had moved to Tulum, Mexico about six years ago. He hadn't lived in Tulum long before he had a spiritual breakthrough and became a Shaman, changing his name from Frank to Inkarrii. It was his chosen name, selected in celebration of his spiritual rebirth. The name Inkarrii was in honor of a Peruvian god and means "Inca king", who founded the mythical lost city of Paititi. Bobby found the whole thing to be silly and he had a very hard time calling Frank Inkarrii.

The change had happened almost overnight. Frank left as a clean-cut Midwestern-type guy and came back with long beaded braids and clothing which literally could have been costuming for *Lawrence of Arabia*. You know the look - flowing gauzy linens of white and beige. The whole costume was supposed to portray a bohemian sensibility but ended up just looking like another trend for posers who are desperate and grasping for some type of belonging.

Inkarrii liked to believe he was a spiritual teacher who was put on this earth to open minds and change lives. Never mind the fact his retreats and ceremonies came with a hefty price tag for those who came to Tulum looking for answers as to why they were so fucking miserable in their lives. Bobby found it somewhat humorous that people would think the jungle held the answers for escaping their misery. What was different about the jungle from their own backyards? Wasn't that the lesson of the Wizard of Oz? You will not find contentment and belonging unless you can find it in your own backyard? Why the search for something within oneself by traveling somewhere else? It made no logical sense to Bobby.

The last time Bobby saw Frank/Inkarrii was a few years back. At that time Inkarrii had begun, what he called, administering good medicine in the jungle in the form extracted frog toxins and ayahuasca. One retreat he was very proud of offering was his weekend of inner silence and meditation. He would take people into the jungle, and they would pay him upwards of five hundred dollars apiece to sit in the hot jungle without any electronic communication and not saying a fucking word. They basically paid Inkarrii to sit in complete silence and sweat their asses off. Bobby wondered why people didn't realize they could have done this as easily in the backwoods of Missouri on a hot August day without ever stepping off a plane in Tulum. Aside from the fact that they could have saved themselves airfare and five hundred bucks.

Yes, Bobby thought Inkarrii was a complete trip. It wasn't as if he didn't like Inkarrii, after all he was a very likable guy. Bobby thought Inkarrii was weird, strange, opportunistic and more than a little full of shit. But regardless of all he could find wrong with Inkarrii, Bobby found him surprisingly likable. A complete fucking contradiction.

Bobby smiled looking at Jane. He could tell this was something Jane really wanted to do so he replied, "Okay, let's go."

Chapter 21
Party

The party was in full swing by the time Jane and Bobby arrived at the downtown loft where it was being held. Washington and Lucas avenues in St. Louis were known as a trendy district where old buildings and warehouses had been turned into loft apartments with high ceilings, large windows, concrete pillars and brick walls. The centerpiece of the loft neighborhood was a funhouse-type place known as the City Museum. A fun place with a playground and Ferris wheel on the roof and an old airplane in front turned into an oversized jungle gym. Everything about the place was made from recycled objects. What was once one man's trash had become the City Museum's treasure. The loft where the party was being held was practically next door and the neighborhood was always buzzing with excitement. It seemed even more energized than usual to Bobby as their taxi pulled up.

Jane and Bobby jumped out of the taxi right in front of the City Museum and took the short walk over to the entrance of the loft building. They had left their cars at Jane's place because street parking was usually scarce, and lot parking was very expensive in the loft district. Over the years, the neighborhood had lost some of its rebirth luster as the crime was moving in and businesses were closing and moving out. Taking a cab was simply less complicated and if they decided to drink or get a little high, they would have a guaranteed designated driver to usher them safely home.

They both could see and hear the party on the fourth floor from the outside of the building. Through large windows they could see a wall size projection screen flashing colorful images as lights and bass filled the air with electric energy. Strangely-dressed people were coming in and out of the building. Some of them were laughing and some of them were clearly stoned. Jane and Bobby entered the lobby and got into the elevator as a group of bohemian-looking girls got out, stumbling and giggling. One of the girls turned around and smiled at Bobby. He smiled back sheepishly and flashed her a quick peace sign as the elevator door closed. The elevator rose quickly and in a very short moment the doors opened with the increased sound of people and the pulsing bass of EDM.

Jane and Bobby followed the sound down the hall and to the left where the door was continually opening and closing with people coming and going. Each time the door opened they would get a whiff of palo santo, sage, incense and marijuana which would rush out into the hallway. Jane walked through the door as if she owned the place, grabbing Bobby's hand as she worked her way through the crowd, searching for her cousin. Bobby had always admired Jane's confidence in these situations. She just belonged everywhere she went without a second thought or trepidation coming to her mind. Jane was just simply what he thought of as socially fearless.

Bobby saw there were people dancing with their hands in the air. A lot of the men were shirtless, and he also noticed a lot of the women were as well, with bare breasts bouncing with complete and total abandon. He continued with Jane as she worked their way through the large open space. In the back left corner of the room Jane had spotted Inkarrii who was sitting on a large expanse of Indian-looking pillows with a group of people who were smoking a hookah. Inkarrii saw Jane immediately and jumped up to greet her with a huge hug. Jane let out a squeal of delight as Inkarrii grabbed her.

"Hey there hippie chick!" he said smiling, breaking the hug so he could look directly into her face.

Inkarrii's beaded braids bobbed over and around his bare shoulders and the numerous beaded necklaces around his neck. Bobby had to laugh to himself because everything about Inkarrii seemed to be beaded. Bobby was sure beneath the thin gauze pants he was wearing you would find an unshaved and beaded bush. By the look of all the piercings he had all over his body, Bobby was sure this guy had to have a Prince Albert piercing to accentuate his guiche piercing. Bobby knew the type. He had sex with this type before and he knew there would almost always be hidden piercings. Inkarrii was barefoot and was sporting a beaded bracelet on one ankle and toe rings on both of his feet. The man was nothing but a walking, talking, beaded, pierced and tattooed Tulum gringo cliché.

Jane interrupted Bobby's thoughts, "You remember my friend Bobby from a few years ago when you visited."

Inkarrii looked at Bobby with a stoned-kind-of-thinking look, "Oh yeah, I remember you bro. You have an incredible aura man. Yeah, I remember who you are. Namaste bro."

Bobby reached out to fist bump his hand but instead Inkarrii went in for a deep and uncomfortably long patchouli-scented hug. Bobby had a thing about his personal space being violated without invitation and he felt his body flinch in reaction to the hug. A long uncomfortable moment. Inkarrii finally released the hug, standing back to look at Bobby like he was some kind of long-lost friend.

"It is so good to see you bro. Long time no fucking see,' Inkarrii said smiling while looking Bobby in the eye.

Bobby forced a polite smile and nodded in return. Inkarrii offered them a seat next to him where he had been sprawled on large pillows when they walked up to greet him. He cleared a space for them, shooing some of the hookah smokers away.

"Give me some space so I can catch up with these guys."

Jane and Bobby sat with him on the pillows. Inkarrii sat between them with his legs folded and offered them some of the hookah. Bobby politely declined while Jane anxiously puffed away. To Bobby's relief, Inkarrii did most of the talking, monopolizing the conversation. For the most part, Bobby didn't need to do anything but nod. He found Inkarrii to be boring, as cliché after cliché rolled out of his mouth. Bobby had heard all this love and light shit before. He thought Inkarrii was too full of himself for someone who was supposed to be so spiritually wise.

Inkarrii was a self-proclaimed lover of life, energy and light. Bobby, on the other hand, was proclaiming Inkarrii to be mostly full of shit and himself. It was clear to Bobby that Inkarrii thought he was far superior to anyone around him. The guy stank of fucking narcissism and Bobby despised a narcissist. Inkarrii spent a lot of time trying to convince Bobby to believe he was this enlightened being of the universe who could take his followers on guided spiritual journeys to find the essence of how they fit into the grand design of things. In truth, Bobby felt Inkarrii couldn't find his way to a bathroom, let alone enlightenment.

Inkarrii was living some kind of costumed fantasy which was a way he found to make a fast buck. People would pay big money to someone claiming they could give them the keys to the universe and enlightenment. Yes, there was a time when Bobby was able to overlook all of Inkarrii's faults, but it was clear that he had gotten much worse over the past few years and even more full of himself. Bobby thought it was almost as if Inkarrii felt he was not only some type of modern-day guru but a jungle-loving messiah.

"I do most of my real work with people through the use of good medicine. You ever done anything like that Bobby? Have you ever connected to the source through good medicine? I know Jane has, but have you?" Inkarrii asked in a quizzical manner.

Bobby wasn't sure how to answer. "I've smoked some weed and dropped ecstasy a few times. Well, maybe more than a few times. But I don't think I have ever done anything like you are talking about," Bobby replied politely, trying not to seem too impressed.

"You have never turned on to turn up?" Inkarrii asked, as Bobby replied shaking his head no.

Bobby had to laugh to himself because he had done the musical *Hair* a few years back and he was sure that was a line taken right out of the script. Bobby felt that everything about Inkarrii was bottled, branded and bogus.

Inkarrii spoke to a topless girl who was laying a few feet from his feet on a pillow and said, "Hey baby, bring me over some of the Pope."

Bobby wasn't sure what he had asked the girl for, but the girl eagerly and obediently jumped to her feet without a thought, her bare breasts bouncing as she went. She headed over to a guy who was DJing the whole scene behind a makeshift stage with sound boards and mixing equipment. Without hesitation, the DJ reached over to a wooden box, pulled something out of it, and handed it to the girl, who ran back to Inkarrii excitedly.

Bouncing Boob Girl handed Inkarrii three black oblong capsules with silver crosses imprinted on them. Inkarrii reached toward Jane to hand her one, but Jane declined saying she wanted to be aware for Bobby in case he needed her because enlightenment could sometimes be intense for some people the first time. Bobby was a little more than aggravated at Jane because she referred to him as 'some people'. For God's sake, he was more like her fucking brother than just simply somebody. In fact, whatever this was, Bobby had decided he was even more determined now to show he could not only do it, but handle it like a pro. Besides, through all his bluster and posturing he did feel a little more at ease knowing Jane was going to keep her wits about her. After all, they were in the middle of a wild party scene which was getting wilder with each passing minute.

There were now some people dancing completely naked in the center of the room. Bouncing penises were now dancing without abandon along with bouncing breasts, which Bobby found humorous. The whole idea of exhibitionism was something Bobby found hilarious. To him, it seemed like no big fucking deal. He never understood people feeling somehow free just because they shed their clothes publicly. If you wanted to be naked then do it at home. Bobby found enough naked freedom from laying on his own couch. He really didn't need to dance with his junk flopping about in a room full of strangers.

Inkarrii leaned over and handed Bobby a pill with a knowing smile and kept one pill in his hand for himself. He handed the third capsule Jane had refused to Bouncing Boob Girl. Bobby waited, holding and looking at the black capsule in his hand. He examined the metallic silver cross that had been stamped upon it. It seemed harmless enough to him as he looked at it. It was almost pretty and inviting in a weird sort of pseudo-religious way.

"Normally, I would use the pure and purified medicines from the jungle, but Man fears the real medicine from the jungle. Man fears the enlightenment it could bring to the world. The good medicine was given to the world by Pachamama, or who you might call Mother Nature. We are given everything we need in nature and within the world to learn and expand. This is our purpose here. This is what we are here to do." Inkarrii held up his black capsule, looking at it as he continued to speak.

"Man, overall, doesn't understand or comprehend and will try in earnest to stop the spread of Pachamama's gifts. Unfortunately, I cannot travel with my medicines from the jungle. Even though they can stop me from bringing my medicines across the border, they cannot stop me from teaching here with effective alternatives. They cannot stop me from opening minds. This medicine is what is known as Black Pope. This is an equally effective alternative medicine. It is a synthetic of sorts but infused with great mind-expanding capabilities. It is a great source of DMT and so much more. I can use this as a tool when I am here in the US, giving people the exact thing the Man had tried so desperately to keep from them. Bro, the Pope will open you up to the universe and the gifts Pachamama has to offer. Man is unable to stand in my way, even here in this country. Enlightenment will not be contained by boundaries. Enlightenment will find a way." Inkarrii reached across Bobby for a bottle of kombucha sitting on a small table near him.

Inkarrii handed the glass of kombucha to Bobby as if he were handing him a communion goblet in church. He began to chant some spiritual mumbo-jumbo Bobby couldn't understand as he indicated for Bobby to take the pill and wash it down with the drink. Jane looked on with encouragement as Bobby placed the pill on his tongue like a communion wafer and took a drink from the glass as if it were communion wine. Bobby found it all a little scary and amusing at the same time because he had no other basis for comparison, other than a fucked-up version of communion. Inkarrii stopped chanting, took his pill and washed it down. He then encouraged Bobby to relax and lean back on the pillows as he did the same.

At first Bobby wasn't feeling anything out of the ordinary. The naked dancing people were growing in numbers as clothes seemed to be shed continually. Inkarrii stood up and dropped his pants to join in. Bobby noticed that indeed Inkarrii was sporting a Prince Albert and smiled to himself with the satisfaction of getting it right. Bobby watched as the naked crowd danced and flirted with each other with the music. Men dancing with women, men dancing with men, women with women. They were all entranced in the rhythmic beat moving in unison.

Inkarrii stepped into the center of the dancing with his hands reaching toward the sky. The naked dancers surrounded him like a flock of birds, reaching out for him as they danced. They were worshiping their naked guru who was obviously getting more than a little sexually aroused as the Black Pope began to work its intoxicating magic through his veins. Bobby had to admit, he himself was feeling a tingling within his own body as he lay back even further on the pillows to take in the scene.

The music, the lights, the abstract visuals on the huge screen added to the whole scene as it continued to throb and pulsate along with the beating of his heart. A beating he was now hearing quite loudly through his ears. A beating and vibration he could feel coming alive within his body. His heart felt connected to the beat, and he could feel the rest of his body slowly responding, becoming one with the rhythm. Bobby felt reality slipping further and further away from him, almost as if he was falling down a deep colorful vibrating hole in the floor. He felt himself sinking.

Inkarrii looked over noticing Bobby was beginning his ride with the Pope and came over to speak with him to help guide him through the opening of the spiritual door. Bobby wasn't too far gone yet. He could understand the words Inkarrii was speaking to him. He also saw Inkarrii was sporting a huge erection as he leaned over to speak to him. Bobby found a weird humor at watching the pierced member bobbing up and down comically almost in front of his face.

Inkarrii knelt on all fours as he moved in closer to speak and guide Bobby. There was nothing sexual inferred by any of it for Inkarrii. Inkarrii just felt no shame about the body the universe had given him to house his soul. Inkarrii viewed his sexual organ as a source of power. A wand of energy. Energy which was causing it to be rock hard in the moment. Inkarrii viewed his body as a tool - he had lost all bodily hang ups years ago.

"That's it, bro. Lay back and relax. You are among friends. You are beginning to ride the Pope, and everything will be okay. Close your eyes for a moment and just breathe. Listen to your heart as you breathe in and out. Feel the air as it enters and leaves your body. How are you feeling bro?" Inkarrii quizzically asked Bobby.

"I'm doing good," Bobby mumbled, giving into the trip and letting himself go.

He could feel himself letting go and he was not frightened by it at all. It felt good as the calm washed over his body. Inkarrii leaned in even closer to Bobby. He could feel Inkarrii's breath as it washed over his face. A warm breeze, Bobby thought.

Not unpleasant at all.

Soothing.

Bobby opened his eyes and looked at Inkarrii's face. The face looking back at him had white glowing eyes.

Glow had now possessed the Shaman.

"Bet you're feeling really fucking special right now," Glow's voice hissed and crackled. His rancid breath made Bobby's eyes start to water.

Immediate fear rose in Bobby. He knew he was in deep danger and there were very few options left for him to escape. He needed to get out of there. He needed to get as far as he could away from the possessed Shaman. The only thing he could think of to do was run.

Bobby, without warning, shoved the Shaman away from him with both of his hands as hard as he could. Inkarrii's naked body rolled off the pillows with his head smashing onto the floor, knocking him unconscious. His followers immediately began screaming and crying as they quickly circled like ravens around their guru's unconscious body, giving Bobby the perfect moment to RUN.

Jane screamed as she tried to stop Bobby, but he was already ahead of her. Bobby bumped and pushed his way through what seemed like a never-ending crowd. Everyone he looked at had been possessed with white glowing eyes.

GLOW WAS EVERYWHERE.

Bobby could hear Glow's growling and hissing voice all around him and behind him as he struggled through the crowd toward the front door. Bobby looked over his right shoulder to see who was following him and how close they were. He immediately spotted Jane moving frantically through the crowd. He locked eyes with her for an instant.

JANE'S EYES WERE GLOWING WHITE TOO.

Bobby went wild at the sight of his now-possessed friend. He fought like a caged animal, violently pushing and shoving his way through the crowd. He heard a strange sound that seemed to rise above everything else as he fought. He then understood it was his own screams he was hearing. He could also hear Glow not far behind him hissing and howling his name in a game of cat and mouse.

Bobby made it to the door. He ran out into the hallway, without stopping or hesitation he ran toward the elevator screaming the entire way. He was praying the door would open because he didn't want to take the fucking stairs.

"Please God don't make me take the fucking stairs."

Besides, he didn't even know where the stairs were. He looked over his shoulder and saw an EXIT sign, indicating the stairwell. Too late anyway, because the fucking stairs were behind him, and he knew he was not turning back. Bobby knew he had to continue forward because Glow was not far behind.

He could hear the hissing and growling as people he passed in the hallway were changed - possessed by the traveling Glow.

There was no going back. To his relief the elevator door was opening in front of him as he drew nearer to it. Bobby violently pushed past a group of people who were exiting the elevator. All of them were seemingly stunned as they stepped into the chaos of the hallway.

Bobby threw his body to the back wall of the elevator as the door began to close. The last thing he saw before the closing of the doors were Jane's angry glowing white eyes with Glow's hissing, screaming voice coming out of her snarling mouth.

When the elevator doors opened onto the lobby floor, Bobby didn't hesitate. He ran out of the elevator even before the doors had fully opened. The lobby was full of people and in an instant all eyes were upon him.

ALL WHITE GLOWING EYES.

They were all screaming at him as he fought toward the lobby doors. All in Glow's taunting growling voice.

"Run Bobby run."

"We are having a fucking good time now."

"Are we having fun yet?"

"Namaste bitch."

Person after person Bobby confronted had white eyes and Glow's hissing voice, which drove him closer and closer to the exit until, finally, he made it through the glass double doors and out into the street.

Once outside, Bobby saw a side street to his left that separated the two main avenues. Bobby instinctively knew that Washington avenue would be his best route for escape. Bobby made a mad run for it. Glow's soldiers continued to confront Bobby as he ran further down the side street onto the sidewalk of Washington avenue.

Once he reached Washington avenue, Bobby halted at the curb of the sidewalk and turned to see if he was still being followed. There he saw no one but Jane who was running toward him down the alley. Bobby began to cry as he heard her voice.

It was Jane's voice he was hearing and not Glow's.

He could see she was frantic and crying. She was calling for him to stop and wait. Jane just about reached where he was standing and with a blink, Jane's eyes switched back to Glow's.

WHITE GLOWING EYES.

Bobby knew he had been tricked. He knew he had to move quickly before she could reach him

- before Glow could reach him. Bobby stepped off the curb and onto Washington avenue.

An oncoming city bus slammed into his body propelling him forward and throwing his body down onto the pavement. Bobby could hear the brakes squealing as the bus's back tires rolled over his abdomen. Bobby screamed out in pain. Pain like he had never felt before in his life. A pain that ripped through him as he felt his body being crushed. He looked over to see Jane standing on the curb, also screaming.

The number twenty bus came to a screeching halt in front of his brutally crushed and broken body. Jane ran toward him, dropping to her knees. She looked into his eyes with tears streaming down her face. Bobby saw it was just Jane. No Glow. No white eyes. It was clear to him that he had been played and Glow had just won the game.

From his dying lips Bobby struggled to say just one word, "Glow."

<u>Chapter 22</u>
Doubt

Alex found parking about a quarter mile away from the scene. The traffic was backed up on Washington all the way to Jefferson Avenue. Alex quickly got out of his car and began running toward where Vincent had told him he was waiting with Jane. Alex already knew Bobby was dead. He arrived where the police had the street blocked off and an STLPD officer stopped him, not letting him enter. Alex had to plead with the cop over and over to call Vincent on his radio. The cop finally gave in, just to shut him up. To the cop's surprise he was instantly told to accompany Alex through the scene to where Vincent was waiting with Jane.

The scene in front of the event and banquet space, Windows on Washington, was complete chaos. The flashing red and blue lights bounced off the closely located buildings and made the street pulse like some sort of fucked-up disco. Alex saw a body was covered in the middle of the street and he knew without question it was Bobby. The officer directed Alex toward the side street where Vincent and Jane were waiting. Jane, sitting on the curb, jumped up immediately when she saw him enter the street and collapsed into his arms crying. Alex looked over her shoulder and saw Vincent watching them with a sympathetic look.

Alex spoke, not letting go of Jane, "What happened to Bobby? Can you tell me what happened to Bobby?" Alex asked with his voice quivering from the tears forming in his eyes.

"There was nothing anyone could do for him, Alex. He was gone by the time the paramedics got to him," Vincent knew it was best to try to answer the question as compassionately but directly as he could.

Alex helped Jane to sit back down on the curb. She reached upwards towards him crying and Alex took her hands, assuring her he was going nowhere.

"I'm not going anywhere. I am staying right here with you. Give me a moment to talk with Vincent," Alex said.

Normally Jane would have questioned the casualness of Alex's reply. She would have wondered why Alex would call the detective by his first name. Why hadn't he called him Detective Rossi? She would have noticed and questioned how easily the name rolled off Alex's lips. But this wasn't a normal situation. She wasn't in her right mind, and it went by her without much thought.

Alex took a few steps over to where Vincent was waiting to speak with him. He could tell by how stiff Vincent was standing that the whole scene had him uptight and worried. Alex had seen Vincent when he had dropped the detective act and let himself be human. He knew, in this situation, he would be dealing with the detective and not a friend. He could tell by Vincent's stance this conversation was going to be all business. Alex was not sure if he was going to let the stiff detective act play out between the two of them. They were way past the whole professional thing.

"Well, what happened? Can you tell me?" Alex asked, not sure if he really wanted the answer.

It was one of those moments when Alex understood that, once the words were spoken, they would never be able to be taken back. Alex knew in his gut that whatever happened to Bobby could also happen to them.

"I can tell you what we know at this point. We know Robert Winchell was attending a party at this adjacent building in one of the fourth-floor lofts. We know, while at this party, he was given a controlled substance," Vincent began to explain in his best just-the-facts demeanor.

Alex cut him off.

"Wait. What? What kind of controlled substance - because the Bobby I knew did nothing more but drink and smoke some weed from time to time." Alex was clearly disturbed by the idea of a controlled substance, because that was just not the Bobby he knew.

"Alex, he had taken a street drug known as Black Pope, which is a highly potent and strong DMT synthetic mixed in a cocktail with other very strong narcotics. This was already confirmed by Jane Moore, who personally watched him take it." Vincent tried to remain calm and selective with his words because he knew this was hard for Alex to hear.

"Black Pope? DMT? Jane, is this true? Did Bobby take something at this party?" Alex had turned to Jane for confirmation.

Jane nodded with a shameful yes and Alex turned back toward Vincent, clearly surprised by her response.

"Alex, he had a bad trip. I have one victim who has been taken to the hospital with a severe head wound and concussion. I have two other victims with broken bones from being pushed violently to the ground. Robert Winchell was the cause of all these injuries as well as the accident which caused his own death. Witnesses, which include Jane Moore, also saw him taking the drug Black Pope. They saw him run out of the party from the building. Jane Moore saw him on the sidewalk of Washington Avenue where she said she tried to stop him, but he turned and ran into the street where he was hit by a city bus. That is what happened, Alex." Vincent stated the facts as directly as he could because he could already tell Alex was having a difficult time accepting them. Sometimes blunt and to the point was the best way. Sometimes it was the only way.

"Is this what happened Jane? Bobby was just high and got out of fucking control. Tell me Jane. Is that what fucking happened?" Alex said angrily, not fully believing what he was hearing.

Jane shamefully nodded yes again and began sobbing loudly. Alex turned back to look at Vincent, who was waiting.

"I don't believe this. I have known Bobby for years and this wasn't the Bobby I know. This is not something Bobby would do. Vincent, you know it wasn't the drugs. You know it wasn't because I told you. I told you. You know it was Glow. You know because I told you he was trying to kill us. It was John Glow," Alex broke down into uncontrollable tears.

Vincent walked over and put his arms around him, letting the detective act drop because he could tell this was too much for Alex to handle. Vincent stood holding Alex in his arms with his head against his chest, feeling his sobbing body shake. He just stood there for a few minutes holding Alex and letting him cry. Holding onto him to ease the pain Vincent knew was growing within Alex. Vincent knew the tears would help to wash away some of the shock. He needed to give him a moment to cry through the initial shock of it all. In this moment, Vincent was no longer the detective, but Alex's friend.

Vincent held onto Alex tightly as he continued to cry. When the tears began to subside, Vincent broke the hold, standing back in front of Alex to look seriously into his eyes. He took a deep breath because he knew he had to try to talk some sense into Alex. He desperately needed to bring Alex back to a place of reality. He needed to confront Alex's idea of Glow.

"Alex, I know you believe in Glow. I know you do. You even had me believing in him too for a moment. It was just for a fleeting moment Alex, because I know the difference between what is real in this world and what is just a nightmare built out of our fears to help us handle some pretty fucked up shit this life hits us with. Alex, you have been given more than your fair share of fucked up lately. I completely understand that, but your nightmares are just that. They are nightmares. The boogeyman does not come out of your dreams to harm you, rape you or kill you when you are awake. It is just your imagination trying to cope, Alex. Glow did not kill Bobby because Glow is not able to kill. There is no such thing as demons, djinn or genies roaming the earth. It is fantasy. The things of books, Alex. The drug Black Pope killed Bobby, not John Glow." Vincent said with as much understanding as he could convey but the truth was, Robert Winchell's death was caused by his own actions and not that of some sort of imaginary djinn.

Alex couldn't believe the words that were coming from Vincent's mouth. This was the one person outside of his small group of friends Alex was convinced that believed him. All the trust and faith Alex had in Vincent and his ability to help them went out the door in that moment. In an instant, Alex lost all trust in Vincent and the anger grew within him as he looked into Vincent's pleading face.

"I should have known better than to believe a fucking cop was really going to help me. At the end of day, I should have known that behind that suit was nothing more than a fucking St. Louis cop. What is even worse - you are the token gay one. The one who they use to betray all of us. Goddamn me for believing you were any different than the rest. Damn you for making me believe you were different because you are not different, Vincent. In fact, you are even worse. Fuck you. Fuck everything about you. May I take Jane and leave now or do you want to put us under arrest and interrogate us some fucking more." Alex spoke loudly as people were starting to look toward him and take notice.

All Vincent could do was nod to him and motion for him to go.

Alex walked over and helped Jane to her feet, saying nothing more. They were leaving and no one was going to stop them. They were leaving because they had done nothing wrong.

Vincent stepped to the side and let them pass. He knew there was nothing he could say now. But he also knew, because he cared for Alex, he needed to be truthful with him. He had to say to Alex what he believed to be true. He understood the power of his own nightmare. The difference between the two of them is that Vincent understood it to be nothing more than a nightmare caused by the suggestion of a very scared and confused young man. Alex needed to face the facts. He liked Alex. He liked Alex a lot and that made this moment even harder for him. Vincent felt, in this moment he lost something valuable to him and, as confused as it made him feel, it emotionally hurt. Vincent sadly watched Alex round the corner with an arm around Jane who was crying - and then they were gone.

Chapter 23
Lawnmower

It was a hot day. It was one of those hot and humid kind of days St. Louis was notorious for. The kind of day when the air was so wet with humidity the heat literally stuck to your skin. Spring had come and gone quickly. With the changing of the season, Chuck was hopeful things might change for all of them as they went into the summer months.

The Glow nightmares had stopped suddenly for Chuck after Bobby's death and funeral even though he knew they had continued for Alex and Jane. Chuck hadn't seen much of them over the past few weeks, and when he did, they were both very quiet and withdrawn. Chuck thought they had the look of prisoners of war. Seriously, it was not as strange as it sounded. In a strange and fucked up way Chuck thought they had all been fighting an unwinnable war. For whatever reason, a relieved Chuck was glad he was no longer fighting that war. Chuck felt he had escaped whatever it was that had been haunting, hurting and raping him.

Glow was now leaving him alone for whatever reason and Chuck was being very careful not to draw attention to himself or provoke the nightmares to return. He felt as if it was some type of victory. He wondered if somehow Paul or Bobby had given him this as a gift from the other side. Chuck knew that was a crazy fucking thought, but then again nothing seemed too impossible anymore. The one thing all of this did for Chuck was to open his mind to possibilities he had never considered before. He felt like he had been given a frightening window into the universe and what he saw there scared the literal fuck out of him.

Opened minded now? Yes. Stupid? Fuck no.

Bobby's funeral had been held in his hometown of Washington, Missouri. It was a very nice funeral. Bobby had very kind and loving parents and it was hard watching them bury their son and his friend. It all seemed so senseless to Chuck. The idea that Bobby had taken a drug like Black Pope was hard enough to handle. There were some tense moments between Bobby's parents and Jane. Understandably so, hell, Chuck even blamed her somewhat, but he would never voice it or let it show. Besides, he could see she was living in her own private hell with it and was beating herself up enough. Jane would carry that guilt with her for a very long time.

It was hard for Bobby's parents not to blame Jane for his death or at least, in their mind, not doing enough to stop it. Rational or irrational, they were grieving parents. It was not unusual behavior from parents when they lose a child, no matter how old they are when that happens. Nonetheless, twenty-two was way too young for anyone to die. And no one deserves to go out the way Bobby did.

The coroner told the parents the initial impact of the bus did not cause the injuries needed to take his life. He could have recovered from those. What killed him were the injuries he received when the back wheels of the bus rolled over the center part of his torso. Chuck would never understand why the gruesome details were necessary to tell the grieving parents. Chuck thought just telling them he was hit by a bus was sufficient enough information. No additional details needed. Chuck was sure they got the point with, *hit by a bus.* The image of that statement is enough without needing any further details.

Chuck walked around the back of his house. He grabbed his hand mower and gas can. Heading into the front yard, he waved at some of the neighborhood kids playing in the street. Chuck looked up and saw that hanging from his front porch gutter was an annoying string. One single red string. Probably from the fucking kids across the street and their balloons.

But why red?

Chuck wasn't sure how the string had gotten there but it was out of place, and it bothered him. It bothered him a lot. Chuck reached up and tried to pull the string down with his hands, but it didn't budge. He tried a few times without any luck. Chuck couldn't believe how strong this one piece of red string was. It was taunting him, screaming inside his head to be taken down. Pissed off, Chuck went into the house to look for some scissors to cut it down.

Chuck stomped into the house through the front door. Then stomped through the living room. Through the bedroom. Back into the kitchen where he opened, and began to frantically search through, his junk drawer for scissors he knew were there. Chuck had everything you could ever need in this drawer. There were twisty ties, batteries, a multi-head screwdriver, even a few condoms, but no fucking scissors. He was getting frustrated. Then he saw the long lighter he used to light the charcoal for his BBQ grill. That's it. He would burn the motherfucker off.

Chuck took the lighter in his hand. Back through the kitchen. Through the bedroom. He stomped through the living room once again and out the front door onto the front porch. He clicked the lighter and held the flame up to the string and burned it off with a great sense of satisfaction and accomplishment. He placed the lighter down on the ledge of the porch and walked back toward the waiting lawnmower and gas can.

Chuck wiped the sweat from his forehead. Man, was it a fucking hot day! He took his t-shirt off drying himself off and threw it over onto the porch. He filled the lawnmower with gas, set the gas can on the sidewalk, and started the engine.

The lawnmower came to life, drowning out the sounds of the neighborhood children playing in the street. One of them had opened one of the fire hydrants a few houses down and they were jumping in and out of the water. The old neighbor was yelling at them - she was going to call the police. The kids laughed at her and continued splashing. They knew from living in the city that it would take the police or fire department a while to get there to shut off the flowing water from the hydrant because they would have more pressing calls to handle than a group of kids having fun at the city's expense. By the time they arrived the kids would be bored and would have moved onto something else. It was this never-ending game the kids played with the old woman who spent more time paying attention to what they were doing than she did her own life. You know the kind of stay-off-my-lawn type? Yeah, that was her.

Chuck laughed to himself as he drowned the noise out with the roar of his mower. He began slowly traveling up and down his front yard in neat overlapping rows cutting his grass. The air filled with the sweet scent of mowed grass as he went. Chuck loved the smell of a freshly cut lawn. It was one of those smells he wished they could bottle for those cold, dead-of-winter St. Louis months. Freshly cut grass instantly brought memories of summer quickly to mind. Before he knew it, he had mowed his entire front lawn. In this moment, in the heat of the day, Chuck felt he was lucky that all of his grass and lawn were in the front of his house. The backyard consisted of a garage and concrete. That was it. There was not much room back there for anything else at all. So, once he finished cutting the front lawn, he was done. Grass was cut and the chore could be checked off of his list.

Chuck switched off the lawnmower and headed inside for a drink. His entire body was covered in sweat. He walked through the front door. Through the bedroom and once again into the kitchen. The cool breeze from his air conditioner felt good on his body as he downed some new ice-cold sports drink he had in the refrigerator. One of those unnaturally blue kind of drinks whose flavor he could never quite put his finger on. It tasted like blue something-or-other is what it fucking tasted like. At least that's what he thought. He laughed at the idea of what the taste of blue would be and if a color even could have a taste. Well, if blue had a taste this is how fucking blue was supposed to taste. Blue was fucking delicious.

He put the bottle back into the refrigerator and headed back through the kitchen. Through the bedroom. Through the living room and then out to the front yard to put away his supplies. When he got there, he heard a high-pitched, sickening kind of voice. He knew instantly who it was. It was Carol. The married neighbor lady from across the street. Carol was about forty or so. Nosey. Bothersome and always horny. Chuck was sure her husband hadn't satisfied her in years. Carol was the neighbor whose house was constantly under repair. She was notorious for answering her door in her string bikini to welcome any repairman that was unlucky enough to draw the short straw for her call. Carol kept the plumbers and washing machine repairmen in work. How could they complain - and besides, her flirting was harmless. A bother, but harmless none the less.

Chuck was sure she must have heard his lawnmower and came out into the front yard to attempt one more time to 'get her some of that', Chuck thought as he giggled to himself. He looked across to her front yard. There was Carol, half-assed watering her yard, hoping he would come out so she could be neighborly and say hello.

"Hey there Chuck. How ya doin' hon? It sure is a hot one out here today. I am all sweaty over here all by myself. Dale is gone fishin' and won't be home until tomorrow." She said as she hosed down her bikini-topped scantily covered chest.

"Doing just fine Carol. Thanks," Chuck said trying to look busy around the mower and sidewalk.

"You been workin' out? Have you been workin' on your chest, hon? I would say it sure does look like you have been workin' on your chest and things. I see all of those muscles and stuff." Carol said flirtingly.

She dropped her hose and bent over to pick it up with her string-bikini-bottomed ass facing the street and Chuck. Chuck knew this was his chance to make a break for it.

"Nice talking to you Carol." he said as he made his break for the safety of his house.

She didn't even have time to stand back up and say goodbye before Chuck was inside the coolness of his house, closing and locking his front door. He would wait a while and go pick up his things out of the front yard later. Maybe by then Carol would have moved on to someone else, or, fired up the dildo Chuck was sure she kept in her bedside drawer. A huge dildo, he was sure. Battery-powered. Something like a big pink sexual jack hammer for sure. He found it amusing that most female sex toys were pink. Like the sheer pinkness of them made them somehow feminine and less kinky. Yeah, he was sure Carol's huge jackhammer dildo would have to be pink.

The air conditioning felt good. Chuck walked through the living room into his bedroom. Turning on the fan, he laid face-down on his bed with his shorts still on and legs and shoes hanging off the side of the bed. The cool air from the fan felt good as it moved from side to side and up and down over his sweaty body. It was cooling it and drying it at the same time. The sound of the fan's motor as it moved back and forth was somehow to strangely relaxing and hypnotic. Chucks eyes began to get heavy. Then to close. Then to sleep.

Chuck was lying on a lounge chair on a beach somewhere in Mexico. Someplace familiar. Chuck remembered this place. This was a place they had rented a few years back in Akumal which sat between Playa Del Carmen and Tulum. They had rented this apartment in a brightly pink and blue colored building which sat right on the shore of the Caribbean Sea. It was a huge apartment on the lowest floor with a double glass door which opened onto a BBQ patio, no more than fifteen or twenty feet from the water.

Chuck heard some commotion coming from behind him.

He turned around to see Alex, Paul and Bobby coming out onto the patio laughing and joking. Chuck got up off the lounger and walked over to them. Bobby was getting the charcoal ready to grill some burgers. Alex and Paul were standing there watching him as they all chatted back and forth, drinking some beers.

Paul walked over to Chuck, sensing he was somewhat confused by the whole dream. He was confused by it all, but Chuck knew he was dreaming. None of it mattered to him though because this was a good memory.

"Hey, you doing okay?" Paul asked, smiling.

"I 'm doing fine. I sure do miss you," Chuck replied seriously.

"I know you do. I miss you too," Paul said reassuringly.

Chuck was loving the fact that he was getting to relive this place in his dream. That had been a great trip they had taken together. This was before any of the nightmares had begun. In fact, this was the last trip they had all taken together. Even though he knew it was a dream, it was nice to relive the moment.

"This was a nice trip, wasn't it?" Chuck asked Paul.

"It was. Do you remember this day?" Paul asked.

Of course, Chuck remembered this day. It was so hot, but the sun had felt so good on his body. So good he had fallen asleep holding his beer, waking up when the guys came out to the patio.

"I got sunburned and you told me that I should throw some cold water on it to cool down before it got much worse." Chuck said to Paul as the other two were busying themselves around the grill.

"That's right, that's what I told you," Paul said with a knowing smile on his face.

"You said that we needed to get some more beer and ice in the large tub we were using as an open cooler. You told me it would be a good idea to dump the water on my sunburned body to cool it down." Chuck said smiling sheepishly.

"I never thought you would actually do it, but you did. Go over there and do it now. This is the memory, and you can't go changing it now." Paul laughed as he spoke.

Chuck, laughing, walked over to the large bucket which was now nothing but ice water where the ice and beer had been before. He picked it up with both hands and he dumped the cold water over his body. The shock of the cold water shot through his body. He let out a sound that was not quite a scream but more like a shocked puppy than anything else. It was enough to get the other two boys to turn around and look at him along with Paul.

"That was the coldest water I thought I had ever felt in my life. It took my breath away so I couldn't even scream. I remember I stood there shivering," Chuck said as he stood shivering in the dream just like he had in real life.

He was taking in every second of this dream and memory. He didn't want to miss anything about it.

"And then I asked you if you had a lighter for the grill?" Bobby said to Chuck looking at his shivering body with a smile.

"I remember looking around for it and I couldn't find it at first. Then it was Alex who reminded me," Chuck said remembering.

"I said to you that I thought you set the lighter down on the ledge of the wall right over there." Alex said pointing toward the wall and the lighter.

Chuck walked over to the ledge and picked up the lighter into his hands and walked over to the grill where he tried to light it. It didn't light.

"It didn't light at first. Then I tried again, and it didn't light. It was on the third time when it finally lit, and I was able to light the fire." Chuck walked over to the BBQ and did exactly what he said. On the third try the lighter lit and he put the flame to the fire, and it roared to life as he stood back.

Then something came into the dream that wasn't part of the memory. There was a noise he had not heard on that day and the noise was getting louder and louder. Chuck could feel himself getting hot and hotter. He was sweating and the heat washing over his body was becoming unbearable. He looked toward the sea thinking he would run into the water. He thought the water would help him cool down, but he stopped when he saw Glow was standing in the water laughing at him.

The noise he was hearing became louder and LOUDER.

IT WAS A SCREAM. IT WAS HIS SCREAM!

Chuck woke up standing in his front yard. He had been sleepwalking. He had sleepwalked out into his front yard and poured gas over his head, dousing his entire body. He had then ignited the gas with the lighter he left on the ledge of the porch.

Chuck was now burning alive as he screamed.

The neighborhood kids were gathered in front of him watching him burn, not knowing what to do as someone ran for help. Carol came running out of her front door with a blanket to put out the flames. She wrapped the blanket around him, but he was already dead as she felt the skin peel off of his body when he fell to his knees and then onto the ground.

<u>Chapter 24</u>
Trauma

Vincent wasn't sure how to handle the scene before him in the front yard of Chuck's house. The whole neighborhood was now facing the horrific trauma from it all. Vincent looked across the street as an officer finished taking the statement from the neighbor Carol, who was now sitting on her front porch crying.

"She said, he was completely engulfed in flames. She heard his screaming and looked out her front window and saw him burning. She did the only thing she knew to do which was to grab a blanket and run to help. She wrapped the blanket around him. As she did, he stopped screaming. He went to his knees and then he went down. She said she thinks he was dead before he even hit the ground. I questioned the kids as well. A few of them said they saw him come out of the house. He acted strange. One of them said he looked like he may have been sleepwalking," the officer said with a quizzical look on his face.

"Now that would be a fucking thing, I tell ya. Doing something like this to yourself in your sleep. That is some messed up shit, I tell ya. The kids said he walked over to the gas can next to the lawnmower and he poured it over his head. They said he acted like it was cold. Like it was a shock. Ya know, like those people use to pour cold water over their heads as a challenge. Yeah, they said it was like that. Like it was really cold, ya know. They said he was also talking to himself but really could not make out what he was saying. That is when he walked over to the lighter and lit himself up. Fucking thing for those kids to see," the officer said shaking his head.

Vincent looked up from his notes nodding in agreement.

It indeed was a fucked-up thing for the kids to see. Vincent thanked the officer for the information, reminding him to put every detail in his report when he filed it. Yes, it was a hell of a thing to see. Vincent worried it might stay with the kids. Something like that was not likely to go away too quickly and could cause nightmares. It would be a while before the kids who lived on Shenandoah Avenue would be able to forget the day Chuck Parker set himself on fire. That was one thing Vincent was sure about. This was the type of thing urban legends were made from. A horrific story that would be told over and over. Added to as the years passed. Chuck would become infamous and the thing of nightmares for any kid living in the neighborhood. Yeah, they would be talking about the man in flames for many years to come.

"You better be good, or the Burning Man will come to get you," they would be told for many generations to come.

There really wasn't a whole lot left for him to do on the scene. It was all pretty cut and dry. Vincent winced at his poor choice of words, cut and dry. Everything was in place as described in the testimonies that had been taken on the scene. How Chuck Parker carried out the act wasn't at issue.

What was at issue was, why? It was pretty fucked up and a horrible way to die. Vincent was sure when the toxicology report came back, they were going to find Black Pope in Chuck's system. Vincent was beginning to think that there was nothing unusual about any of these cases at all. The common denominator seemed to be drug related. Black Pope was notorious for causing paranoia and irrational behavior. The department had seen scenes like this playing out all over the city. People who 'rode the Pope' were doing crazy things, and it was causing huge problems.

Vincent had lined it all up in his mind as he watched them begin to prepare Chuck's body for transport. He had to walk away toward his car because there was one thing you would never forget once you smelled it and that was burning flesh. It stayed with you. Almost like the smell itself was burned and imbedded in your nostrils for days to come.

Vincent went over all of the cases within his mind. The medium had DMT in her system. Let's not forget one of the main active ingredients in Black Pope is DMT. Paul had no signs of drugs in his system at the time of his death. However, everyone he came in contact with that evening said he was acting irrationally, including the door man who was not connected at all with the others. The doorman was a complete outside observer, which held a lot more weight with his testimony.

Vincent decided what they had seen was Paul going through a serious withdrawal. That would explain why no drugs were found in his toxicology. Vincent was sure this drug was Black Pope. The horrible withdrawal was why it was so hard to get the Pope off your back once you were hooked. For most people it only took one capsule, one time for the addiction to set in. Once the craving for the Pope was set into motion it would require the next fix and then the next. The withdrawal of the Pope was severe and just as immediate. These people would go from high to withdrawal very quickly. There was not an in between. You were either flying high or you were slammed down. Think of the worst possible addiction. Black Pope was easily a hundred times worse. That is what Vincent believed happened to Paul and Ellis. He already knew Black Pope was involved in Bobby's death, and he was sure he would discover it was involved in Chuck's as well.

Vincent decided to try to give Alex a call. He hadn't talked with him since the night of Bobby's death. It had ended badly between both of them that night. It wasn't as if he didn't want to talk to Alex, but he wasn't sure if Alex wanted to talk to him. Vincent knew anger was a part of grief and Alex McAllister had been given more than his share of it in a very short time. Vincent could completely understand why Alex may have turned to something supernatural for an explanation. As ridiculous as it may have sounded, Vincent got it. It was easier for Alex to make up a boogeyman than to face the fact everyone around him was falling apart due to their own addictions. Vincent had seen denial before. It was not as uncommon as you would think.

Alex's phone went straight into voice mail. Vincent was disappointed, but not surprised at all. He didn't bother leaving a message. Chuck's death was not something he wanted to leave on voice mail. Vincent knew Alex would hear about it soon enough and so would Jane.

Vincent had thought of Alex a lot over the past few weeks. He couldn't help but think how life might have been different if they had met under different circumstances. Of course, Vincent knew he was attracted to Alex. It was obvious there was a sexual energy between them. This bothered Vincent as well because he knew it was something he could never act upon. Vincent was doing everything he could do to save his marriage, not destroy it with a fling with some younger guy. There was also the age difference. There was almost a ten-year difference between them, for God's sake. This mattered to Vincent, even though age difference wasn't something gay men usually got hung up about. There were a lot of gay couples who had ten- or twenty-year differences in age and for them it was no big deal and it worked out fine. But Vincent was way too practical for that. Vincent had this idea he wanted to grow old together with someone.

Vincent and his husband Tim were only six months apart in age. Vincent could see them in their eighties sitting on the porch looking back on their life together. Having that kind of history mattered to Vincent. But he could have been Alex's friend. Nothing stopped him from being Alex's friend. Then of course there were those couples who would bring a third person into their relationship. Vincent had always been too much of a prude to even consider a three-way or a polyamorous relationship. Besides, he had heard if you had a three-way you might as well add a fourth because if you didn't someone was going to always feel left out or neglected. Even when thinking about a three-way, Vincent would connect immediately to the emotion of the idea and try to correct it. That was the key to everything about relationships with Vincent. It was all connected to, and with, emotion.

Besides, Vincent wasn't sure if he wanted to share, or trust sharing, his friendship with Alex with his husband Tim. Tim could sometimes be very judgmental and he could see something happening between Tim and Alex that would ruin their friendship for good. Of course, there was always the possibility Tim could fall in love with Alex. Vincent knew his hours were crazy and he wouldn't want to leave Tim and Alex alone together for too long. But he had to wonder to himself if it would be Alex he would worry about coming onto Tim or Tim coming onto Alex? They were both obviously very good-looking men. Vincent could see the sparks flying between the two of them. The idea he would even think of such a thing bothered him. It bothered Vincent a lot. Of course, he would be able to trust them. How could he not trust his husband? He knew Tim loved him and would never do anything that would, or could, destroy the love between them. And of course, the whole hypothetical idea of it all was ridiculous because, in truth, Alex McAllister didn't want to see or to talk to Vincent ever again.

"The body is ready to move. The scene is secured and taped off," one of the officers said to Vincent as they walked up to his car.

Vincent thanked them and commended them for a job well done. He was getting ready to leave when Chuck's neighbor Carol came running over to him from across the street.

"Hey there detective. I really don't understand any of this. My neighbor Chuck was one of the good ones. You know, a nice guy who never bothered anyone. I just don't understand why he would do something like this. It doesn't make sense," she began to cry falling onto Vincent who reluctantly put his arms around her to comfort her.

Vincent felt sorry for her because he knew she had been through a hell of a lot. Of course, it made the situation more awkward that she was wearing a neon yellow string bikini. My God this was St. Louis and not someplace like Miami, or even Cancun. Vincent felt Carol's hand slide down his back and placed firmly on one of his buttocks. Vincent politely removed her hand before stepping away.

"I have no answers for you at this time as to why. If you can think of anything else you need to tell us, here is my card. You just call this number, and I will add to your statement - whatever you need to add. Now please excuse me I am late getting home to my husband. He doesn't like it when I am late," Vincent said to her as he handed her a card and got into his car.

He left bikini-clad Cougar Carol standing in the street as he drove away. He wasn't sure but he thought he heard her ask, "Husband? Are you a homosexual, hon?"

Whether she had indeed said it or not wasn't important and neither was the obvious shock he left her with - standing in the middle of the street with her mouth gaping open in surprise.

"Well, I never," Vincent could hear her saying within his mind.

"Well, I bet you have," Vincent laughed because he knew in fact, Cougar Carol most definitely had.

Chapter 25
Alone

Jane was very tired. She was working a job managing a bar/restaurant called Patrick Nolan's in the Bevo Mill area of St. Louis. It was a good place that drew nice crowds. Regular crowds who were loyal to the business and those who worked there. Jane was the night manager. Even though she was so tired from a lack of sleep, it helped that she didn't have to work mornings. She could caffeinate and energy-drink-it-up through most of the day and be ready to head out to work at four. Even at that, Jane had to call in sick more days than she would have ever done before. Her boss didn't question her too much because they could look at her and tell something serious was going on in her life.

Jane began to look drawn and overly thin. There were dark circles under her eyes. Her hair had even begun to fall out in handfuls every time she took a shower. They also noticed there were several bruises and scratches on her body. Her boss tried to talk to her about the marks, but Jane simply shut him down by walking away. She knew her boss thought it was maybe a boyfriend or something along those lines. Her boss would never believe Jane was being attacked in her sleep by a monster named John Glow and she didn't want to get into the conversation or even begin to offer an explanation. Sometimes there were some things that were better left unsaid, and this was one of those things. Everyone at her work knew she had tragically lost three of her friends. Two of those required her to go to a funeral.

Jane hated funerals but went anyway because she knew they would want her there. Both funerals were very different. Bobby's funeral was incredibly sad, with a closed casket. Chuck was cremated, for obvious reasons and was given a memorial service. The cremation just finished the job he had started on his own. Jane tried to cling closer to Alex through it all. But after Chuck's death, Alex really began to push her away. She could completely understand why. After all, she blamed herself for the whole mess. If she hadn't tried to show off with the spirit board on that first night, then none of them would be where they were right now. The other three would be alive and they all would be living somewhat normal lives.

Well, as normal of lives as anyone could expect. Jane convinced herself of this and Alex let her do it, even though, deep down, Alex knew it wasn't true. Ellis was killed before the spirit board incident and not after. Alex felt it was himself all along who was the reason for the attacks, but, when it came to Jane, he kept that to himself. Alex knew he had always been Glow's target, but he kept that to himself too and let Jane believe it was her. Jane had no clue as to what Alex felt was the whole truth of it. Was it fair to Jane? Of course, it wasn't fair to her, but Alex no longer had the energy or the desire to set the record straight.

Nothing was going to bring back the closest friends he ever had in his life. Jane could believe what she wanted to believe. Even if she hadn't been the initial cause of it all, she sure in the hell had helped move it along.

Jane set the security alarm for the building and quickly headed out the back door of her work where her car was waiting. She put the key into the ignition and tried to start it. It didn't start. She tried again. The car just didn't seem like it was sparking.

"Come on and fucking start," Jane said hitting both hands on the steering in a half pissed and half praying gesture, looking at the heavens as if God himself had the time to come down and start the car for her.

Jane tried once more and to her relief the car reluctantly turned over and started idling. She knew she needed a new car but with everything else going on in her life a new car was the last thing on her mind.

Jane thought of her cousin Inkarrii and wondered if he was finally able to return to Tulum. He had spent four days in the hospital for his injuries from the whole scene with Bobby. After he came out of the hospital, the STLPD informed him that he needed to stay around for a few weeks until they finished the investigation and cleared him to leave the country. It made sense to everyone because, after all, there were drugs involved. However, the only drugs which were actually found at the scene were the ones already in Inkarrii's and Bobby's systems. The DJ had stashed away his supply of Black Pope long before the cops had arrived. So Inkarrii had been essentially grounded to stay longer in the city than he wanted to. Jane heard the investigation had completed and hoped he had been able to fly home by now. She didn't want to call him because she felt like it was another tragic circumstance that she had caused through her own actions. It was as if Jane almost thrived on self-blame in these situations in her life. It was a fault of hers she needed to correct. She was always stepping in to take the blame for everyone's fuck ups. Have some guilt? Just unload it onto Jane Moore because she would gladly accept it. She wore that shit like a badge, and it was guaranteed she would wear it there until the end of her fucked-up days. Jane Moore was not going to change. She was firmly stuck in her ways.

Jane pulled her car out onto the street. She really wasn't paying attention to where she was driving. One of the ways she had tried to avoid the Glow attacks was to take long drives at night. It wasn't as if they didn't also happen during the day - because they did. But the day attacks appeared to be less violent and were easier to handle. At least that was the way it seemed to Jane, which in truth could have been nothing more than her own rationalization which gave herself permission to sleep. So, when it was dark, and she was not working, she drove. Listening to music and guzzling energy drinks which she found could be bought in supersized cups at popular all-night gas station/convenience stores. This was how she was surviving. She really had no idea how long she was going to be able to keep it up. She had looked in her dressing mirror this morning and the person she saw looking back at her shocked her. She had aged a whole decade in the process of a few months. She looked not only tired, but older. She knew she felt older as well. More than older, Jane felt broken down and ready to be discarded.

Jane saw a news report on one of the bar's televisions talking about people who were addicted to the drug Black Pope. She had stopped to listen to the story because she knew that was the drug Inkarrii had given to Bobby. The story interviewed some of the Pope junkies in the city and it was really shocking how bad they looked and how the drug had changed them. Jane was sure, after watching the report, that everyone she knew had to think that was her problem as well. It was no secret her best friend Bobby had been riding the Pope the night of his accident. But Jane really didn't do drugs. Sure, there was a few ayahuasca ceremonies she took part in with Inkarrii when she was visiting Tulum. That was different because that wasn't to get high at all. She did it in order experience her own ego death in order to be reborn into her higher vibrational self. Did it work? Maybe it did for a while, but it didn't take long for her old ways to settle back in, leaving her once again the same old Jane everyone not only knew but expected.

"Look at what that fucking got me," Jane said laughing as she turned up the volume on her car stereo.

It was a nice night out and Jane was just blindly following various streets and avenues. She had her windows down and the warm breeze and fresh air felt good. Well, as fresh as it could be in the middle of the city. She was enjoying herself and the time to think. Moving back to St. Louis from Chicago had been hard on her. Running into Bobby and hooking back up with her longest and best friend was good. It seemed to have made everything easier to handle at first. Then, of course, it all began to unravel when the nightmares began. It seemed everything had turned toward the worst in an instant and without warning. One day they were happy and the next day they were in hell.

Jane wished she could go back to change that first night at Chuck's, or even better, if she hadn't even gone with Bobby to Chuck's house at all. Jane knew it was an unrealistic wish because she couldn't undo what had already been done. She knew there was no one in the world out there who was granting wishes for her. The good wishes for Jane had already completely dried up. At least that is the way she felt in the moment. Jane knew she had to make sacrifices for every single step she took in this life. No one was going to do it for her. Of that, she was sure. She also knew her life was never going to be easy again. Jane felt like some type of cursed trade. Fucked, used and cursed. Cursed, yeah that was it, Jane felt cursed.

Jane was humming along to an old song playing on the radio. She was listening to the classic FM station KSHE 95 classic rock radio on her stereo. It was funny she didn't usually listen to FM anymore. Streaming was way more convenient, and she could control what she heard. But tonight, she felt like jamming to old school was the way to go, even with the commercials. She heard a familiar guitar riff, and she turned it up to sing along with an old song about the Reaper. Maybe Glow was the Grim Reaper himself? Alex told her his theory about the djinn and how he felt Glow was one of the ancient beings. Jane was open-minded enough, and she believed whole-heartedly in some weird fucking shit, but seriously, she had a very hard time believing some ancient fucking demon like genie had some type of cosmic vendetta he was playing out against them. Besides, genies grant wishes, and the only thing John Glow did was to take things away. But in truth, even though Jane didn't want to admit it to herself, she knew it was a possible explanation. However, the thought that it was some type of ancient being scared her even more than the not knowing. How would she fight off something older than Christ himself? It was easier for Jane to label Alex's idea crazy than to face the helplessness of the frightening possibility it was a djinn. She was not prepared to fight anything older than Christ himself. So, out of the necessity she filed it all away in her minds folder marked 'Crazy Shit.'

She kept singing along with the old song on the radio when her car began to shake and then cut out, and then, die. She was lucky she had been near a curb, so it was easy to pull the car over as it cut out one last time coming to a complete halt. It was dark and silent inside the car. Not only had the car stopped, but it had completely shut down. Jane wasn't a mechanic or anything close to one, but she knew enough to realize she either just blew a fuse or her alternator had gone out. Whatever the specifics of her mechanical crisis, she knew, above all, she was completely fucked.

"Fuck," Jane said, shoving the car into park and banging her hands on the steering wheel. This was the last fucking thing she needed.

She could feel the anger rising to her face as she looked out the window to see if she could tell where she was. She reached for her phone to look at her map app for her location. Her phone had been low when she left work, and she had plugged it in to the charger in the car. Her phone should have charged quite a bit by now, but the instant she clicked the side button to turn it on, it shut down. Her phone battery was fucking dead. It didn't charge at all.

"Goddammit," Jane said once again pounding her hands onto the steering wheel. She hadn't a clue where she was. It was night. Her car wouldn't fucking start, and her phone was dead as well. What in the fuck was she going to do?

"Looks like I am going to have to walk," she said to herself, grabbing her purse and getting out of the car. A few more choice curse words were muffled by the sound of her slamming door.

Jane began to walk, not sure where she was headed. She could see lights on one of the side streets and she followed it out of a residential area onto a more commercial street. Well, sort of commercial. It was old commercial with some businesses with a whole lot of boarded-up windows and closed buildings. The moment she saw this street she knew she was in deep trouble.

Jane had somehow driven to the North Side of the city. St. Louis can be a very dangerous place to live and one of the most dangerous places in the city was its North Side. The area had once been a nice place for families to live and grow, but it had turned into an actual war zone over the years during the time when everyone was leaving the city for a better life in the county. This was no-man's land. A modern-day wild fucking west where lawlessness and chaos reigned supreme. Out of all of the areas she could have been in the city of St. Louis, this was the absolute worst possible place for Jane to be. Let alone a place for her to be stranded. Jane Moore was in serious danger.

Jane knew her safest bet was to stay in the light as much as possible and eventually she would end up at a gas station or somewhere to call for some help - or at least a cab. Her stomach sank when she realized she wasn't even sure if she would be able to communicate the location of her car. She kept walking, looking to see if there were any street signs at each intersection, but each corner had nothing but flashing yellow lights. There wasn't a person, or even a car, anywhere to be seen. It was just after three in the morning, and no one was coming to save Jane from her own stupidity. She was going to have to get herself out of this mess on her own. She hoped that maybe, just maybe, a cop would drive by and see her and stop. She knew she was hoping for a lot because there truly was no one anywhere to be seen or found. This was as much of a blessing as it was a curse because in this part of the city you had no idea who that someone could be, even if they did show up. Jane knew she was in danger, but she also knew she had to focus on moving forward. She had no time for fear. Fear wasn't going to help her out of this mess.

Jane continued walking, passing the boarded-up windows and broken-down storefronts. She listened to the sound of her feet as they hit the sidewalk when she walked. She used the rhythm of her footsteps to keep herself moving forward at a consistent pace. Then, in an instant, she heard another set of footsteps sounding in the offbeats of her own. There was someone walking not far behind her.

Jane could feel the panic begin to set in as she stopped and turned around to see a man with his hands in his pockets and a black hooded sweatshirt over his head. He stopped walking when she stopped. Jane couldn't see his face, but she knew in an instant she needed to keep moving. She continued walking again, listening to the footsteps as she went. She could hear that whoever it was behind her was keeping a steady pace with her. Jane would speed up and the sound of his footsteps would speed up as well. Jane would slow down her pace and the sound of his footsteps would also slow down. It was clear, by this point, she was being followed. Jane stopped and heard his footsteps stop. Jane turned around to look at the man who was still there standing about a half-block away.

"Is there something I can do for you?" Jane asked nervously but the man beneath the hoodie did not move.

"Are you following me for some reason?" Jane asked as her voice quivered.

The man in the hoodie remained silent - not answering.

"Can I call the police for you? Do you need help of some kind?" Jane asked him.

She held her dead phone up, trying to get him to respond. At least he might think she had a phone to call for help if he tried anything with her. But he just stood there, quiet and unmoving.

Jane turned around and began to walk faster, listening as the man behind her kept up with her rhythm.

Then she heard his footsteps go into double time.

He was coming closer to her.

Not knowing what to do, Jane stopped to face him once again.

He stopped as well.

He was only a quarter of the block away this time. Jane could see him quite clearly under the streetlamps and the flashing yellow lights of the intersection just ahead.

"You need to leave me alone." Jane began frantically searching through her purse for a small can of pepper spray she always carried with her.

She finally found it and put it up for the mysterious man to see.

"This is pepper spray, dude, and I promise you, it will fuck you up. I don't want to use this on you but if you come any closer, I promise you that I will," Jane was pointing the pepper spray in his direction.

She could see her own hand shaking but she couldn't stop it. She was worried that it showed him her weakness and the last thing she wanted at this moment was to appear weak. Showing fear in the city was the weakest sort of thing you could do. Fear said, take advantage of me. Fear said, do to me what you will. Fear was a way of showing you were vulnerable, and the one thing Jane hated was the feeling of being vulnerable.

She heard the man mumble a few words that she couldn't make out. He spoke too softly for her to hear.

"What did you say? I'm sorry, I couldn't hear you," Jane said with her voice still quivering and her hand still shaking.

The unmoving man didn't answer.

Jane started to say something else but stopped when she saw the man had begun to slowly move his arms up toward his bowed head and onto each side of his hood. He began to pull the hood slowly back revealing long stringy hair.

He began to slowly raise his head revealing white glowing eyes.

Jane knew it was John Glow and she knew this time she was not dreaming. This time she was wide awake. She could now see his crazed face as he slowly grinned at her and said one word - calmly and to the point.

"Run," Glow said, smiling wickedly.

He remained unmoving. He was waiting for the full impact of Jane's situation to slowly sink into the gravity of the danger she was in. It only took a moment before he heard her scream as she turned on her heels and began to run down the street.

The chase was on.

Jane ran as fast as she could. She knew Glow was behind her. She was trying to do everything she could to get away from him. She would run up to every building that looked like it might be occupied. She would bang her fists on the door screaming for help but help never came.

She had to continue moving as Glow was following slowly and deliberately behind her, waiting to pounce. Jane ran down the street toward another intersection with a yellow flashing light. She turned, looked over her shoulder and saw Glow was steadily coming up behind her. She almost fell as she veered quickly onto a dark side street at the intersection.

She was hoping if she did it fast enough, she could gain some distance from him. It bought her no time at all. Glow was still there behind her, and he was advancing.

Jane ran down the street, screaming through the occasional spotlights from the burning streetlamps above that were becoming and less and less frequent as she ran.

The further she ran the less light there was.

The further she went into a city of deserted homes and broken streetlamps the darker the night was and the less she could see in front of or behind her.

She could barely make out what looked like a neighborhood park ahead. She ran toward it as fast as she could. Into the park she ran and down a hill toward an opening barely visible in the distance.

Maybe she would be able to hide there? Maybe there she would be able to find some safety? She turned around one more time to see Glow was still behind her and then she lunged toward the opening to get away.

Her feet came out from under her, and she felt herself falling through the air. She screamed as her body came down hard on a dark concrete staircase and then she began rolling down the long flight of stairs.

The last thing Jane felt was the breaking of her neck.

Lights out.

Jane's body would be found the next morning. She would be found broken and alone at the foot of the stairs in the park only a few feet away from one of the few remaining pay phones in St. Louis. She was almost there but just not... quite... close... enough.

<u>Chapter 26</u>
Broken

Vincent stood at the foot of a concrete staircase located in the middle of Murphy Park in North Saint Louis, looking down at the lifeless body of Jane Moore at his feet. The call had come in from the pay phone located not far from her body. An anonymous male had reported finding her. Vincent looked into her lifeless eyes, which, even in death, showed the terror that her last moments had held. He recalled those eyes from the day of Robert Winchell's demise, and how, through her tears, he could see the fear, sorrow and guilt she was feeling.

Jane was sprawled out at the bottom of the stairs with both of her legs on the steps and her torso and head laying on the concrete landing below. It was clearly obvious her neck had been broken from the fall. Vincent looked up the staircase at one of the crime scene investigators dusting the top railing, hoping to find any possible leads from any prints they lifted. Vincent could not help but notice it was a long way up to the top of those stairs and for Jane Moore he knew that fall had to seem even longer on her way down to the bottom.

Vincent stood there looking at her body and the terror of frozen death within her eyes with a deep sense of sadness. He had too many questions racing through his mind. What was Jane Moore doing in Murphy Park at night by herself? The STLPD patrol had easily found her car a little more than half a mile away, parked in a section of the city which was pretty much deserted. The area where her car and her body were found looked like a bombed-out neighborhood after a horrible war. Jane Moore had been alone. Alone at night in this part of the city was something no one ever wanted to be, and it just made no fucking sense.

It was hard to believe, when you looked around at the devastation of North St. Louis, that you were standing in the middle of the United States. It was a place that lay home to squatters, junkies and gangs. The amount of crime which took place there was, and had been, so out of control the news media had just stopped reporting on it and the police were very slow to respond - if they could get anyone to respond at all. It was no-man's land and the only reason to be there was to look for trouble or to be the trouble itself.

The fact that Jane Moore's body was amid all this urban desolation raised way more questions than it answered. There were just too many questions to even begin to think this was somehow an accident. Rational explanation would tell Vincent she had been pushed down those stairs. But then again nothing rational had come up with anything surrounding this group of friends and their untimely deaths. Vincent was now looking at six deaths, and even though some of the cases had been closed, he knew he could be on the edge of reopening all of them. Once again, there was one common denominator between all these deaths.

There was one suspect and one suspect alone. And that suspect was Alex McAllister. Vincent immediately made the call to have Alex McAllister brought in for questioning. He wasn't giving Alex the option this time. This time he was just going to have him picked up and brought in. Vincent turned back to Jane Moore and said a quick prayer for her under his breath. He wished for her to find some sort of peace in her death. He walked away to his car with his head down, thinking. He had already begun to get himself mentally ready to question Alex.

Vincent reached the station just as they were bringing Alex in through the back. He stopped at his office to gather his notes and to prepare for the questioning which lay ahead. After about a half hour or so he found himself looking into the interrogation room through a two-way glass mirror.

There was a small table in the room. A chair on one side and another chair on the other. There was one camera in the corner hanging from the ceiling to record the interview and there was an overall surveillance camera hanging from the opposite corner. Alex McAllister, appearing somewhat shaken, sat in one of the chairs with his hands on the table facing the first camera. Vincent knew the officers had to tell Alex why he was being brought in for questioning, so he was certain that he was informed of Jane's death. Vincent took a deep breath and walked into the room. He took the seat directly across from Alex.

"You have the right to remain silent," Vincent began speaking. These were the first words he spoke to Alex, and they cut through the room with an echo, breaking the silence between the two of them. Alex appeared shocked to hear them coming from Vincent. This was the second time that day these words had been spoken to him.

"You have to fucking be kidding me?" Alex said over the top of Vincent speaking,

"Anything you say can and will be used against you in a court of law. You have the right to an attorney. If you cannot afford an attorney, one will be provided for you." Vincent continued in an emotionless and functional manner.

"Come on. You know I've done nothing wrong here." Alex insisted over the top of Vincent's speaking.

Vincent paused for a moment, let Alex finish his sentence and then continued, "Do you understand the rights I have just read to you? With these rights in mind, do you wish to speak to me?"

"Do I have any fucking choice, Vincent? Have I ever had any fucking choice whether I speak to you or not?" Alex looked painfully into Vincent's eyes as he spoke.

Vincent could tell he was fighting back tears.

"Do you understand the rights I have just read to you? With these rights in mind, do you wish to speak to me?" Vincent repeated slowly and somewhat angrily to Alex.

"Yes, I will speak with you. I have nothing to fucking hide and you know it," Alex said defiantly.

Vincent knew he was going to have to keep a serious and professional tone. He knew he could not show any emotion toward Alex at all. His questions were going to be direct and to the point. They had to be, and it was not going to be easy. Vincent knew, in doing so, he was going to be hurting someone who he had grown to care about.

Right or wrong, that is the way it had to be. Short and to the point.

"Can you tell me your whereabouts early this morning between the hours of 1:30 a.m. until about 8:00 a.m.?" Vincent asked, looking directly into Alex's eyes.

"I was at home. I would like to tell you I was sleeping, but, as you can tell by the fresh bitemarks up both of my fucking arms, that wasn't going too well," Alex said while pulling up his shirt sleeves to show the marks on the inside of his arms.

Vincent forced himself not to react. He knew Alex was trying to gain his sympathy and he couldn't let that happen. Not this time. He couldn't let Alex control the narrative because there were some serious fucking questions that needed to be answered. Vincent found himself wondering if Alex was involved in some kinky S&M type of relationship. One where they would get off biting, scratching and hurting each other. Vincent knew this was not out of the question either. People in the world were into some crazy things. Bitemarks and scratches would seem pretty damn vanilla in some circles.

"Is there anyone who can vouch for the fact that you were indeed home between those hours? Maybe the person who left those marks on your body?" Vincent asked.

He knew the possibility of that was slim, but it still had to be stated for the record.

"You know I live alone. You know I am not seeing anyone. You know that all of my friends are dead at this point, and I haven't spoken to my parents in a few days. The answer would be NO, Vincent. I have no one who can verify I was at home between those hours," Alex paused, thinking for a moment, which seemed somewhat odd to Vincent.

"I did order a pizza for delivery about ten, but that is outside of the time frame you are asking about. So no, Vincent. No. There is no one who can vouch for me and as far as I can see there is nothing wrong with that. All of this is really fucking ridiculous, and you fucking know better." Alex replied, irritated.

Vincent could see Alex's cheeks redden as he gave his answer. Vincent examined Alex's face and was struck by how changed Alex's features had become over the past few months. He looked drawn and sick. Vincent hated thinking the cliché, but Alex looked like some type of a prisoner of war. Alex had PTSD written all over his face. The dark circles under his eyes told the story that the lack of sleep had been obviously taking a toll on him. He was skinny and drawn.

Vincent was well aware what stress, and the lack of sleep could do to a person. But what was all of this truly being caused by? Was Alex being haunted by some kind of guilt? Was Alex going through some kind of horrible withdrawal with his body needing a fix? Was it possible Vincent was looking at someone who had some kind of psychotic break? Was the psychosis becoming worse with the passing of days as the body count was rising? There was also the possibility that Alex McAllister was nothing more than just a victim like the others.

"You do know Jane Moore was found dead this morning in Murphy Park in North St. Louis?" Vincent asked Alex directly and completely without any type of feeling or emotion showing.

"Yes. I know," Alex replied softly in an instant show of emotion. A knee-jerk type of emotion that wasn't easily forced and showed vulnerability. Tears began to stream down his cheeks.

Vincent gave Alex a moment to settle down. When he was sure he could, and should continue, he asked, "Alex, did you kill Jane Moore late last night or early this morning?"

Alex looked at Vincent with an instant hatred, not only for the question being asked but this was also coming from someone Alex thought he could trust. The tears continued to flow down his cheeks as Vincent's words cut into him. How stupid he had been to trust Vincent.

"No. I did not kill Jane. I did not kill Jane or Ellis or Paul or Bobby or Chuck. You know I didn't. How fucking dare you even suggest it. You know better," Alex said angrily.

"Am I under arrest, Vincent? Is this where this is heading? Are you going to try to pin all of this on me so you can just close the file and move on? Am I your easy solution? Answer me, Vincent. AM I UNDER FUCKING ARREST?" Alex said screaming as he stood with his hands clenched into fists. Vincent remained calm and unmoving.

"No. At this time, you are not under arrest." Vincent replied without emotion.

"Then I am out of here. The next time you decide you want to talk to me about this you will be talking with me and my attorney. Is that fucking clear enough or do I need to say that part slower so you can fucking understand it? Fuck you and fuck me for putting my trust in you and thinking you were different. I should have known better. Can I go now?"

"Yes," Vincent replied emotionless getting to his feet.

<h1 style="text-align:center"><u>Chapter 27</u>
Rage</h1>

Alex left the police station full of rage. How dare they fucking try to pin all of this onto him! My God, he was the fucking victim here too. Why couldn't they see that? Why couldn't they see there was a force at work here that was trying to destroy him? He had told Vincent about Glow. He had shown Vincent the marks on his body. He had told him everything, including the gory details of the horrific rapes. How dare Vincent sit there and try to put the blame at his feet! He had nothing to do with Jane's death and he was damn sure had nothing to do with any of the other deaths.

Alex flagged a cab down in front of the police station. He gave the driver the address and sat back in the seat trying to settle his nerves and calm his anger.

Everything was filling him up and emotionally he knew he was very close to losing complete control. He looked out of the window of the cab at the scene of other cars passing by, running along with their daily lives. Alex knew he was in serious trouble, and he had no idea how he was going to get himself out of it. He had no clue even where to begin to turn for help. Vincent was his help. Vincent had not only just betrayed him but the cruelest part of it was letting Alex believe he had cared. Alex wondered how he could have ever been so fucking stupid to allow a cop to convince him that he had his back. Even worse, Alex, at one point, thought he might have even been falling for Vincent. Alex thought that just maybe there could be something more between the two of them. All of it had now been washed into the gutter. Alex, at this particular moment in time, never felt more alone.

"Is it cool enough for you Sir?" the driver inquired about the temperature inside the car.

"Yes, thank you," Alex responded while still looking out the window.

The coolness inside the car did feel good on his hot skin. In some ways, it was having a calming effect on him and he sunk deeper into his seat. He had thought about going home to live with his parents for a while. Maybe take a semester off of school. As soon as he thought it might be a good idea, he would see the glowing white eyes in his mind which would remind him that he would be putting his parents in serious danger as well. He had tried very hard to keep his parents out of it and not let them in on what was happening. He knew they had to be way more worried than they pretended to be when they talked to him. They knew his friends were dead.

In Chuck's and Bobby's cases, the media did an excellent job covering the stories. If it bleeds and burns it always leads the news. Of course, his parents knew drugs had been involved in at least one of the deaths. Alex was sure they were most likely working behind the scenes at this very moment to set up his intervention. You know, birds of a feather, and all of that crap. Sometimes his parents would jump to the worse possible conclusion where he was concerned. Alex couldn't understand how they could have so little faith in him and, even worse, how little they actually knew him. Of course, he was sure they were whispering to each other behind his back on how their little boy had grown into a full-blown junkie. Of course, they were as wrong as they could be, and in truth, they had no idea what was actually ripping him apart. They were most likely thinking rehab, when what Alex really needed was something more along the lines of an Exorcist.

The driver said something which brought Alex out of his deep thoughts.

"Pardon me, I didn't quite understand what you said," Alex replied, still looking out the window without moving. He didn't want the driver to see he had tears in his eyes.

They were sitting at a light waiting for it to turn green.

"Everyone bringing you down, Alex?" The driver asked once again, as they continued to wait. This time Alex heard him quite clearly.

"Wait a minute, how did you know my..." Alex turned to look at the driver in the front seat of the cab. He didn't finish the sentence.

Reflected back at him in the driver's mirror were glowing white eyes.

Panic washed over Alex in a huge tidal wave of fear. He fumbled with the handle and struggled to open the cab door. He was shaking so bad he couldn't get the fucking car door open. He began throwing his body violently against the door trying to escape from the glowing of those eyes. Finally, the door gave way as Alex fell out onto the street.

The traffic light had turned green. The driver, also possessed by Glow, got out of the cab and was screaming at Alex over the roof of the car as the traffic began honking and swerving around the cab and Alex. Alex was on his feet now, running.

"Where do you think you are fucking going?" Glow's voice was screaming at him through the white-eyed possessed cab driver.

Alex heard the squeals from slamming brakes as another car plowed into the cab throwing the driver into the path of an oncoming delivery van. Alex just kept running as cars piled up and pandemonium exploded behind him.

Alex was running frantically through the streets. He was trying desperately to get home. He needed to get home.

He looked ahead and there was an old woman sweeping her front porch. She looked up at him with white glowing eyes, laughing. He kept moving past her as fast as he could.

Then, at the next corner, a kid was coming out of a bodega. Alex didn't see him until he was right on top of him. He saw the boy's white, glowing-eyed, laughing face as he knocked him to the ground. Alex didn't turn around. He just kept on running.

He passed more possessed versions of Glow as he ran hysterically. A man, a woman, a nun - all with white eyes – laughing. Alex began to shut the world out around him. He focused on nothing else but running and the passing pavement in front of him.

Finally, he saw his apartment ahead. Alex knew he would have just a very short time to grab a few things before the police would come looking for him. He bounded into his building, taking the stairs and running down the hall. Inside his apartment he shoved some cash, cards and few things he might need into a backpack.

The last thing he did was to grab Chuck's pistol that Bobby had given him for safe keeping. Alex knew very little about the pistol, but he did know how to take the safety off, which he did. He also knew it was loaded and he would have eight shots if he needed it. Alex was completely irrational at this point.

Survival was the only thing on his mind. He was going to survive as long as he could, and he was going to do whatever it took to do just that. Alex made an irrational plan in his mind that he would use the pistol to shoot John Glow if he needed to. Alex had already convinced himself, in the moments packing his backpack, that if Glow was able to come out of his dreams, then Glow was able to die. That is when Alex made the dangerous and foolish decision that he had no choice but to kill John Glow if he got the chance. He would shoot to kill.

Alex hurriedly locked his apartment and headed down the stairs and out the front entrance. A police cruiser was pulling up out front as Alex quickly moved down the street and over to an alley, allowing him to disappear unnoticed into the city. He wasn't sure where he was headed. He just knew he was on the move.

He passed by numerous people as he went. Each time he would pass someone he could feel the gun in his pocket, waiting. But now that he was armed there were no white glowing eyes following him. There was no John Glow waiting and Alex began to laugh because he was sure he had it all figured out. As long as he had the gun, he would be safe.

When he was far enough away from his apartment, he slowed his pace in order to not look too suspicious. But he knew he needed to keep moving. He kept walking and walking. Once he got thirsty, he stopped for some water and a few protein bars. Just enough supplies he could fit into his backpack. The whole thing seemed ridiculous to Alex at this point. He felt like he was ten again running away from home. He smiled thinking about it because he wished it was all a bad dream. He wished he was ten again.

The realization of everything hit him once again. He knew if he was going to live, he had to see this through. He had no other options. He was either going to survive this on his own terms or he was going to end up dead like the others. He was going to fight and knew this was the way. He knew he had it figured out. Alex knew in his heart the only way he was going to survive this was to kill Glow and the only way to do that was to wait for him to appear once more. Alex knew he needed to shoot to kill. He needed to shoot John Glow.

<u>Chapter 28</u>
Talk

Things with Alex had quickly gone from bad to worse. At the moment, no one had any idea where he was. It had been over twenty-four hours since the chaos at the intersection where Alex was not only spotted but filmed fleeing the cab and the scene. Alex had not contacted his parents and was not at his apartment when the officers arrived there to see if he was home.

The death of the driver at the intersection was an accident. An accident that could have been avoided, but now that Alex was on the run it didn't look good for him. Not good at all. None of this made any rational sense to Vincent, who just needed some answers. It was clear to Vincent from looking at the tapes Alex was running from someone. Vincent knew there were two possibilities.

The first possibility was that Alex was running from someone he had messed with. Maybe drugs were involved? It was not out of the question for the drug element to go after an associate they see getting questioned by the police. If it were something like this, they would go to great lengths to shut it down and neutralize who they would consider a possible snitch. It was how the street worked, and Vincent was quite aware of what could happen. He worked a case a few years earlier near Compton Avenue where a couple had been beheaded in their apartment for no other reason than someone told the drug element they had been seen talking to a cop in a cruiser. Of course, the couple had been dealing drugs. But everyone knows that loose lips sink ships and there is no room in crime for a snitch. No questions were asked. Off with their heads and it was a done deal.

The second option seemed more likely to Vincent, which had to do with Alex's mental health and stability. Vincent thought it was most likely Alex had a complete break with reality and was now running from the nightmare figure within his imagination. Vincent realized Alex fully believed in the existence of John Glow. He also knew Alex had been able to plant the idea of Glow into his own imagination and dreams. The mind is a complex thing which is not fully understood. Vincent believed Alex could have set Glow loose by feeding it with his own imagination and that of others. This kind of mass hysteria had been documented time and time again. The Salem Witch Trials were the result of mass hysteria. The idea of the unknown and the supernatural has fed hysteria concerning everything from werewolves to alien abduction. Vincent felt it was very likely this was wild hysteria he was dealing with here. Most likely a mass hysteria-type event which was being fueled by some strong hallucinogens.

Black Pope had some serious side effects, one of those being extreme paranoia. Add paranoia to hallucinations and you had serious trouble on your hands. There was a reason the CIA and Defense Departments had attempted to harness the powers of LSD and DMT for use in their programs. They wanted to control people and populations. They knew drugs like these worked. They knew it was possible, with the use of these drugs, they could meet their objectives. The substances they used had effects on individuals that were not much different than Black Pope's. Except, in Vincent's understanding, these current synthetics were maybe light years ahead of what the CIA had experimented with, and more than likely, a hell of a lot more dangerous. Very little was actually known about the full effects of Black Pope on the body and the mind. It was scary how fast it hit the streets and how fast it spread with frightening speed.

Mass hysteria mixed together with Black Pope would be a serious problem, especially with someone like Alex who was good at planting ideas in another's subconscious. Vincent could testify to it himself, but in his case, he was able to distinguish reality from nightmares when it came to Glow. However, it was a lot easier to throw out all reason and reality for those who may have had severe drug addiction. A nightmare figure like John Glow would give an addict a perfect way to place the blame for their addiction on something or someone else other than themselves. It gave their guilt an out. This was classic addiction behavior and Vincent was very sure it was close to what he had been observing with this misfit group of friends.

Alex was so unassuming that he was even able to wiggle into Vincent's heart and conscious. Almost as if he could read Vincent's deepest secrets and insecurities. Vincent was sure of it. Whether Alex was aware of it or not, either way, he had a talent for getting under and inside the skin of others. That is the only reason Vincent could begin to understand how he could have started to emotionally fall for Alex so quickly. But what if he was wrong? If he was wrong, then that would mean Vincent was no better than the junkie looking for somewhere to place the blame for his feelings.

Vincent's cell phone rang, and he looked down to see it was an unknown number. He answered it anyway figuring it would be just another sales call or something along those lines.

"Hello, Vincent Rossi speaking."

"Vincent, I had nothing to do with that cab driver getting hit. I was just trying to get out of the cab," Alex was talking quickly and nervously.

"Alex, we know that. We just wanted to know why you were seen fleeing from the scene. We have cameras at every major intersection throughout the city. Trust me, we saw what happened and just wanted your statement," Vincent replied calmly in attempt to talk some type of reason into him.

"I didn't mean to knock that kid down when I was running," Alex said crying. "Vincent, you know me. Right? You know I wouldn't hurt a kid, right?"

Vincent was somewhat stunned to hear Alex's scared voice. Vincent instinctively understood this was a cry for help. He knew Alex was reaching out to him because he had nowhere else to turn.

"Alex, you didn't hurt a kid and if you did, we would know. You might have run into some kid, but you didn't hurt them because there was no report or call. All we want from you is a statement about what happened in the intersection. Why don't you come into the station so I can take your statement and then you will be free to go?

Everyone is worried about you." Vincent said knowing he had to handle this situation carefully.

"I'm not coming into the station again, Vincent. We have been down this road too many times before. It never ends well for either of us." Alex said, catching Vincent off-guard with the use of the word 'us.'

This gave Vincent hope that, just maybe, he hadn't completely lost Alex and there was still an opportunity to get him the help he needed.

"Then how about I come to you? Where are you and I will come to talk to you there." Vincent said feeling like this just might be the angle that would work.

"Okay," Alex surprisingly agreed after a short pause to consider it, "But it is going to be in a public place. I would feel much safer in a public place."

"We can do that. Tell me where to go and I will be there right away, by myself, and we can get all of this settled." Vincent said, knowing he was gaining some type of trust. He could tell Alex was running scared.

He was also sure it wasn't the STLPD Alex was worried the most about. Alex's fear of Glow was much stronger than his fear of the police. With the police, Alex had become defiant. With Glow, Alex had become paranoid and frightened. Vincent was sure of this. The most important thing was to find Alex first and then they could figure out how to get him the serious help he needed.

"I am in Forest Park at the ball fields. There is a men's softball game getting ready to start. You will find me at the ball diamond closest to the parking lot. You know where that is?" Alex said willingly, trying to meet Vincent halfway.

"Yeah, I know where that is. Stay right there. I am on my way," Vincent replied anxiously.

"Alone. You come alone or I will know, Vincent. I promise you I will know if you are not alone. I will be out of here and you will never hear from me again if you don't come by yourself," Alex replied sternly, making sure Vincent completely understood his rules of the game.

"I will be alone. I promise you that. I am on my way," Vincent hung up his cell, already in his car. He was, at most, only ten minutes away from the ballfields.

Softball was a big deal in Forest Park during the summer months. The evenings were mainly saved for the men's games. It would be mostly adults there with a lot of beer flowing. St. Louis was a beer town where nothing happened that wasn't sponsored, paid for or advertised by one of its breweries. This participation guaranteed the beer would flow - and flow it did - in cups, buckets and full coolers. Vincent knew the scene and knew the drill as he headed to the park.

<u>Chapter 29</u>

Pandemonium

Alex pulled his ball cap down over his eyes as he walked toward the ballfield. He was nervous because he was putting a lot of his trust into Vincent. He felt the last time he put his trust in him it didn't turn out too well at all. But at this point he didn't have much of a choice. He had to try.

People were busily walking about getting ready for the next men's softball matchup to begin. Alex could smell the popcorn being popped at the concession stand. People were lining up and walking away with snacks, and of course, beer. Lots of beer. Alex walked by the awaiting line of thirsty, anxious people and further into the huge complex of ballfields. It was a very warm summer evening. Alex had his hoodie tied around his waist and the pistol concealed under his shirt, securely tucked into the back of his jeans. He was glad to see there were not too many children running about. It was mostly a thirty-something crowd by the looks of it. Business leagues mostly. Most of the city's major corporations had leagues that would face off against each other.

Alex looked nervously around as he walked toward the nearest field. He needed to make sure he wasn't being followed. So, he would walk forward for a bit then he would turn and change direction for a few minutes to the side or back. He did this to slowly work his way to the seating located by the field. In this way, he felt he would be able to spot anyone following him. After a while his nerves began to ease somewhat because he was sure he wasn't being followed. He stood next to the field, watching as the men's game began.

Alex knew Vincent would be there soon and he liked the idea of being in the middle of something normal. For the first time in a very long time, he was letting himself feel normal and that felt good. He was sure he hadn't been followed and felt, since he was armed, Glow was going to keep a good distance. After all, Alex was sure he had it all figured out. Once Alex armed himself, Glow went away. The pistol was the deterrent he needed. The pistol tucked into his jeans was the crucifix he had been searching for.

Alex had broken into Chuck's now-deserted house last night to rest. He knew of no other place to go, and he was sure Chuck's house was a place no one would expect him to be. He jimmied the lock on the back door and spent the night sleeping on Chuck's bed with his clothes and shoes on and the pistol in his hand. For the first time in months, he had been able to sleep. It was a deep sleep. When he woke hours later, he felt even more sure he had figured out how to handle Glow. That is also when he also decided to try to reach out to Vincent, but he needed to figure out where and how. He decided he would wait until it was almost evening and head to the park near the ballfields. He had already been there when he called Vincent.

When Vincent offered to meet him, Alex was more than willing. Alex believed Vincent when he told him he just wanted to get a statement from him about the taxi accident and the accidental death of the driver. Alex was even more relieved that there had been no report filed about the boy he had knocked to the ground when he was running. Alex took a deep, cleansing breath as he watched the first batter strike out at the plate. Normal was feeling damn good. Safety and the feeling of having it all figured out was even better.

Alex looked toward the pitcher who was on the mound waiting for the next batter to step up. The pitcher was kicking the dirt. The next batter stepped up and he was tapping his bat onto the plate and then he drew the bat back, readying for the pitch.

The pitcher looked down and as the pitch was released from his hand Alex saw the pitcher's GLOWING WHITE EYES.

In a rush of panic Alex knew exactly what he needed to do. He reached behind his back, pulled the pistol out from his waistband and pointed the gun straight out in front of him, taking aim at the pitcher. The shot echoed throughout the ball field as the bullet made a direct hit into the center of the pitcher's forehead. There was a dead silence as the pitcher stumbled and fell onto the mound, dead.

PANDEMONIUM.

The batter at the plate turned to look at Alex in an instant, screaming. The batter was now Glow-possessed as well. With great force and anger the batter lunged toward Alex.

Another shot rang out and Alex dropped the batter to the ground with one hit.

The crowd began to surge in a panic to get away from the deadly danger that was playing out in front of them. Mass panic and chaos filled the air with the noise of screams and the sound of stampeding feet. Alex ran in the direction of the fleeing crowd, instead of away from them, thinking his odds were better going with the confusion and fear of the crowd rather than away from it. He felt his ball cap fly off his head as another one of the players pushed him to the ground. Glow was moving quickly now from one person to the next and this player was the latest of fast-moving possessions.

Alex was looking into Glow's glowing white eyes as he tried fighting off the large muscular body on top of him. The Glow/Player was trying to get the gun out of Alex's hand but failed with another shot of the pistol.

This time, the shot rang out at a very close range. The attacking, white-eyed player screamed as the bullet ripped into his chest and through his heart.

Alex scrambled to his feet, pushing the now-dead player off of him. He began to run once again, trying to make his way to the exit. Just ahead of him, he saw a woman standing in the middle of the walkway screeching, with her hand pointed straight toward Alex trying to single him out of the crowd. Her screeches were loud, accusing and violent in Alex's ears. She was the next in line for possession.

Alex dropped her white-eyed body in an instant with a shot from the pistol. He didn't stop long enough to see where the shot had hit her, but he could see her begin to fall.

He had to get away.

HE HAD TO GET AWAY FROM GLOW.

Alex turned around and, in an instant, he began to head back once again toward the ballfield. He was now fighting upstream against the surge of the crowd as he went. People were falling and screaming around him.

Vincent had just entered the ballpark complex when he heard the first shot fired. He knew immediately something was going terribly wrong. The second shot rang out and the crowd began rushing toward him.

Vincent was fighting against the crowd, slowly working his way through the surge of screaming and crying people. He grabbed for his sidearm, preparing for whatever he was heading into.

The third shot rang out - closer.

The crowd went even wilder as the screams rose to ear piercing levels. For a moment Vincent lost his footing. He could hear sirens in the distance as he reached down with one hand on the pavement to steady himself. He screamed out in pain as a foot came down upon his hand. Vincent felt his bones breaking. The foot did its damage and was gone.

The sirens were getting closer and closer.

Help was on the way. Another shot rang out just ahead. This time it was very close. In front of him he could see a woman still pointing forward as she crumbled to the ground. This caused the crowd to divide, creating a momentary path through its center, giving Vincent the opportunity to run forward. He could see the softball field ahead.

Vincent saw Alex running wildly toward the field with a pistol in his hand, knocking people to the ground as he went.

"Alex STOP!" Vincent screamed as he reached the field.

Alex was just about mid-field.

"STOP!" Vincent shouted one more time as Alex heard him and stopped with his back still turned to Vincent.

Vincent began to walk slowly toward Alex with his pistol raised. Alex slowly turned around to look at Vincent. He was crying. Alex looked Vincent in the eyes. Vincent stood back as he saw Alex's eyes turning a glowing white.

Alex began screaming wildly like a caged animal as he raised the pistol pointing toward Vincent to shoot him.

A SINGLE FINAL SHOT RANG OUT.

There was a strange moment of silence of shock between the two of them as everything moved in slow motion. Vincent could see the fear on Alex's face and the still-glowing eyes.

Blood appeared and began to grow in the center of Alex's t-shirt as it began to flow from his dying body.

Alex stumbled backwards, falling to the ground as his legs gave out under him. The pistol dropped from his hand as he fell.

Vincent ran forward dropping down at his side. He was trying to calm the dying Alex as he looked into his still glowing, but dimming, white eyes. Vincent was holding Alex's head in his hands as blood began to trickle out of the sides of his mouth.

The white glow left Alex's eyes, and he was dead.

Chapter 30
Autumn

It was a cool brisk afternoon as Vincent parked his car on the side of the street. He stayed in his car for a moment out of respect as a funeral procession passed him by. Once it had passed, Vincent got out of his car, holding a single black rose in his hand. He began to walk up the street and then crossed over onto the grass of Calvary cemetery in St. Louis. Calvary was a huge cemetery which was very easy to get lost in, even if you thought you knew where you were going and the grave you were looking for.

This was the first time Vincent had been there since the chaos of last summer had left Alex McAllister dead. Of course there had been an internal investigation. There is an investigation any time a weapon is discharged, and someone is killed. It was found that Vincent not only acted in accordance with the law, but he had also acted with courage in the face of a dangerous situation. His actions in return saved lives.

Vincent was a hero, but he didn't feel very much like one. Vincent didn't feel so courageous. He still wasn't sure what he had fully witnessed that day. But the fact was, he had seen the glowing white eyes for himself and in that moment everything in the world he knew to be true was gone. Whether he completely understood it or not, Vincent knew John Glow was involved.

When they ran the toxicology on Alex they found no sign of drugs in his system. It was believed by most that Alex had suffered a psychotic break which drove him to murder four random strangers in cold blood.

The whole aftermath of it all had thrown Vincent into a tailspin for a bit. He wasn't sleeping and he was drinking a little more than usual. He had been given a paid leave and, in that time, he slipped deeper and deeper into depression. Vincent's husband Tim became increasingly more and more worried until Vincent finally agreed to seek counseling. Vincent had to admit the counseling helped. It had helped with all parts of his life, including his marriage.

Vincent was still haunted by the fact that he did not fully understand the feelings he had toward Alex McAllister, and he wasn't sure he ever would. He talked with his therapist about it, and he had concluded his attraction and caring for Alex was more about his own need to feel accepted and loved. It was true. Over those months he had felt less and less valued and loved by his husband, Tim. Alex was the possibility that made Vincent feel like he was valued, and that just maybe he could be loved. Of course, Vincent felt he had deliberately sabotaged that as well.

Vincent felt maybe his feelings for Alex were meant to fill something he was missing from Tim, but any feelings of attraction he had toward Alex were never going to replace his husband. Even with these personal revelations and conclusions it still didn't stop his heart from breaking after Alex's death. You cannot simply walk away from someone who dies in your arms like it didn't matter, because it did matter. It mattered very much. He was there to face his own guilt as much as he was there to mourn for Alex and somehow put all of this to rest in his mind.

He saw Alex's name on the headstone ahead. It had been spray-painted with graffiti and vandalized with taunts like COCKSUCKER and KILLER.

Vincent was surprised Alex's family hadn't seen the potential for this type of hate. It would be a very long time, if ever, when Alex McAllister would be left alone to sleep in the peace of his grave. Alex's memory was reduced to nothing more than that of a monster.

Vincent was surprised at how quickly the tears came to his eyes as he stood looking down at the grave. He took a deep breath and then, he began to speak out loud.

"I know it took a long time for me to get here, but I did get here. I am here finally and I'm sorry for that Alex. After you died, I went to a very dark place. Yes, I was feeling guilty. Guilty that I had to be the one to stop you from hurting anyone else. Guilty for stopping you from hurting me. You gave me no choice Alex. I had to shoot. But part of me thinks you knew that. Part of me thinks you wanted to end it and just couldn't do it on your own. I think that maybe you wanted me to do it. If this was case and there is a heaven, I would hope God would consider that," tears were flowing down Vincent's cheeks, stinging in the cool autumn air.

"I forgive you Alex. I do. But dammit, I wish you would have let me help you. You destroyed so many lives and that is something I know I will never be able to completely come to grips with. How could you just blindly shoot innocent people the way that you did? I understand the mental illness part of things. But I really don't think I will ever understand what I was looking at when I saw you that day. Because I did see you, Alex. I saw the pain and the struggle. I saw the white glowing eyes and I saw you fighting against something. I heard the agony in your screams. I saw your eyes change and then I saw them change back as your life left them." Vincent looked down crying while taking a deep breath.

"I am not sure I will ever understand your belief and understanding of John Glow. I guess there are some things in this life which are never answered. Maybe there are some things in this life we are just not supposed to know. Maybe this is the case with your belief in John Glow and the glowing white eyes I saw the moment I took your life," Vincent took a pause through his tears to gather his thoughts.

"I'm sorry it had to be me, Alex. Yet, I'm glad it was me because I know you had someone with you who had compassion for you and someone that cared about you at the moment of your death. I am hoping the fact I was there helped you to be a little less scared for your last moments. I don't know. Sometimes I just think I am talking crazy. You know, the strange thing was, in the moments after your death, the thought that went through my mind. The thought was something, was something from *Romeo and Juliet*. I know how corny that sounds and I haven't told anyone about it until now. I have saved it for this moment and you. The thought was, "I defy you, stars." That was it. Simple. Yes, somewhat corny. But it said everything I was feeling as I lay your dead body down onto the ground. "I defy you, stars," as I raised both of my hands into the air to show I had put down my weapon as my back up surrounded me," Vincent's voice cracked remembering that horrific day.

"I defy you, stars. What do you suppose that means?"

Vincent took the single black rose he was holding in his hand and lay it onto Alex's vandalized headstone. He straightened his back up, satisfied that he at least brought Alex something of caring amid the spit-covered and spray-painted profanity of the headstone. The contrast was striking.

"I brought you this black rose because, when I look at it, I am reminded of you. This is the memory of you I want to carry with me. It says to me that, even in the blackest and most horrific of nights, beauty will find the way. What we experienced together was very dark and horrible. This is my way of letting you know that in the abject terror of it all, I still was able to see the beauty in you. You will always be the black rose in my heart, and I will carry that with me through the rest of my living days."

Vincent heard a wicked giggle as he looked over to a big tree with falling leaves. There he saw a figure of a man in black, with long, stringy hair. Vincent was sure he saw a flash of white eyes as the figure stepped behind the large tree and then was gone.

About the Author

Steven LaChance has been called one of the most prolific supernatural writers of this generation. In 2007, he released the bestselling non-fiction book **The Uninvited**, which detailed the true story of the infamous Screaming House. **Entertainment Weekly**, called **The Uninvited** a true horror classic.

In 2014, Steven released the long-awaited sequel to **The Uninvited, Blessed are the Wicked,** which completed the two-book Screaming House series.

Crazy: A Prayer for the Dead, the Truck Stop Hell story was released for Halloween 2016 and immediately gained critical praise and a large cult following.

On February 8, 2017, Steven published his long-awaited book on the 1949 St. Louis Exorcism case - the same case the blockbuster film **The Exorcist** was based upon. **Confrontation with Evil** was one of the most anticipated true-life paranormal books of 2017. The book was based upon Steven's decade of research into this horrifying case. It revealed new insight and evidence never before shared with the public. It won numerous awards and was featured in the **New York Post** and **The Sun. St. Louis GO Magazine** voted it the Best Book of 2018. Subsequently, the book was released in a Special Edition, which includes new information and photos. The book and Steven were also featured in the **1895 Films** documentary **The Exorcism of Roland Doe.**

On October 8, 2024, Steven released his newest horror novel, **Glow. Glow** is the first book in a three-book contemporary horror series - **Glow, Gorilla and Grace.** These books deal with the effects of evil and monsters living within the current world. All three books comprise one frightening **Modern Monsters** book series.

Steven has appeared on numerous television, film and radio programs worldwide. He has been featured on **NBC News, CBS News, Travel Channel, Chiller, CNN, Destination America, the Discovery Channel, Warner Brothers, Universal, Sony** plus many more. Steven has also worked for the popular television series, **Supernatural.** You can currently see Steven on the **Discovery+** in the Travel Channel documentary, **The Exorcism of Roland Doe.**

Other Books by Steven LaChance:

The Uninvited
Blessed are the Wicked
Crazy: A Prayer for the Dead
Confrontation with Evil

Coming Soon:
From the **Modern Monsters** series:

Gorilla
Grace